THE WHITE KNIGHT

BOOKS BY GILBERT MORRIS

THE HOUSE OF WINSLOW SERIES

The Honorable Imposter
The Captive Bride
The Indentured Heart
The Gentle Rebel
The Saintly Buccaneer
The Holy Warrior
The Reluctant Bridegroom
The Last Confederate
The Dixie Widow
The Wounded Yankee
The Union Belle
The Final Adversary
The Crossed Sabres
The Valiant Gunman
The Gallant Outlaw
The Jeweled Spur
The Yukon Queen
The Rough Rider
The Iron Lady
The Silver Star
The Shadow Portrait
The White Hunter
The Flying Cavalier
The Glorious Prodigal
The Amazon Quest
The Golden Angel
The Heavenly Fugitive
The Fiery Ring
The Pilgrim Song
The Beloved Enemy
The Shining Badge
The Royal Handmaid
The Silent Harp
The Virtuous Woman
The Gypsy Moon
The Unlikely Allies
The High Calling
The Hesitant Hero
The Widow's Choice
The White Knight

CHENEY DUVALL, M.D.[1]

1. *The Stars for a Light*
2. *Shadow of the Mountains*
3. *A City Not Forsaken*
4. *Toward the Sunrising*
5. *Secret Place of Thunder*
6. *In the Twilight, in the Evening*
7. *Island of the Innocent*
8. *Driven With the Wind*

CHENEY AND SHILOH: THE INHERITANCE[1]

1. *Where Two Seas Met*
2. *The Moon by Night*
3. *There Is a Season*

THE SPIRIT OF APPALACHIA[2]

1. *Over the Misty Mountains*
2. *Beyond the Quiet Hills*
3. *Among the King's Soldiers*
4. *Beneath the Mockingbird's Wings*
5. *Around the River's Bend*

LIONS OF JUDAH

1. *Heart of a Lion*
2. *No Woman So Fair*
3. *The Gate of Heaven*
4. *Till Shiloh Comes*
5. *By Way of the Wilderness*
6. *Daughter of Deliverance*

[1]with Lynn Morris [2]with Aaron McCarver

07A

GILBERT MORRIS

the WHITE KNIGHT

The White Knight

Cover illustration by William Graf
Cover design by Josh Madison

Scripture quotations are from the King James Version of the Bible.

Published by Bethany House Publishers
11400 Hampshire Avenue South
Bloomington, Minnesota 55438

Bethany House Publishers is a division of
Baker Publishing Group, Grand Rapids, Michigan.

Printed in the United States of America

ISBN-13: 978-0-7642-0028-1
ISBN-10: 0-7642-0028-3

Library of Congress Cataloging-in-Publication Data

Morris, Gilbert
The white knight / Gilbert Morris.
p. cm. — (The house of Winslow)
ISBN-13: 978-0-7642-0028-1 (pbk.)
ISBN-10: 0-7642-0028-3 (pbk.)
1. Winslow family (Fictitious characters)—Fiction. 2. Fighter pilots—Fiction. I. Title. II. Series: Morris, Gilbert. House of Winslow.

PS3563.O8742W48 2007
813'.54—dc22

2006037951

To all the faithful readers of

THE HOUSE OF WINSLOW novels

In 1986, *The Honorable Imposter,* the first novel in THE HOUSE OF WINSLOW, saw the light of day. At that time, no one could have predicted that the series would go through forty novels in the next two decades.

During these years, I have met many of you who loved the series and have received hundreds of letters from so many who spoke of how the series gave you pleasure—and in many instances was helpful to you.

I wish that I could meet each of you face-to-face to tell you how your faithfulness made the series possible, but since I can't, let me assure you that I have always felt that you and I were partners in THE HOUSE OF WINSLOW.

So I bid a fond farewell to all of you loyal friends of the Winslows. May God bless every one of you!

GILBERT MORRIS spent ten years as a pastor before becoming Professor of English at Ouachita Baptist University in Arkansas and earning a Ph.D. at the University of Arkansas. A prolific writer, he has had over 25 scholarly articles and 200 poems published in various periodicals and over the past years has had more than 180 novels published. His family includes three grown children, and he and his wife live in Gulf Shores, Alabama.

CONTENTS

PART FOUR
September 1941–December 1942

THE HOUSE OF WINSLOW

★ ★ ★ ★

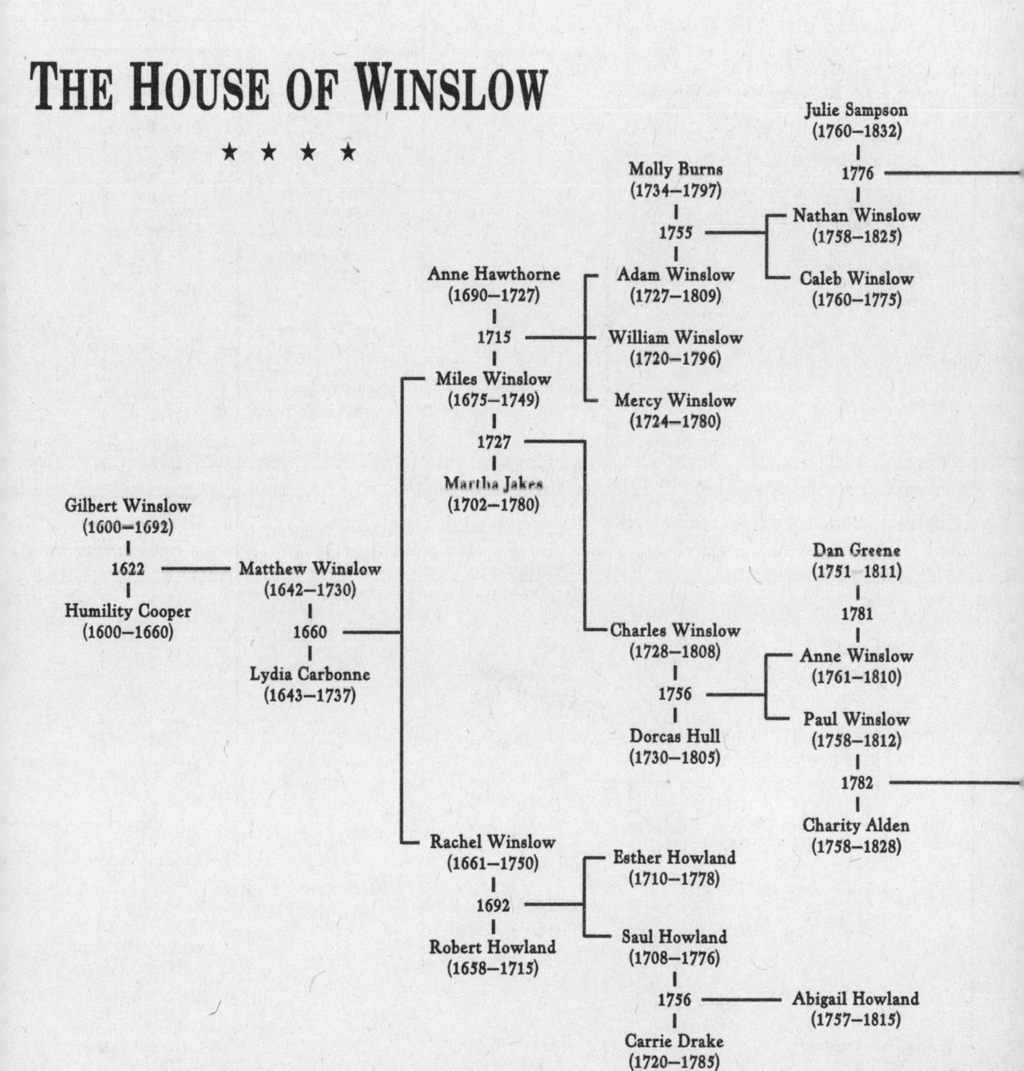

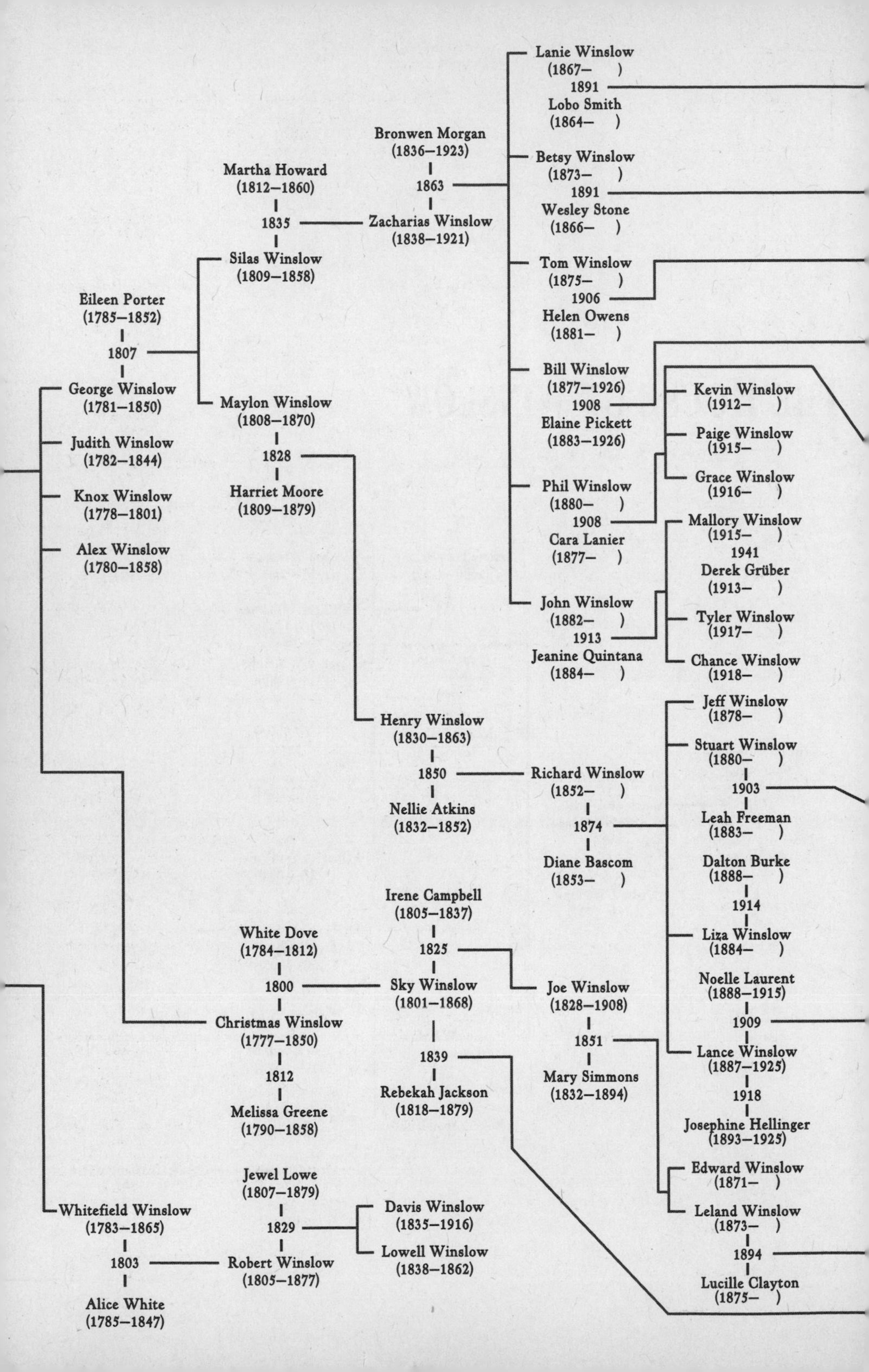

Lanie Winslow
(1867–)
1891
Lobo Smith
(1864–)
Bronwen Morgan
(1836–1923)
1863
Zacharias Winslow
(1838–1921)
Betsy Winslow
(1873–)
1891
Wesley Stone
(1866–)
Martha Howard
(1812–1860)
1835
Silas Winslow
(1809–1858)
Tom Winslow
(1875–)
1906
Helen Owens
(1881–)
Eileen Porter
(1785–1852)
1807
George Winslow
(1781–1850)
Maylon Winslow
(1808–1870)
Bill Winslow
(1877–1926)
1908
Elaine Pickett
(1883–1926)
Kevin Winslow
(1912–)
Paige Winslow
(1915–)
Grace Winslow
(1916–)
Judith Winslow
(1782–1844)
1828
Harriet Moore
(1809–1879)
Knox Winslow
(1778–1801)
Phil Winslow
(1880–)
1908
Cara Lanier
(1877–)
Mallory Winslow
(1915–)
1941
Derek Grüber
(1913–)
Alex Winslow
(1780–1858)
John Winslow
(1882–)
1913
Jeanine Quintana
(1884–)
Tyler Winslow
(1917–)
Chance Winslow
(1918–)
Jeff Winslow
(1878–)
Henry Winslow
(1830–1863)
1850
Nellie Atkins
(1832–1852)
Richard Winslow
(1852–)
1874
Diane Bascom
(1853–)
Stuart Winslow
(1880–)
1903
Leah Freeman
(1883–)
Dalton Burke
(1888–)
1914
Liza Winslow
(1884–)
Irene Campbell
(1805–1837)
1825
White Dove
(1784–1812)
1800
Sky Winslow
(1801–1868)
Joe Winslow
(1828–1908)
Noelle Laurent
(1888–1915)
1909
Christmas Winslow
(1777–1850)
1812
Melissa Greene
(1790–1858)
1839
Rebekah Jackson
(1818–1879)
1851
Mary Simmons
(1832–1894)
Lance Winslow
(1887–1925)
1918
Josephine Hellinger
(1893–1925)
Jewel Lowe
(1807–1879)
1829
Edward Winslow
(1871–)
Whitefield Winslow
(1783–1865)
1803
Alice White
(1785–1847)
Robert Winslow
(1805–1877)
Davis Winslow
(1835–1916)
Lowell Winslow
(1838–1862)
Leland Winslow
(1873–)
1894
Lucille Clayton
(1875–)

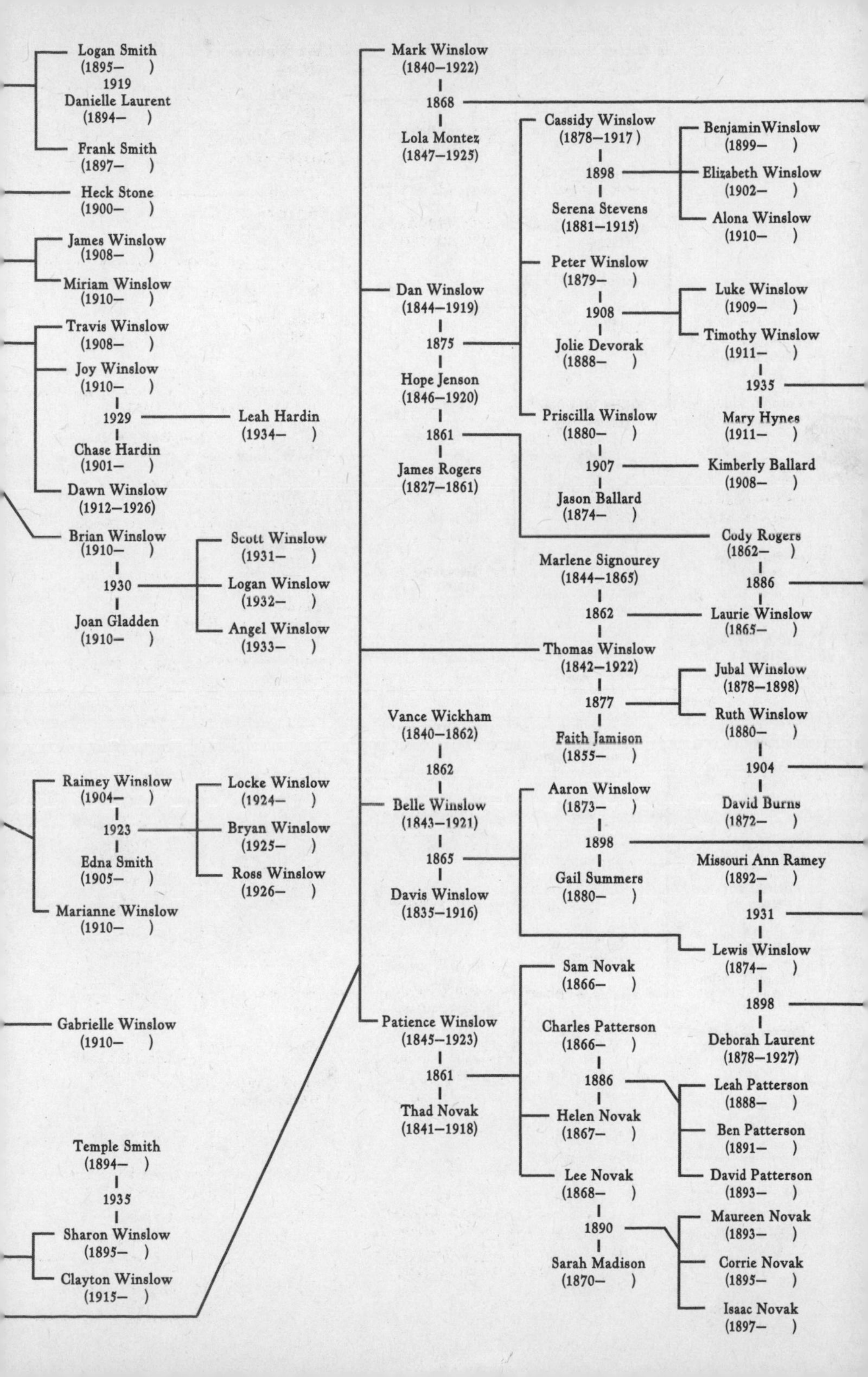

Logan Smith
(1895–)
1919
Danielle Laurent
(1894–)
Frank Smith
(1897–)
Heck Stone
(1900–)
James Winslow
(1908–)
Miriam Winslow
(1910–)
Travis Winslow
(1908–)
Joy Winslow
(1910–)
1929
Chase Hardin
(1901–)
Dawn Winslow
(1912–1926)
Leah Hardin
(1934–)
Brian Winslow
(1910–)
1930
Joan Gladden
(1910–)
Scott Winslow
(1931–)
Logan Winslow
(1932–)
Angel Winslow
(1933–)
Raimey Winslow
(1904–)
1923
Edna Smith
(1905–)
Marianne Winslow
(1910–)
Locke Winslow
(1924–)
Bryan Winslow
(1925–)
Ross Winslow
(1926–)
Gabrielle Winslow
(1910–)
Temple Smith
(1894–)
1935
Sharon Winslow
(1895–)
Clayton Winslow
(1915–)
Mark Winslow
(1840–1922)
1868
Lola Montez
(1847–1925)
Dan Winslow
(1844–1919)
1875
Hope Jenson
(1846–1920)
1861
James Rogers
(1827–1861)
Vance Wickham
(1840–1862)
1862
Belle Winslow
(1843–1921)
1865
Davis Winslow
(1835–1916)
Patience Winslow
(1845–1923)
1861
Thad Novak
(1841–1918)
Cassidy Winslow
(1878–1917)
1898
Serena Stevens
(1881–1915)
Peter Winslow
(1879–)
1908
Jolie Devorak
(1888–)
Priscilla Winslow
(1880–)
1907
Jason Ballard
(1874–)
Marlene Signourey
(1844–1865)
1862
Thomas Winslow
(1842–1922)
1877
Faith Jamison
(1855–)
Aaron Winslow
(1873–)
1898
Gail Summers
(1880–)
Sam Novak
(1866–)
Charles Patterson
(1866–)
1886
Helen Novak
(1867–)
Lee Novak
(1868–)
1890
Sarah Madison
(1870–)
BenjaminWinslow
(1899–)
Elizabeth Winslow
(1902–)
Alona Winslow
(1910–)
Luke Winslow
(1909–)
Timothy Winslow
(1911–)
1935
Mary Hynes
(1911–)
Kimberly Ballard
(1908–)
Cody Rogers
(1862–)
1886
Laurie Winslow
(1865–)
Jubal Winslow
(1878–1898)
Ruth Winslow
(1880–)
1904
David Burns
(1872–)
Missouri Ann Ramey
(1892–)
1931
Lewis Winslow
(1874–)
1898
Deborah Laurent
(1878–1927)
Leah Patterson
(1888–)
Ben Patterson
(1891–)
David Patterson
(1893–)
Maureen Novak
(1893–)
Corrie Novak
(1895–)
Isaac Novak
(1897–)

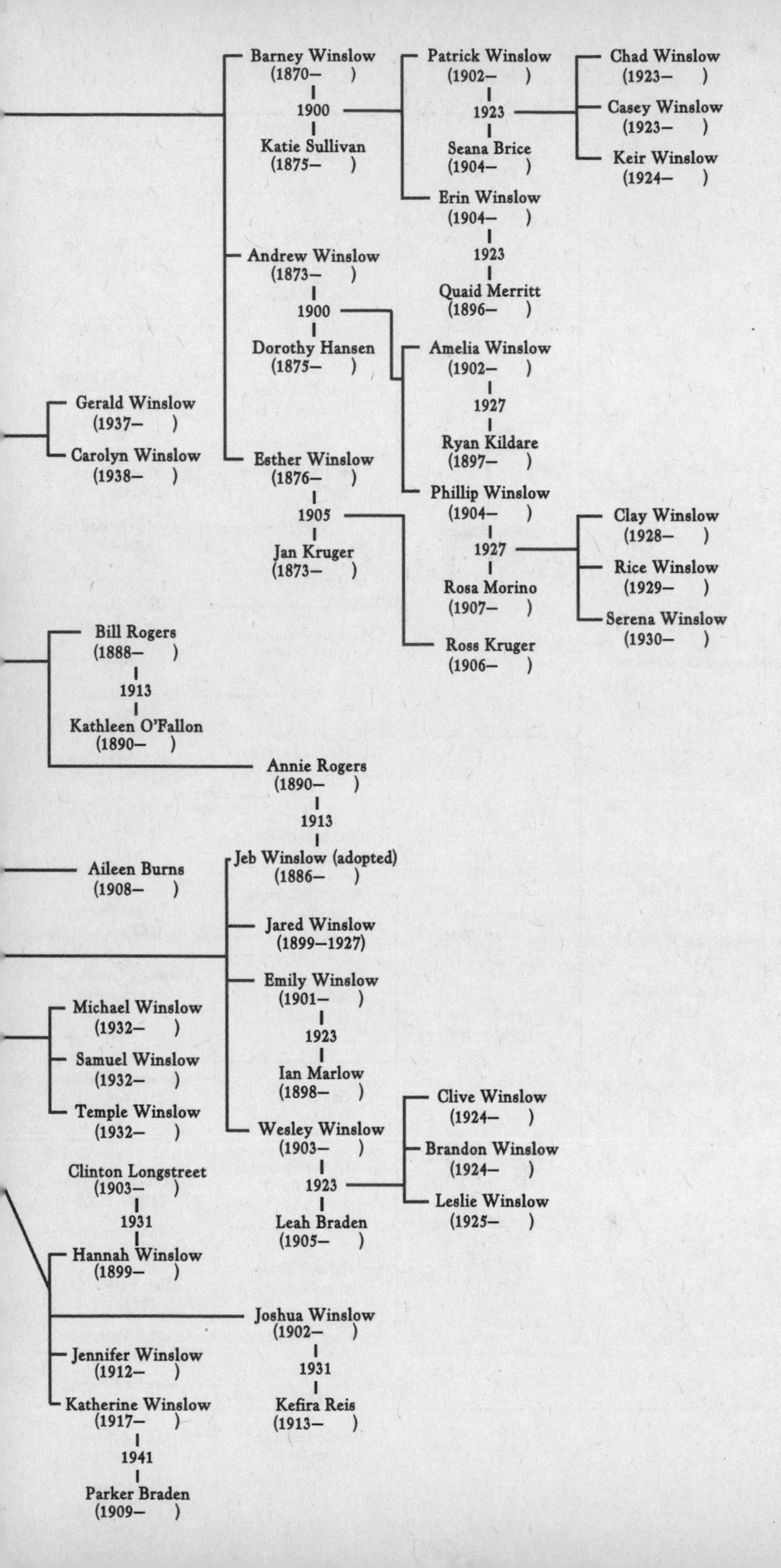

Barney Winslow
(1870–)
1900
Katie Sullivan
(1875–)
Patrick Winslow
(1902–)
1923
Seana Brice
(1904–)
Chad Winslow
(1923–)
Casey Winslow
(1923–)
Keir Winslow
(1924–)
Erin Winslow
(1904–)
1923
Quaid Merritt
(1896–)
Andrew Winslow
(1873–)
1900
Dorothy Hansen
(1875–)
Amelia Winslow
(1902–)
1927
Ryan Kildare
(1897–)
Gerald Winslow
(1937–)
Carolyn Winslow
(1938–)
Esther Winslow
(1876–)
1905
Jan Kruger
(1873–)
Phillip Winslow
(1904–)
1927
Rosa Morino
(1907–)
Clay Winslow
(1928–)
Rice Winslow
(1929–)
Serena Winslow
(1930–)
Ross Kruger
(1906–)
Bill Rogers
(1888–)
1913
Kathleen O'Fallon
(1890–)
Annie Rogers
(1890–)
1913
Aileen Burns
(1908–)
Jeb Winslow (adopted)
(1886–)
Jared Winslow
(1899–1927)
Emily Winslow
(1901–)
1923
Ian Marlow
(1898–)
Michael Winslow
(1932–)
Samuel Winslow
(1932–)
Temple Winslow
(1932–)
Wesley Winslow
(1903–)
1923
Leah Braden
(1905–)
Clive Winslow
(1924–)
Brandon Winslow
(1924–)
Leslie Winslow
(1925–)
Clinton Longstreet
(1903–)
1931
Hannah Winslow
(1899–)
Joshua Winslow
(1902–)
1931
Kefira Reis
(1913–)
Jennifer Winslow
(1912–)
Katherine Winslow
(1917–)
1941
Parker Braden
(1909–)

PART ONE

March–April 1939

★ ★ ★

CHAPTER ONE

"WHY ARE YOU FIGHTING?"

★ ★ ★

Melosa Chavez applied a drop of perfume from a fluted bottle to her forefinger, then dabbed it behind her right ear. She repeated the action on the left side, then held the bottle under her nose, closed her eyes, and inhaled.

"Beautiful!" she exclaimed. "What a fine scent! Only a romantic man such as Luke Winslow would know how much such a gift would please a woman."

Melosa put the bottle down and studied her reflection in the mirror. She checked her ivory complexion and noted the rich color of her cheeks. Her mouth was wider than she would have liked, but it was well shaped and, she had been told, quite provocative. Her eyes pleased her. They had always been her best feature—nearly black, deep set and almond shaped, shaded by thick lashes. She nodded with approval, then reached up and smoothed her black hair, swept up into an ornate hairdo and anchored with a mother-of-pearl comb.

Her gaze wandered down to her pale green dress. It was nipped in tightly at the waist, and she smiled in self-admiration at her tiny waistline and pleasing curves.

"Why are you looking at yourself, Melosa?"

She whirled at the voice of her ten-year-old sister, who must have tiptoed in on little cat's feet. "Isadora, you have a bad habit of sneaking around!"

"I wasn't sneaking."

"Yes you were."

"I just came in to see what you were doing." Isadora was a smaller edition of her older sister, with the same black hair and almond-shaped eyes. She was wearing a white dress and patent leather shoes, and her hair hung straight down her back. "You look at yourself in the mirror so much. I think you're vain."

Melosa's eyes glinted, but then she laughed. "I think you are right, Isadora. I am vain. I will have to ask God to forgive me."

"I'll ask Him too." Isadora nodded. "But I'm not surprised. You're so beautiful it would be hard for you not to be vain."

Melosa went over and hugged Isadora, kissing her on the cheek. "You can be trying at times, but you do have a way of pleasing me. What have you been doing?"

"I've been talking to Luke."

"You shouldn't pester him with your questions all the time."

"That's what Papa said, but Luke said it was all right. He said I could ask him anything I wanted to."

"Luke spoils you and Victor too. I suppose Victor's firing questions at him right now."

"He asked him how many men he's killed."

"Surely he didn't ask him that!"

"Yes, he did. But Luke wouldn't talk about it. He's killed a lot of them, I know. He's shot down lots of those German planes."

"I don't want you to pester Luke anymore with questions like that."

"Why not?"

"It's not polite."

"How am I going to learn anything if I don't ask questions? I have to find out things." Isadora shrugged and tilted her head to one side. "Are you in love with him?"

"That's none of your business."

"You're my sister. If you marry him, he'll be my uncle or something."

"You are always asking about things that have nothing to do with you."

"If he's going to be part of my family, I need to know everything about him."

"It's not polite to ask direct questions like that."

"I think you're in love with him." Isadora moved around to get a closer look at Melosa's face. "What does it feel like to be in love?"

Melosa could not help laughing. "You've got all the curiosity of a cat, but I will tell you this." Her face lit up with a brilliant smile. "It feels very good indeed."

"Is this the first time you've ever been in love?"

"Yes . . . real love, that is."

"What do you mean? Is there a kind of love that isn't real? Like when you let Ramon come calling on you? I knew you didn't like him much."

"You see too much."

"You didn't love him, though."

"No, I didn't."

"But you love Luke, don't you?"

"Oh . . . all right. I'll tell you. Yes, I do. Very much."

"Does he ever kiss you?"

Melosa threw up her hands in exasperation. "What questions you ask, child!"

"Well, does he?"

Melosa looked down at her younger sister. She remembered clearly when she herself had wanted to ask the same questions of some of her friends' older sisters but had never found the courage. Isadora, however, would ask anyone anything.

"Why do you want to know?"

"Because one day I'll have a sweetheart, and I'll need to know how to act, won't I?"

"Yes, you will."

"So . . . does he try to kiss you?"

Melosa put her arm around her sister. "Yes, Isadora, he does."

"Does he respect you? That's what Papa always asks."

"Yes, he respects me."

"I heard what Mama said to you last night. You thought I was reading, but I wasn't. She said, 'You are a pure young woman, Melosa. See that you stay that way!' Are you doing that?"

"Yes, I am. That's enough questions. You go now and tell them I'll be in to dinner in a moment."

"I'll go talk to Luke."

"Don't you dare tell him what we've been talking about. Do you hear me?"

"I won't—at least not unless he brings it up."

"He won't mention it—not to you, anyway."

As Isadora left, Melosa found herself giggling. *That child is impossible! Asking if my sweetheart kisses me.* She touched her hair to be sure it was still in place, then went to the closet to find her shoes. *Isadora doesn't know how right she is. I am in love with Luke, and he's in love with me. If he asks me to marry him, I will.*

"This war is horrendous!" Alfredo Chavez exclaimed in Spanish. He sat across the table from Luke Winslow, waiting for Señora Chavez to put dinner on the table. In his early fifties, Alfredo did not have a gray hair on his head. It was plain where his children got their black hair. He had penetrating dark eyes as well and was in good physical condition. Nevertheless, as he sat in the plainly furnished dining room, he exhibited a nervousness that Luke had noted before.

"War is always terrible, Señor Chavez," Luke replied. His Spanish had improved in the two years he had been in Spain to the point where he could discuss practically anything in the language.

"But this one is at our front door. I don't even know how it came about." He stared curiously at Luke, who was a mystery to him. Physically the Americano was an impressive specimen—he had a handsome face with dark eyes and a generous mouth. He was about six feet tall with a muscular neck and powerful callused hands. His auburn hair had a glint of gold and a slight curl. A fine-looking man!

Two things puzzled Chavez about the young American. One, why was he fighting a war in Spain? And two, how serious was he about Melosa? He didn't feel that he could bring up the matter of his daughter, but he could ask about the war. "Why are you fighting in this war?" he finally asked as he leaned forward, his arms on the table. "This is not your war, not your country."

"No, it's not, but this man Hitler threatens not only your country but the whole world." Leaning back, Luke began to talk about General Franco's attempted overthrow of the Spanish government and how Hitler had seized the opportunity to spread his fascist ideas. He had sent troops, transport planes, and fighter planes to support Franco in his bid to take over Spain, and the poor Republican government was slowly being throttled.

Winslow stretched his legs out under the table and ran his hands through his hair. "If we don't stop Hitler in his tracks, this whole thing will end in tragedy. The British are afraid of him. They've tried to appease him by letting him take over territories in Europe, but that will never satisfy him. The whole world wouldn't satisfy that man! He's proven it over and over. He's clearly a madman, and I came to do my bit to stop him here."

"A very noble deed, Lucio. I think we are losing the war," Chavez said heavily. "Unless things change in a big hurry, our government forces won't be able to hold out."

Luke shot a quick glance at his host. He feared that Chavez was right, but still he tried to be optimistic. "We've had some setbacks, but we'll hope to do better. Try not to lose your confidence. It's a matter of effort."

"What again is the name the Germans give to their air force?"

"They call it the Condor Legion, and it's the big reason why Franco is winning. Hitler sent over some Me-109s—the best fighter planes in the world right now. And the Germans seem to have plenty of them."

"Are they better than our own planes?"

"Oh yes. They're faster and more heavily armed, and their pilots are excellent. Their training program is the best in the world, while our men get very little training."

The Condor Legion was indeed a formidable opponent. They were commanded by Wolfram von Richthofen, cousin of the famed Red Baron, the most successful fighter pilot of the Great War. Under Richthofen were a group of expert fighter pilots, the most successful being Erich Ritter. Ritter had shot down twenty-one Republican planes and was acclaimed all over Germany for his skill. He had painted his Me-109 a solid black with a knight fighting a dragon on the cowling. The media had dubbed him the Black Knight, and the phrase had caught the German imagination.

"I'm afraid for my family," Alfredo said.

"It's true that it's a dangerous situation," Luke agreed.

"What should we do?"

"I think you might want to consider moving farther inland. The German bombers could easily bomb this village." Luke knew the family had deep roots in the northwestern part of Spain and had no desire to leave the area.

"But there is no military target here, Lucio."

"Perhaps not, but it is right in their way, and you never know what they might do next. They may get a notion to simply bomb villages. They've done it before. Think what they did to Guernica back in '37."

Señor Chavez cast a quick look at the younger man. "That was atrocious, the act of beasts! The entire world has condemned that terrible act!"

Luke could feel the anger rise in him at the memory of the Germans' vicious attack. Guernica was a small town without defenses or military importance, its citizens mostly Basque tradesmen. On the twenty-sixth of April, 1937, on a market day, German and Italian forces dropped bomb after bomb on the small town. Some of them were incendiary bombs, and a raging fire swiftly consumed the town. The world was horrified, but the Germans claimed it was a legitimate military target. Some of the Luftwaffe professionals were critical of the attack on Guernica, but the higher-ups claimed that the Basques were not friendly to the Germans and deserved to be bombed.

"You don't think they would do here what they did in Guernica, do you, Lucio?"

"Yes, I think they would. You need to consider moving out to the country, perhaps renting a house in a rural area."

"I will consider it. It would be inconvenient, of course, but I must think of the safety of my family. Why don't those women hurry up?" he said suddenly. "I'm hungry."

★ ★ ★

"Come. You're wasting time, Melosa," Nalda said as she poked her head into her daughter's bedroom. Though heavier than she was when she was younger, Nalda was still the vivacious beauty she had always been. "Dinner is ready. You don't want to keep Lucio waiting."

"Why not? The longer he waits, the happier he'll be to see me. You know that, Mama."

"If you make him wait too long," her mother said with a sly look, "he might find someone else—perhaps Raquel Mendez."

Melosa laughed. "He will not! Not Raquel. He's in love with me."

"Perhaps, but all men need some encouragement. He's a

serious man. Not like Juan Denosa," she said of one of Melosa's suitors.

"No. He's not like Juan."

"Some of these soldiers have no respect for decent Spanish women."

"Most men don't," Melosa said, "but I know that Luke does respect me."

Señora Chavez paused. "You're still a good girl, aren't you, Melosa?"

"Yes, Mama, I am."

"Be sure you stay that way. Now go. Keep him happy. Feed him and flirt with him—that is the way to a man's heart. Do you think he will ask you to marry him?"

"I do not think so—not until the war is over. He's very serious about his work . . . and that's in his favor."

Nalda sighed. "I suppose that is best. Well, come now to dinner."

★ ★ ★

The visit with the Chavez family was a relaxing time for Luke. He enjoyed listening as the family talked about everyday things—Isadora and her brother, Victor, going on about their schoolwork and their friends, and Señor and Señora Chavez discussing the political situation. Melosa was telling Luke about her dream to go to America some day when Isadora started yanking on Luke's arm, her face alive with curiosity.

"Have you had many sweethearts, Luke?" she blurted.

"Don't ask such personal questions," Señora Chavez said at once with a frown.

But Luke only laughed. "Oh, it's okay. The answer is no, not many."

"Do you have any other girlfriends you like as much as you like Melosa?"

Melosa's face flushed and she snapped, "That's another

impertinent question! Now, you be quiet."

Nevertheless, Isadora's eyes were still on Luke.

"No, none that I like half so much," he replied with a wink at the little girl.

Eight-year-old Victor, who was sitting on the other side of Luke, asked, "Will you marry her and take her to America?"

Señora Chavez clapped her hands together. "What a question! You children stop pestering our guest."

But Luke always answered their questions. He had become very fond of them and almost felt as though they were his own siblings. They adored him in return and would rarely leave him alone. "I'll tell you, Victor," Luke said. "It's not the best time for anybody to get married. War is hard on soldiers, you know. It's much better to wait for peace."

"You mean because you might get killed?"

Silence fell over the table, and Melosa was blinking back tears. "Don't . . . don't say that, Victor."

But Luke reached out and smoothed the boy's hair back. "Soldiers sometimes do get killed, son. That's why it's best not to get married during a war."

At that moment the faint sound of airplane engines caught their attention, and everyone looked up at the ceiling.

"Are they ours?" Señor Chavez asked with a worried expression.

"No, not ours," Luke said.

"How can you tell?" Melosa asked.

"These sound like heavy bombers," Luke explained. "Our side doesn't have any planes that big—only fighter planes."

"Are our fighter planes as good as theirs?" Victor asked. "Like the one you fly?"

"No, they're not. So our men have to make up with skill and daring what we lack in planes."

"Are we going to win, Luke?" Isadora asked, obviously frightened.

Luke looked around at the Chavez family, seeing the fear in all of their eyes, and answered the little girl carefully. "I hope so, sweetheart." Determined to lighten the mood, he said, "Let me tell you about a funny thing that happened when we were coming back yesterday. . . ."

* * *

The moon was enormous as it climbed into the night sky. Luke and Melosa had played a game with the kids after supper and had finally escaped to take a walk about the village. It was a pleasant evening, and a light jacket was all they needed to stay warm. The town was quiet except for the sounds of laughter coming from one house. Luke gazed wistfully toward the windows and said, "Whenever I pass a house and hear people laughing like that, I think, They've got everything a person needs."

"Is that what *you* want, Luke?" Melosa asked, desperately wanting to know what was in the heart of this man. Their courtship had begun casually eight months ago but was turning into something more serious. Unlike most American men she had met, Luke was always very courteous with her parents, asking their permission to call on her, taking time to chat with them before the couple left on a date. On their first few dates, one of Melosa's aunts had even accompanied them, acting as a chaperone. Luke had found this amusing but politely accepted their tradition. He had made no attempt for quite some time to even hold Melosa's hand, and the family had been impressed with the tall American. Once when Luke had been visiting with the family, Señor Chavez had asked him, "Why are you so different from other Americans we've met?"

Luke had answered with a grin, "Oh, I've won medals for my politeness and good behavior. I guess I just like the attention." He had winked at Melosa as he said this.

As their courtship developed, Melosa started looking forward to their long walks together, listening to Luke talk about his family in America, playing football in college, and his travels. She was fascinated by the stories and could never hear enough.

Now as they walked along in the bright moonlight, Melosa remembered the first time he had kissed her. They had been holding hands as he walked her back to her house after a concert. When they stopped at her front door, she had thanked him for the nice evening and started into the house when he pulled her back. With a teasing smile he said, "Don't you think that when friends part they should do something more?"

"Something more? Like what? Shake hands, perhaps?" she said teasingly.

"Perhaps even more than that. Doesn't the Bible say to greet each other with a holy kiss?" Before she could think of an answer, he leaned forward and kissed her. She had been kissed before, but this time she could feel her heartbeat speed up as his lips lingered. When she stepped back with her hand on his chest, her eyes were dancing. "I'm not sure that kiss was holy."

"Why, sure it was," Luke assured her, grinning. "But I'll try again if you think it wasn't."

That had been the beginning. Melosa was ready for love, and Luke Winslow was everything a woman could want in a man. He was handsome, fun to be with, honest, and respectful, and had proven his selfless character by coming to fight for a people who were not his own. She had fallen in love with him completely, and now she wondered what would come of it.

The two were holding hands in the quiet village square. On the other end of the square, a man was playing the guitar and singing a sad love song. They listened to it silently, and when the song was over, Melosa felt completely vulnerable, open to whatever her love for this man would bring into her life.

Luke was also moved by the moment. Living each day in the shadow of death, he had often thought about what he would miss in his future if he were to die in battle. One of the things he would miss most would be the love of a woman, and with Melosa's eyes now gazing into his, he pulled her into his arms and pressed his lips onto hers. When he lifted his head after a moment, he realized that she was silently crying even as she clung to him. The dangers of his life flooded his mind and heart, and though he longed to surrender his life to the woman he loved, he was frightened by his own mortality. He feared death but longed for his life to be real, to have some purpose. That purpose seemed to lie in his arms at this very moment, but could he give his life to her when he might not even be here tomorrow?

"You heard what I said earlier about war being a bad time to marry," he whispered in her ear.

"Yes, I heard, Luke."

He pulled away from her gently and looked intently into her eyes. Hesitating at first, he then made up his mind. "If you would marry me when the war is over, Melosa, I would be greatly honored. I love you very much."

She cried out happily and threw her arms around him, laying her cheek against his chest. She held him tightly, savoring the strength of his arms.

"Will you marry me?" he asked again, stroking her hair.

"Yes—I would like to marry you. But we're so different. Your people . . . they would never accept me."

"*Your* people have accepted *me*." He thought for a moment and then said, "After the war I'll take you to America. I know you've always wanted to go there."

"I'm afraid for my family."

Luke did not answer but held her tightly, savoring the smell of her hair and the softness of her body. "America is a big country. There's plenty of room for one fine Spanish family."

And then Melosa lifted her head, and he saw the pride in her eyes. "Come," she whispered, taking his hand, "you must ask my father's permission."

"What if he says no?"

"He won't." She laughed and threw her hands wide in a motion of pure joy. "He will say yes. Come. You must ask him now."

CHAPTER TWO

THE LITTLE FLY

★ ★ ★

Luke strode toward his fighter plane, admiring the paint job as he approached. A knight in full armor, spear poised to strike, adorned the otherwise bright white I-16. He grinned as he thought of how the German pilots of the Condor Legion had dubbed him the White Knight. They were incensed that he had shot down a number of their planes, and they had vowed to bring him down.

Luke turned and waited while the three other pilots from his squadron caught up to him and gathered around him. They had been ribbing him ever since he had told them he was getting married. These men were all that were left of the full squadron Luke had commanded only a month earlier. The other eight were either dead, wounded, or captured by the fascists. One of his best pilots had been a fellow American named Thad Turner, but only three days earlier Turner had been wounded so severely he'd been sent back to the States for medical care. The loss of his men made Luke fiercely determined to keep the rest of them alive.

Roscoe "Streak" Garrison, now his most skilled pilot, was an oversized man with a mop of reddish hair and a pair of bright blue eyes. Everything about him was large, including his hands. It never ceased to amaze Luke how Streak's huge fingers could handle the delicate pieces of an engine. Luke and Streak had played football together in college and had managed to stay in touch since then. When Streak had learned that Luke was going to fight in the Spanish war, Streak had decided in an instant that he would join the effort. Streak was a talented flier and knew when to fight and when to run away—which some of the men he had lost from the squadron had never learned.

"I'll tell you what, Luke," Streak told him, grinning broadly. "I've got this book I'm gonna loan you called *On Your Wedding Night*. It'll tell you just what to do. I'm afraid if you don't read it, you're gonna make a mess of things."

"I appreciate that, Streak. It's just the sort of help I can always count on from you."

"You don't need a book to help you out." The speaker was Nicolai Dubrovsky, a Russian with wild hair and even wilder eyes. His English was bad, and he was an aggressive pilot. He never hesitated to throw himself against any collection of fascist planes no matter what the odds. It was a continual miracle that the Russian had survived this long.

Luke and his squadron used to communicate in Spanish, back when the majority of the group were Spaniards. Now, with two Americans, a Spaniard, and a Russian, they alternated between Spanish and English—and even bits of Russian from time to time.

Luke shook his head, saying, "What do I need, Nick?"

"Just go after her like she was one of those Messerschmitts we're going to be facing today."

"Go in with all guns blazing, eh?" Luke grinned. He had developed a great affection for the Russian but had more confidence in his flying than in his advice to the lovelorn!

"Oh yeah. I have loved so many women I have lost count, and they all keep coming back for more."

"You are an idiot, Nicolai!" Joaquin Varga charged as he broke into the conversation. The man was a true Spaniard in every way. He looked Spanish, he spoke Spanish, he thought Spanish, and he lived for one purpose: to kill the pilots of the Condor Legion. He was small, thin, and wiry, with a pencil-like mustache and glittering black eyes. "Women are like a violin," he said, his voice growing gentle. "You need a soft, sure, but certain touch—like mine!"

Luke stood listening with a smile as the three gave him contradictory and confusing instructions. It was good in his judgment that they had something to think about, for the fight that lay ahead of them was sure to be, as always, grim and bloody. Anything to take their minds off the odds they faced.

Luke was acutely conscious of the other squadrons that were warming up their planes, and he thought about how their numbers had been whittled down too. The air was filled with the sound of coughing engines and men shouting. Finally he said, "Fellows, after we get back, we'll get together for a drink and you can give me more advice. Now it's time to go kill some Germans—as many as we can!"

"Good!" Nicolai agreed with satisfaction. "We go right at them is what I say."

"No. We don't 'go right at them,'" Luke countered. This wasn't the first time they had had this discussion. "We'll do exactly as I say."

"You've always been too choosy about how to kill Germans," Streak complained. "What difference does it make as long as they're dead?"

"The difference is, if we don't do it right, *we'll* be the dead ones. Now, pay attention to me." Luke's tone grew serious. "We don't attack unless we get above them, you got that?"

"Above, below, beside. What's the difference?" The Russian shrugged. "We kill them any way we can—that's the way we do it in Russia, you see."

"Pay attention, Nick. You're not in Russia. We're going to fly at the absolute maximum today. When we see the enemy down below us, then we go in. We stay out of dogfights if at all possible."

"Why?" Varga asked, his eyes flashing. He made a handsome figure as he stood in the sunlight. "We can outfly any of the stupid Huns. The White Knight must be bolder."

"There'll be more of them than there are of us. That's the one thing we can be sure of. What we need to do is come out of the sun together in close formation, then fire together. We knock down a plane and then run like the devil."

"That's no way to fight a war," Varga protested. "We need to attack when we see them."

"No!" Nicolai said. "We can only get four that way."

"We can always get four more." Luke lowered his voice, letting them know he was serious. "I don't want any dead heroes, do you hear me? I want some live cowards who will kill the enemy, run away, and live to fight another day."

Streak shrugged his beefy shoulders and said in a sour tone, "If we just had some better airplanes than these little flies, we wouldn't have lost so many men." The Spanish liked to call the I-16 the *mosca*, or little fly, while the Nationalists called it the *rata*, or rat.

The Germans flew the Messerschmitt Bf-109, which was, in all likelihood, the finest fighter plane in the world, and Hitler had sent a large number of them to fight in the Spanish war. Luke had learned to respect the airplane and the men who flew it. He despised their politics, but the German pilots were probably the best trained in the world. Germany had been forbidden to have an air force after the Great War, but in secret they had taught young men to fly by using gliders and had later managed to build a formidable air force despite the limitations imposed. Now Hitler had no fear at all and was building an air force in exactly the same way he had built a magnificent army.

"They've got better planes, but we're better men," Luke said. "Now, remember. We get above them. You stay on me, and no flying off to become heroes. When we sight the enemy, we go down, hit them, and run."

"Is crazy." The Russian shook his bushy head, and Luke knew that Nick would disregard everything he'd been told and do exactly as he wanted once the madness of battle had seized him.

"All right. It's time to go," Luke said with grim finality. "Good hunting."

Luke watched as the three pilots jogged to their planes, then climbed into his own, patting the side affectionately as he did. He loved his white plane with the knight on the side. He had argued about it with Streak many times. "They'll pick you out and come for you first, Luke," Streak had argued. "They know you've shot down more planes than any of us, and you'll be their number one target."

"Exactly what I want. I want them to know who's killing them," Luke had replied. He climbed into the mosca, a low-wing monoplane with retractable landing gear and an enclosed cockpit, and went through the procedure of getting the engine started. When it caught and roared, he eased the machine forward with a touch on the throttle. The cockpit was as narrow and uncomfortable as a designer could possibly make it. There were few instruments. Those that did exist were poorly arranged. The controls, however, were sensitive, and the featherlight ailerons gave a high rate of roll.

Taxiing out into position, Luke felt the thrill he always did just before a takeoff. The mosca was responsive to his touch, and he gave it full power. He knew the plane well. It was an agile airplane and had an outstanding climb capability. It was faster than most fighters, except for the Messerschmitt, and at ten thousand feet it could go as fast as three hundred miles an hour. Unfortunately, there were flaws. The acceleration was surprisingly poor in a dive, and its rigidly mounted engine caused the whole airplane to vibrate and rattle, which made it a poor gun platform. It was all a pilot could do to hold the plane steady when firing at the enemy.

Despite these aspects, the I-16 did well against German and Italian fighters, and to everyone's surprise proved to be more than a match for the Bf-109. As he left the ground, Luke started into a steep climb. Glancing around, he saw the other three were staying right with him. *They're all good pilots or they'd all be dead,* he thought, fully realizing the odds were stacked against them.

As they climbed rapidly, Luke allowed himself to think about Melosa for just a moment. His engagement had surprised him more than anyone else. He hadn't been planning to ask her to marry him, but while holding her on that romantic night, it had seemed to be the right move. He knew his odds of living through the war were not great. After all, he had been living on the brink of death for the two years he'd been in Spain. He had seen many of his fellow fliers meet death in gruesome ways and knew that such a fate was always close at hand. At times he wondered if he was crazy or if his idealism had unbalanced his mind. When he first came to Spain, he had done so with high hopes and had joined an international group of pilots, all of them convinced they would win the war.

Now, however, Luke knew with dead certainty that Franco was going to win this battle, which meant that Hitler would win as well. The futility of such thoughts dulled his senses, and he shook himself to put his mind on the fight before him.

The planes reached their maximum altitude, and the search began. Luke's eyes roved constantly, searching for the enemy—not only down below but also above, where the Messerschmitts could operate at a higher ceiling. He also checked the mirror he had mounted to his left. The quickest way to get killed was to let the enemy get behind you. The mirror was an innovation Luke had brought to the Republican air force. Many of the pilots who had rejected the idea were now dead.

Luke's squadron flew for half an hour without spotting anything. Then finally Luke spotted a group of black dots below—deadly black dots. He counted six of them and was happy they were not flying in their usual groups of twenty or thirty. "Just right for us," he muttered, smiling grimly. He waggled his wings to catch the attention of the other fliers, then pointed down. They were close enough he could see the wild excitement on the faces of Nicolai Dubrovsky and

Joaquin Varga. Streak edged in close to him, looking as nonchalant as ever. There was little battle madness about Streak Garrison. He was merely an efficient killing machine.

Luke led the three into a good position, then motioned downward. He threw his plane into a steep dive and concentrated on the six dots far below. They grew larger as his dive took him closer, and he noticed with a thrill of excitement that one of them was painted jet black.

"Ritter!" he cried out and his heart beat faster. He was glad he had instructed his pilots to leave Erich Ritter alone.

The wind whistled like a banshee as the four aircraft fell upon the enemy at top speed. He hoped the other three had picked out different targets, for there was no point in all four of them shooting at the same plane. The Messerschmitts were flying steadily on, but suddenly their formation changed, and one of them swung into a position over Ritter's plane. Disappointment enveloped Luke, but he shook his head and put his sights dead center on the plane guarding Ritter. *I'll have to kill him to get to Ritter,* he thought.

He pulled the trigger and felt his plane buck as the four machine guns spat out lead. The tracers revealed his fire was slightly behind his target, so he inched the plane up, holding it firmly while his bullets struck the Messerschmitt, doing a dance from the tail to the cockpit. He saw the pilot's head explode as one or more of the slugs hit him, and the plane veered away and headed for the ground.

As he banked around in a steep curve, he saw that Streak had downed his plane and was following, and that Nicolai and Joaquin had made hits but had not downed their targets. They had both disobeyed his instructions, and Luke watched them whirl around and fly at the remaining four planes.

Having no choice, Luke motioned to Streak, and the two of them joined in the fray.

A dogfight in the air is one of the most disorganized activities on the face of the earth. No one knows what moves to make in an aerial battle. It's a hellish confusion, with planes exploding so violently they seem to shake the skies in their fury.

Luke went straight for Erich Ritter's black Messerschmitt while Ritter was pouring his lead into Varga's plane. Despite Luke's attempts to get in range to shoot at Ritter, the Black Knight had already performed his deadly work. His fire struck Varga's plane in the nose, and at once a white plume of smoke began to pour out. Varga tried to lose Ritter, but there was no losing the best pilot in the entire Condor Legion. Varga would be a dead man if he didn't get out of his plane.

Even at a distance too far for true shooting, Luke began to fire at Ritter's plane. He must have made some hits and startled Ritter, for the black plane suddenly broke off, bearing left, leaving Varga's plane headed for earth. For one instant, even as he flashed by, Luke saw that Varga was slumped over and knew that the young man was dead. A fierce anger raged in him and he stayed after Ritter, firing in short bursts. The one thing the rat could do that was superior to the Messerschmitt was turn more sharply. This had been the secret of Luke's kills. Once he got on the tail of a 109, he could not be shaken off. The only hope the enemy had was to outrun him, for the 109s were faster.

Ritter made one turn, and Luke caught a clear image of the German's face. Ritter was staring at him, and in that brief instant, the two men's eyes clashed.

And then the 109 straightened out, and with his engine fully open, he simply ran away from Luke. Desperately Luke fired all of his ammunition, but the attempt was futile as the Black Knight moved out of sight. Then he saw that the rest of the German squadron had been shot down by Nicolai and Streak, so the fighters came together and Luke led them home.

When the three landed and got out, Streak and Nicolai came right over to Luke. "That Ritter!" Nicolai shouted, his face pale with anger and his eyes filled with a killing light. "I will kill him! You will see me kill him!"

"No. *I* will kill him if it's the last thing I do," Luke Winslow said between clenched teeth.

CHAPTER THREE

A Picnic to Remember

★ ★ ★

"I'm so sorry to have to bring you this terrible news about your son."

Whenever Luke had to visit the family of one of his downed pilots, he felt utterly inept. What could one say to parents who had put their hopes in a promising son, a son who was now gone forever? As Luke stumbled over his words, he saw the pain and anguish in the eyes of Señor and Señora Varga. He wanted desperately to get away, but he forced himself to accept their teary invitation into their home. Varga had been a favorite of his, and his own heart was heavy with the loss.

"He was a favorite in the squadron," Luke said in a husky voice as he sat in an easy chair. "Always cheerful, taking extra duty, never complaining. A fine pilot and everyone's friend. It is a personal tragedy for me and for the men in our squadron."

Señora Varga leaned forward, drinking in his words as though listening to a eulogy of her son would return him to her in some way.

Señor Varga was obviously trying hard not to show his

emotion. Still, underneath the sadness in his eyes there lurked a seething hatred. His words burned as he looked upward as if to see the battle that had killed his son. "This accursed war!" he raged. "It kills the best of our young men."

"It seems the most valiant are taken while lesser men sometimes survive," Luke agreed.

"We have lost the best of our family."

"I know it's of little comfort, but he died bravely."

The man sank back into his chair and sighed. "It was kind of you to come, sir."

"I wish I had come with better news."

As the trio walked toward the door, Joaquin's mother asked Luke a question that surprised him.

"Our son was a Christian, Señor Winslow. May I assume that you are a believer as well?"

Everything went blank for Luke. He wanted to lie, but somehow the words stuck in his throat. He knew he was not a believer, yet he did not want to tell the grieving woman the truth. He hesitated, then said, "My family have been believers for many generations." There it was. The lie was out. True enough, many members of the Winslow family had been exemplary Christians, but Luke was not among this group.

He left the house quickly and drove his car to Melosa's home, but the woman's question continued to haunt him. *"May I assume that you are a believer as well?"*

Actually Luke Winslow did not know why he was not a Christian. He had been brought up by his parents, Peter and Jolie Winslow, in a Christian home. He knew his only sibling, Tim, had accepted Christ. Luke had always thought he would consider Christianity when he was older. It wasn't something a young person needed to be concerned with.

Even as he drove toward Melosa's house, he thought of his family, including his uncles, aunts, and grandparents on both sides of his family. Some of them had been ministers. Practically all of them had been followers of Jesus Christ. *What have I got in place of their faith?* he wondered. *I've missed my way and don't know how it happened.*

When he reached the Chavez house, Luke managed to put the troublesome thoughts aside. He knocked on the door harder than usual, and Isadora opened it, her face lighting up when she saw him.

"Lucio!" she cried. "Come in. Melosa says we're all going on a picnic!"

"That's right. Are you all ready?"

Victor came running in, his eyes bright. "I'm taking my baseball and glove. You will teach me how to pitch like Joe DiMaggio, yes?"

"Yes, I will. I'm not quite as good as DiMaggio, but I'll do my very best."

"Have you ever seen him play?"

"No, I haven't."

"When I go to America, I want to see him!"

"I'd like to take you to a game."

Melosa and her parents came into the room, arms loaded.

Luke greeted Melosa with a kiss on the cheek, and in a short time the entire Chavez family was crowded into the car, along with plenty of food and drink. "Where shall we go?" Luke asked. His heart was light, and for the first time in many days he was thinking about other things besides airplanes and killing.

"Let's go down by the river, Lucio," Alfredo Chavez said from his seat in the front. Melosa sat between him and Luke. "We will eat and drink and play ball and perhaps catch a big fish."

"I haven't been fishing in a long time. I might not remember how. Maybe you'll show me, Victor." Luke flashed a grin at the boy in the back seat.

"Yes. I am a great fisherman, aren't I, Papa?"

"Very good, but you had a good teacher."

"Yes, you are the best fisherman in Spain!"

"Well, *one* of the best, son."

Luke followed Señor Chavez's directions and a half hour later pulled up beside a small river. It was shaded with trees on both sides and meandered across the green fields of the countryside. "This is a beautiful place." He turned to Melosa. "Is this where all your sweethearts bring you?"

She laughed, her eyebrows arching and her lips pursing delightfully. "That is for you to find out."

"Let's eat! I'm hungry," Isadora exclaimed as she jumped out of the car.

"I think you have a tapeworm," Luke said.

"A tapeworm? What's that?"

"It's a disease people get that makes them eat all the time."

"I have no such thing!" Isadora said as she helped her mother unload the food. The group was soon seated on a blanket in the shade of a massive tree, devouring their picnic lunch.

When he'd had his fill, Luke stood up, patting his stomach. "If I keep on eating I might burst. Come on, kids. Let's go catch some fish."

Alfredo dug the tackle out of the car, and soon Isadora and Victor were fishing with Luke while Alfredo and his wife sat under a nearby tree. After a while Melosa got tired of watching and convinced Luke to take a little walk with her. He took her by the hand and they walked a short distance down the riverbank. When he put his arm around her, she whispered, "Be careful. Mama is watching."

"Well, I'm her future son-in-law. I've got my rights."

"You're not to hug me—not in public."

"Then we'll have to go off and find someplace private," he said with a wink.

She wriggled out of his grasp and hit at him playfully. "You are an awful man! A true gringo!"

"I must be if you say so."

"I want to know if you've had many sweethearts."

"Hundreds!"

"You're boasting!" she protested.

"The truth is always best."

The two sat down and continued teasing each other, enjoying the perfect day, watching the children as they fished. "You know," Luke told Melosa after a short silence, "I've promised to take the kids to America someday."

"Yes, they told me. Isadora said you would take them up into the Statue of Liberty."

"Yes, I did. I promised a lot of other things too. It'll take a lot of doing to keep all those promises."

After a while Isadora and Victor grew frustrated that they weren't catching any fish and went off exploring. Luke noted that Mr. and Mrs. Chavez were dozing. He got up and whispered, "Come on. Let's find that private place."

Melosa smiled at him and shook her head. "You are the most terrible man."

"No, I'm a wonderful man."

"You are spoiled," she said as she stood up.

"Me?"

"Yes, all Americans are spoiled."

"I suppose that's true. My mother spoiled me, and I hope my wife will spoil me even more."

Melosa's eyes flashed. "Maybe you will learn to spoil your wife. A good Spanish husband spoils his wife, you know."

The two wandered downstream, following the bends of the river. They finally stopped and sat down on the edge. Melosa took off her shoes and waded into the shallow water. "I've always liked wading in the river, ever since I was a little girl."

"A turtle may bite your toes."

"No. That's never happened to me."

"If I were a turtle, I'd bite your toes. I may anyway."

Melosa shook her head. "No biting is allowed between an engaged couple." She sat down next to Luke and said in a far more sober tone, "I still worry, Luke."

"About what?"

"About your family."

"Why are you worried about them?"

"They may not like me. My English isn't very good, and they may think I'm too different since I'm Spanish."

"You don't have to worry about them. Why, one of the most prominent Winslows, a man named Mark Winslow, became vice-president of one of the biggest railway companies in the world. He married a woman named Lola Montez. You can guess what nationality she was."

"She was Spanish?"

"Yes. A beautiful woman. I've seen her portrait. Everybody loved her, from all accounts."

"Tell me more about your family."

Luke leaned back onto his elbows. "I have to tell you that I'm probably the black sheep of the family."

"What do you mean by that?"

"Most of the other Winslows are far better people than I am."

"I don't believe that." She leaned over and put her hand on his cheek. "You're a good man."

"I'm not as good as I should be."

"I don't believe you."

She suddenly pulled his head toward her and kissed him. Her lips were soft and he detected the faint odor of her favorite perfume. He sat up and put his arm around her, holding her close, and finally, when she drew back, he whispered huskily, "I do love you, Melosa. I never thought I'd get married."

"Why not?" she asked. "Doesn't every man want to get married?"

"I've been kind of a rolling stone, wandering everywhere but never finding a place to settle down. My brother and most of my cousins know where their place is. Many of them are successful and making a mark in the world."

"You're making a mark too. You've come over to fight for liberty for a people not your own. That's a wonderful thing—you are a hero, Luke."

He grinned. "Keep bragging on me," he said. "I'll take all the compliments I can get. My self-esteem is very low at the moment. I need to be reassured that I'm a fine fellow."

She pushed him away teasingly and the two fell silent again, watching the water flow by.

"How long do you think the war will last?" she asked after a time.

"Not long, and I'm afraid we're not going to win it either. I'd really like to go back to the States when it's over."

"Shall we marry as soon as the war is over?"

"Yes, I think that would be best, and then I'll take you home with me. After we get settled, we'll send for the rest of your family."

The thought pleased Melosa. She leaned against him, and the two sat there, enjoying the quiet of the woods and the sibilant murmur of the river at their feet. For once there was no drone of war planes overhead or the sight of their contrails across the sky.

★ ★ ★

The afternoon passed much too quickly for Luke, and at the invitation of Señora Chavez, he gladly went back to their home for supper. After they had eaten, he and Melosa went outside to talk. Darkness had now enveloped the earth, and they sat shoulder to shoulder on the back stoop. He turned toward her and said to her sadly, "I've got to get back." She leaned against him, and he bent toward her and kissed her. She clung to him desperately, whispering, "I wish we were already married. I hate to think about waiting for such a long time."

"I don't want to wait either, but I really don't think it's right for me to marry while I'm on active duty."

"You're right, of course. I love you, Luke. I always will."

"I'm glad, Melosa."

"Tell me you love me!"

"You know I do."

"Yes, but a woman likes to hear a man say it."

Luke spoke the words, holding her tightly. "I've got to go," he said huskily. At that moment a shudder of fear ran through him. He thought he had left fear back in the cockpit of his plane, but here it was, and he could not understand it. He was afraid for his future. Now he had something to dream of and to hope for . . . which meant he had something to lose.

"Oh, be careful, sweetheart!" Melosa whispered desperately. She kissed him one more time, and they walked to his car. "Don't let anything happen to you," she said, her eyes fixed on him. "I would die if anything did."

"I'll be fine," he said. "Don't worry about me." He smiled at her and climbed into the car. As he pulled away he glanced back, watching her wave good-bye. He waved back, even though she could not see him in the darkness. There was no moon, and the fear that had come to him rose again. He shook his shoulders as if to rid himself of something irritating. "What's wrong with you, Winslow?" he muttered. "Don't tell me you're becoming a sissy in your old age!"

★ ★ ★

The squadron was not called out for the next two days, which was highly unusual. They were all on standby alert, however, and could not leave the airfield. Luke was getting edgy and nervous and was unable to shake off his fear.

Finally, almost in desperation, he said, "Streak, I'm going to go up and take a look around. Something's wrong."

"I'll go with you, Luke."

"No. You stay here."

"You need a backup."

"I won't be doing any fighting. If I see any 109s, I'll tuck my tail and run. I just feel that something's wrong."

"I feel that most of the time!"

"You keep your eye on things around here, Streak."

"Watch your back."

"I'll do that."

Luke climbed into the I-16 and started the engine, and fifteen minutes later was looking down on the earth. He searched for enemy formations but saw nothing unusual. It saddened him to see the beautiful countryside below him so scarred by war.

He flew until he was running low on fuel, and then at two o'clock he turned back toward the field. He had not gone far when he spotted a large formation of enemy bombers headed west. They were escorted by numerous 109s. There must have been at least thirty of them. Even if Luke had had the remains of his squadron with him, it would have been suicide to attack those formations. He suddenly realized they were not headed on a mission; they were returning from one. He carefully stayed in the clouds until they disappeared, then increasing his air speed, he headed for the airfield, planning the battle that was coming.

Just before they disappeared he caught a glimmer of black. "That's Ritter's plane," he said bitterly. "One day it'll be just me and him, one on one."

He arrived back at the field and taxied up to the hangars. As he jumped to the ground, he saw Streak running toward him. "I didn't see anything up there except a big formation of bombers," Luke told his friend. "They've been on a raid, I think."

"Luke . . ." Streak said nervously, then suddenly broke off.

"What is it?" Luke knew that Streak Garrison was a hard man to unsettle, but something had done the job. "Tell me, what is it? What's happened?"

"It's not good news, Luke."

The fear that had been troubling Luke for several days now became more powerful. A horrible possibility occurred to him, one he didn't even want to contemplate. "What happened?" he finally had to ask.

"Those bombers you saw bombed the town where the Chavezes live."

"But there's no military target there."

"I know that. There wasn't one in Guernica either, but they bombed it anyway. I haven't gone over there myself, but people are saying it's bad."

Luke tore away from Streak and broke into a run. Still in

his flying gear, he jumped into his car and drove like a maniac toward the Chavez home.

They're all right. They have to be all right. He forced the thought into his mind, but it seemed to flutter and ignore his will. He had been afraid in action before, but this was a different kind of fear, one he could not control.

When he was halfway there, he saw smoke rising and he gasped. He had not seen Guernica after it was bombed, but he knew that sixteen hundred civilians had been killed or wounded in the senseless raid.

As soon as he came in sight of the town, his worst fears were realized. People were carefully moving through piles of burning debris, searching, he assumed, for survivors. Houses, buildings, and shops were scattered around as if a giant's hand had swept across them. He could drive no farther because the road was blocked by debris. He shut the engine off and jumped out and ran, dodging timber and brick. The sound of women wailing and men cursing filled the air. He passed a man who was sitting on the street, holding a small child in his lap. Tears were running down his face, and he was crying, "My baby—my little Ricardo!"

When Luke got within sight of the Chavez home, he froze. The house was almost completely flattened. All the walls but one had collapsed, and smoke was still rising from the fire that had consumed the house. The one remaining wall stood blackened, held in place by a few skeleton timbers burned almost in two.

Like a madman Luke Winslow began throwing broken bricks and beams aside as he struggled to find his fiancée. His hands were soon bloodied, but he paid them no heed as he desperately called her name. "Melosa—Melosa!"

★ ★ ★

Before long a small man appeared at Luke's side and silently helped him search. By the time the sun had set, they had recovered the bodies of the entire Chavez family. Luke had laid the bodies side by side as he found them and covered them with blankets the stranger had brought with him. Luke knew as long as he lived he would never forget the nightmare ending for these people he had come to love as a family.

"I'm so sorry, señor."

Luke turned toward the man who had helped him dig. He could not answer the man but could only stare dully in his direction.

"I know you cared about this family. They were such fine, fine people." The man looked at the family that was now stretched out under blankets—three larger forms and two smaller ones. "I heard that you were engaged to the young woman, Melosa. My wife mentioned just last week that Melosa told her that she loved you very much."

Luke could take no more. He turned away blindly, and the darkness closed in on him. It was not just the lack of sunlight that enveloped him but a darkness that reached his spirit.

The war had suddenly become a personal tragedy, and as Luke stumbled away from the forms hidden under the blankets, he knew for the first time what real hatred was.

CHAPTER FOUR

LUKE'S REVENGE

★ ★ ★

Colonel José Valdez left his desk and stood at the window, peering out as the young pilot in his office spoke haltingly. As he listened, he was watching a flock of sparrows scuffle in the dirt, fighting over crumbs. *Even birds don't agree,* Colonel Valdez was thinking sadly. *How can we humans expect to do any better?* The thought troubled him, and pulling his shoulders back, he turned to face Roscoe Garrison. He knew the men called him Streak, despite the fact that there was nothing really fast about Garrison—except when he was flying. The big man was clumsy and seemed to have little coordination, but once he got in the cockpit of a fighter plane, that did not seem to matter. Valdez listened more intently now as Garrison stammered out his thoughts.

"Luke is just not the same man he used to be," Garrison was saying. "I'm sure you heard that his fiancée died about three weeks ago, and he seems to be taking it awfully hard. I want to help him, but I just don't know how."

"I heard it wasn't just his fiancée who died but her entire family."

"That's right, Colonel. He was real close to that family. He loved the young woman. He told me it was the first time he'd ever been in love."

"Tell me what seems to be the problem now, Garrison."

"Well, Luke's always been a careful man. Back when we played football together in college, I was always in favor of just busting into the other team, but guys like Luke were smarter. They analyzed the situation, came up with more creative maneuvers. And that's the way Luke was with his flying—at least that's the way he used to be. But all that's different now, and I don't like it."

"What sort of change are you talking about?"

"He seems to have lost his caution is the best way I can put it." Streak shrugged his beefy shoulders and chewed on his lower lip, his face troubled. "When he sees Germans, he just goes right at them with no hesitation, all guns blazing. He doesn't think and plan like he used to—he doesn't even give the signal for the rest of us to follow."

"That's not what I've heard about Winslow. He's always been a careful pilot."

"That's not true anymore, sir. I'm telling you he's changed. He used to spend a lot of time studying situations, figuring out how to keep his men alive and himself too, of course. But now it's like he . . ." Streak halted and ran his hand through the stubble of his red hair. "It's like he just doesn't care about anything anymore."

The colonel slapped both of his hands down on his desk. "He needs to go on leave."

"He sure does, Colonel."

"I'll see to it."

"Good! It's not safe for him to be flying anymore—not until he gets a handle on this thing."

Colonel Valdez stood. "We'll miss his leadership, no question about that."

"He can't lead if he's dead, sir."

"You think it's that critical?"

"Yes, sir, he's crazier than that Russian Dubrovsky—which I never thought I'd hear myself say. He doesn't care about anything at all. He's going to get himself killed, and that's no lie."

"All right, then. Thank you for coming to me, Garrison."

* * *

As soon as Luke Winslow walked into Valdez's office, Valdez saw the changes in the man. Valdez had always liked the tall, rangy American, which was unusual for the colonel, who as a rule did not like Americans. But Valdez had seen in this man an attention to duty. It was obvious Winslow hadn't come to Spain merely for adventure, but because he truly believed in the Republican cause.

Winslow had lost a little weight, Valdez thought, but all of them had during these hard days of fighting. There was something different about his mouth and eyes. His mouth seemed tighter, and there was a slight tick in his right eye, revealing a nervousness that had never been a part of Winslow's makeup. Valdez leaned back and motioned to the chair in front of his desk. "Have a seat, Lieutenant."

"I'd just as soon stand, if you don't mind, Colonel. I get enough sitting in the cockpit."

"As you will." Valdez tried to think of the best way to approach the matter. He did not know what to say about the death of the man's fiancée or her family, so he made no attempt. "I'd like you to go on leave, Winslow, starting today."

"There's no need for that, Colonel. Besides, I wouldn't have anywhere to go."

In his other encounters with the man, Luke Winslow had always had a smile on his face, but he was not smiling now. His face was like stone . . . or steel. Luke apparently hadn't understood that the statement was not merely a suggestion.

"Look, Winslow, there's no point mincing words. Your men tell me you're acting crazy up there. You're not yourself. I want you to take a few days off. Or better yet, go home. This war is lost anyway. We both know it."

"Maybe not."

"Don't be foolish! It's clear that we can't hold out much longer."

"If you say so, sir."

"So take a few days off."

"I'm not finished here yet, sir. I'd like to stay until the end and do what I came for."

"That doesn't make any sense. Everything's falling to pieces. Franco has won. Our armies are in full retreat, except there's no place to retreat to." Valdez's tone was bitter.

"Are you leaving, sir?"

"This is my country. I will stay here with my people and do what I can."

"Franco won't treat you gently. You know that."

"That's my problem. Look, Lieutenant," Valdez said, urgently feeling a need to salvage something of the laughing man who had come from the States, "you've got a life back home. Get back to it. You're a young man with your entire future ahead of you. You need to do something with your life. This war is a lost cause."

"I don't have anything," Luke said flatly.

Colonel Valdez could not meet the man's eyes. "I know it's hard that you've lost the woman you love, but life must go on."

"Must it? I wonder why."

"That's no way to talk!"

"It's the way I feel, sir."

Valdez threw his arms apart in a gesture of futility. His voice grew louder as he said, "I could order you to go home."

"Please don't do that, Colonel. I want to stay with this conflict until the end."

"Stay for what?"

"I made a little promise to myself. I'm going to knock Erich Ritter out of the sky."

"That's foolish!"

"I suppose it is."

"And it's dangerous."

"Yes, I'd say so."

"He's the best pilot in the Condor Legion, Winslow! He's a cold-blooded killer."

"I think I can beat him."

"That's not possible! We have so few planes. If you did meet him, you'd be overwhelmed."

"All I need is one clean shot at him, and I intend to get it. I'm not leaving until I do."

Why, he's insane, Valdez thought. *He's suicidal.* But he knew there was nothing he could say to change the man's mind. Sighing heavily, Valdez slumped into his chair and shook his head. "You're a fool, Winslow. Do you know that?"

"You're probably right, Colonel."

"Can I say anything to change your mind?"

"No, sir."

"I give up, then."

"May I go?"

"Yes. Get out of here. But don't forget—if you change your mind, I'll help you get out of the country."

Winslow did not even answer. He turned and shut the door quietly behind him. Colonel Valdez stared at the door, then yanked a drawer open and pulled out a bottle. Pulling the cork out, he did not even bother to pour the liquor into a glass but put the bottle to his lips and drank three big gulps. It hit him like a hammer. He shuddered, then shook his head. "What a waste! What an awful waste!"

★ ★ ★

The war ran down slowly at first and then quicker every day. From their overflight, Luke and his men could see the Republican army scattering with the triumphant army of Franco pursuing them. The Germans sent out such enormous flights of fighters and bombers that there was no hope whatsoever of three pilots attacking. They simply watched and waited to catch stragglers, which did not occur for over a week.

Finally one afternoon Luke went over to Streak, who was working on his plane alongside two mechanics. "That fly is a wreck," he said.

"Pretty much." Streak nodded sadly. "But it's all I've got, so it's gotta fly."

"You think they'll ever get it put back together, Streak?"

"They claim they can. What's up, Luke? You look like you've got something on your mind."

"I'm going to take another look around."

"Wait until tomorrow. This heap will be flying by then."

"No. I'm going now. Where's the mad Russian?"

"Drunk. He can't fly. He can't even walk." Streak's eyes narrowed. "You're not going by yourself, are you?"

"Yes, I am. I'm tired of hanging around here."

Streak argued, but Luke would not listen. The bulky pilot followed Luke all the way to his plane and laid his hand on his arm. "Don't do it, Luke. There's no point in it."

"It's something I have to do, Streak."

"Look. Colonel Valdez told me that the war's over. He said he'd help you and me get away."

"Yes. He told me that too."

"Well, let's do it."

"It's not over yet. Somebody said a thing ain't over until the fat lady sings."

"That fat lady's already sung!" Streak exclaimed. "Franco has won. We've lost. Get that in your head! Let's get out of here and get back home."

"I'll think about it. You may be right. But I sure would like to get one shot at Ritter."

"Stay away from him."

"I can't promise that."

"You'd better!"

Luke pulled his arm away, climbed into the plane, and five minutes later was pulling up into a steep climb. Wind whistled past and the sky was an ominous gray. The little fly

Check Out Receipt

Whitchurch-Stouffville Public Library
905-642-7323
www.wsplibrary.ca

Thursday, October 18, 2018 6:04:23 PM

Item: WS527234
Title: The Icecutter's Daughter
Call no.: FIC Peter
Due: 08/11/2018

Item: WS531684
Title: The quarryman's bride
Call no.: FIC Peter
Due: 08/11/2018

Item: WS135383
Title: The white knight
Call no.: FIC Morri
Due: 08/11/2018

Total items: 3

You just saved $57.97 by using your library. You have saved $2,575.52 this past year and $3,048.75 since you began using the library!

trembled as Luke pushed the throttle forward to the ultimate. He gained maximum altitude and then began patrolling. There was not much point looking down at the earth. Franco's armies were victorious there, so he searched the sky for planes. For over an hour he saw nothing, and then as he banked, a tiny movement caught his eye. He had the sun at his back, so he knew they could not see him, and he descended slowly to get a better look. He practically jumped in his seat when he could finally distinguish that there were three planes directly below, and the one on the left was jet black! As far as he knew there was only one black plane in the Condor Legion, and that was Erich Ritter's.

"I got him!" Luke whispered.

He would get only one chance at Ritter. The 109s could easily outrun him, as Ritter had already shown, so Luke knew he had to get him on the first pass. Ignoring the other two planes, he pushed the stick forward and put the black airplane in his sights. The plane screamed, dropping at full speed in a sharp dive. Luke knew he had to get as close as possible—if the bullets didn't knock Ritter out of the sky, he would ram him. It was a thought that would never have occurred to him earlier, but in his present state of mind, it seemed perfectly logical.

I don't care if it kills me! He had barely slept since finding the bodies of the Chavez family. His despair had turned to a deep seething hatred—all of which was now aimed at Erich Ritter.

The black 109 became large in his sights, and he was confident that none of the German pilots had spotted him. He was coming from their rear and out of the sun.

When Ritter's plane seemed to fill the windshield, he pushed the button, and the I-16 began to tremble and shake as if caught in a wind. Even with the shaking, at this distance it was almost impossible to miss. He raked the plane from tail to nose cone. He saw the bullets striking and tearing fabric, and he hoped he had nailed the pilot. When he saw the engine begin to pour out white smoke, he knew he had hit the plane hard. He turned sharply, missing by only a few feet, and then pulled away. He knew the other two 109s would be all over him immediately, but he just didn't care.

He did a loop and saw at once that the canopy had opened on Ritter's plane. The plane flipped over on its back and the pilot dropped out. He watched as the man fell and the parachute opened.

Luke had heard of pilots shooting men down who were parachuting, and he had never thought he would be tempted. But everything was different now. He flipped his plane over and dived straight toward the figure floating down. He slowed his plane, ignoring the approaching enemy planes. He got a good look at the man falling under the white canopy. It was Erich Ritter, all right. Ritter was facing him, and in the brief moment that Luke closed in on him, he saw no fear on Ritter's face. The hatred Luke felt was oddly mingled with a sense of admiration for the man's courage. Ritter knew he was dead, but he still seemed to have no fear. The German actually smiled at him!

Luke's finger was on the trigger, an inch away from sending the slugs into the man's helpless body. But somehow the smile changed that. At the last possible moment, Luke flipped his plane over and missed Ritter's body by no more than a few feet. He pulled up out of a dive, filled with anger. "Why did I do that!" He knew he would regret his actions. He would have had no qualms about killing Ritter in a dogfight, but somehow the thought of killing a helpless man caused something in him to rebel.

Suddenly the windshield shattered in front of Luke's eyes, and he felt his plane jerk as bullets struck it. He took one wild look over his shoulder and saw the two 109s coming after him.

I gotta get out of here!

He twisted the mosca into a tight turn, but even as he did so, he felt the controls loosen and knew that something vital had been hit.

There was no way to outrun the two, for they were faster

than the mosca and obviously quite determined, so he would have to outmaneuver them.

Luke put his plane into a screaming dive straight toward the earth. He spotted a plowed field below, and he did not even bother to lower his landing gear as he headed for it. The 109s followed until it got too dangerous to continue. Luke pulled up at the last possible moment to avoid crashing into the earth. His plane struck with a ripping, tearing sound. He braced his hands against the instrument panel as the plane skidded across the earth and hit a fence that tore the cowling off. Then his right wing crashed into an ancient shed and sent the plane into a wild careen. The sound of metal bending and crunching filled Luke's ears.

It'll be a miracle if I come out of this alive!

Even as the plane screeched and tumbled, Luke could not help thinking, *I could have killed him, but I let him go.*

Finally the plane came to a stop, and Luke hung there upside down, held by his safety belt. He shoved the canopy back, released the catch, and fell to the ground flat on his back. He lay motionless, the wind knocked out of him, then slowly got to his feet as he got his breath back.

He smelled fire and then noticed that a flame was coming out of the engine, and he ran. When he was barely twenty yards away, an explosion knocked him flat. The plane had burst into a ball of fire, and Luke lay there covering his head. After he realized he was okay, he rolled over onto his elbow so he could see what was going on. Flames danced across what remained of the aircraft, and finally they seemed to be dying down.

Getting to his feet, he staggered away from the wreckage and started in the direction he thought the airfield might be.

He studied the sky and saw no sign of Erich Ritter or his parachute. The 109s were still circling over the wreck of his own plane. He felt strange and disoriented by what had happened and wondered how in the world he would find his way back to his base.

He had not walked more than five minutes when suddenly two vehicles filled with soldiers appeared over the crest of a hill. They pulled up on either side of him, and the soldiers boiled out, laughing gleefully and keeping their rifles trained on him.

"Put your hands in the air!"

A lieutenant got out and was pointing a pistol at Luke. "You are a prisoner of Generalissimo Franco," he said in Spanish. "Do not try to get away or you will be killed. And that would give me great pleasure!"

Since there was nowhere to run to, Luke simply stood there while two of the soldiers came closer and began prodding him with their guns. They forced him to get into one of the trucks. As he climbed in he turned around, and one of them struck him in the forehead with the butt of his rifle. His world was filled with glittering stars of the most brilliant colors Luke had ever seen, but they soon faded to a soft, dull blackness.

CHAPTER FIVE

The Prisoner's Fate

★ ★ ★

Luke was jerked out of a semiconscious state by rough hands and a voice shouting, "Get up, gringo!"

He managed to open one eye, but the other was swollen shut. He reached up and felt dried blood caked over his left eye. He winced, and the pain was sharp enough to pull him up straight. Someone shoved him off the back of the truck, and he fell sprawling and once again felt a kick in his side that took his breath.

"Get up!"

The soldiers were grinning as they stood around him, and the lieutenant once again had a pistol pointed at him. At the man's gesture, Luke slowly got up.

"So, you are a norteamericano."

"Yes."

"You came over to interfere in my country's fight for freedom. You will be shot."

"I'm a prisoner of war."

"You are a filthy spy!"

"No, I'm not a spy."

"Shut your mouth!"

Luke did as he was told, which seemed to anger the lieutenant even more. He slapped Luke in the face and then again with the back of his hand, and the pain bore through Luke's head.

"You will have a fair trial," the man said with a wolfish grin, "and then you will be shot. Lock him up. And you do not have to treat him with gentleness."

The soldiers all laughed, and two of them dragged him toward a shed. One of them yanked open the door and shoved Luke inside. He sprawled full-length, and the stench of the place almost gagged him. It had obviously been used as a pen for animals, and the odor was overpowering.

The lieutenant followed the other soldier inside. "Light the lamp so he can see his home until we shoot him."

A blue spurt, a lighted match, and then the lantern was lit and hung on a nail. The faint yellow beams revealed the squalid interior. There was no furniture, only remnants of straw along the walls and dried mud on the floor.

"Enjoy yourself, Yankee."

"I'll do my best."

"Don't worry about the accommodations. You will not be here long." The lieutenant laughed again and kicked Luke in the thigh. "Come. Let him think about standing in front of a firing squad. The gringos are all godless. We'll send him straight to the pit—where all filthy traitors go!"

"Lieutenant Garcia, let me have a few minutes with him." The guard, a burly man with a cruel, wolfish face, obviously wanted to have a go at the prisoner.

"No. That's enough for now." He grinned. "But maybe we'll come back later and have some fun."

The lieutenant waved the guards out, and Luke heard the door close. His ribs ached and his head was killing him. There was nothing to sit on except the filthy floor, so he simply pulled himself over to the wall and sat up, leaning against it. Closing his eyes, he knew a moment of despair. *Well, at least it'll be quick,* he thought. *It doesn't take long for a firing squad to do its work.*

★ ★ ★

General Wolfram von Richthofen was listening as Erich Ritter told about his harrowing afternoon. Ritter had landed safely and been picked up by a patrol. He had immediately reported to the commanding officer of the Condor Legion. The general was a full-faced man, heavy in body and feature, his cleverness revealed by intelligent eyes. Some had suggested he had achieved his rank because he was related to Manfred von Richthofen, the Red Baron of the Great War, but this was not true. He was intelligent and had learned his trade well. He was now studying Erich Ritter carefully, his eyes hooded.

"I'm surprised that he managed to get you, Major. You don't usually have much trouble with the enemy. How did he get the best of you?"

"He came from behind and above me—out of the sun. I didn't know there was a plane within a hundred kilometers until the bullets started hitting. It was too late then."

"It's a wonder he didn't kill you immediately."

Erich Ritter shrugged. He was a handsome man, no more than five ten but with a strong, lithe figure. He could have served as a poster boy for Adolf Hitler's ideal of a true Aryan. He had startling blue eyes, and his blond hair lay in a slight wave off his forehead. "I suppose it was a miracle. But you haven't heard the rest of the story."

"What happened?"

"I was lucky enough to get out of the plane and my parachute opened. That's always a miracle to me." Ritter smiled slightly. "But as soon as it opened, I looked up and there he came. I was as helpless as a man can be."

"That must have given you quite a shock."

"I was a dead man, General. Winslow was coming straight at me. Of course, my men were getting after him as quick as they could, but there was no time. I hung there and knew that I was dead. I was certain it was all over for me."

General von Richthofen smiled. "Did your whole life flash before your eyes, Erich?"

"As it happens in books?"

"Yes."

"You know, it really did. I thought about when I was a boy shooting my first stag in the Black Forest. I thought about growing up, about things I did when I was just a young boy, you know?"

"You didn't have that much time."

"No, I didn't, General. And I could see him. The muzzles of those guns . . . They looked as big as eighty-eights!"

"I've often wondered what I would do if I knew I was going to die in the next few seconds."

"There's nothing to do," Ritter said simply. "I gave it up and then I think I even smiled to think it would end like this. I always thought I'd die in a dogfight, and here I was as helpless as a rag doll. Not at all what I had expected."

"How did he miss you?"

"He didn't miss me."

"What's that?"

"No, sir, *that's* the miracle. Winslow didn't even fire. He turned the plane over and missed me by a few feet. I just hung there, shocked to be alive."

"Why did he do that?"

"I have no idea, General. No idea whatsoever."

"What happened then?"

"The two pilots with me shot him down. I assume he had a crash landing, but of course, I didn't see it. I landed in the branches of a tree and got hung up. I had to cut myself down, but I was pleased to find that I didn't have a scratch."

The pilot sat back in his chair. "Too bad about Winslow. He was a brave man. I would like to meet him."

A slight smile played around the lips of the general. "I think that can be arranged."

Ritter looked at his commanding officer. "What does that mean, sir?"

"It means we captured him after he crashed. He's in pretty

good shape considering what he went through. Lieutenant Garcia is holding him now."

Erich Ritter's eyes were wide. "I can't believe it, but I would like to meet him."

"Go on over. I'd like to meet him myself, but I don't have time right now."

"I'll go at once if you don't mind, General." Erich Ritter saluted and left the general's headquarters at a quick pace. He called for a driver, got into the vehicle, and said, "I want to talk to Lieutenant Garcia's prisoner. Do you know where he's holding him?"

"Yes, sir, I do."

"Take me there at once."

"Yes, sir."

The driver took the words *at once* seriously and Ritter had to hold on, but he did not mind the rough passage. The driver drove like a madman, perhaps to impress the famous Erich Ritter, the Black Knight, as he was called by many. He pulled the truck up and slammed his foot onto the brake, throwing Ritter forward.

"Shall I wait for you, Lieutenant?" the driver asked.

"Yes."

Ritter got out and was met almost at once by Lieutenant Garcia. Garcia saluted smartly, and Ritter returned it.

"It's good to see you, Major. I suppose you've come to see the prisoner."

"Yes."

"I hoped you might come."

"Where is he?"

"We have him locked up safely. He won't be getting away." Garcia was curious. "The rumor is that he shot you down before he himself crashed, but I suppose that's a lie."

"No. It's the truth."

Garcia was shocked. "I can't believe an American could shoot you down, sir."

"You can believe it, Lieutenant Garcia. Now let me see the prisoner, if you will."

"Yes, sir. Right this way."

Ritter followed the lieutenant, aware that soldiers were watching him and talking behind their hands. He turned to Garcia, asking, "Has he given you any trouble?"

"No, no. We gave *him* trouble, Major." Garcia laughed. "I wouldn't mind being in the firing squad myself when he's shot."

"Why would he be shot?"

"Because he's a traitor, of course."

"He's not a traitor. He's a prisoner of war."

"But, sir—"

Ritter cut off the lieutenant's words quickly. "Just take me to him, Garcia."

Ritter followed the lieutenant to what appeared to be a cow shed. He stopped and stared at it. "He's not in there, is he?"

"Oh yes. He's there, all right. He can't get away."

When the man shoved the door open, Ritter stepped inside, and the feeble light of the single lantern was so dim he could not see for a moment. The stench was terrible, and he looked around, narrowing his eyes. He found a figure sitting against the wall, but he could not make out the man's features. "Lieutenant Garcia!" he barked.

"Yes, sir?"

"Why is the prisoner in this place?"

"So that he won't escape, sir."

"Turn that lamp up!" he commanded.

"Yes, sir." Garcia turned the lamp up, and as the light increased, Ritter gasped. The man's face was half covered with blood and he had a terrible wound over his left eyebrow. He was filthy and did not move, though he watched Ritter with his good eye.

Ritter stepped forward and bent over. "I am Major Erich Ritter. You are Lieutenant Winslow, I assume?"

The answer was feeble, but the one eye that was open looked back defiantly. "I am."

"You are the pilot who shot me down?"

"Yes."

Ritter stared at the face. He could not see much about it for the dirt and the blood. "Can you stand up?"

"I think so."

Erich watched as the prisoner got to his feet. "Come with me."

Erich stepped aside and watched as the prisoner, carefully holding his side, stumbled out. He followed him and turned to Garcia and said shortly, "I'm taking your prisoner, Lieutenant."

"But, sir—"

"I will have something to say about your actions. We do not treat prisoners of war like this. I hope you've enjoyed your rank. You're not likely to have it long."

The two approached the vehicle, and Ritter asked Winslow if he could get in.

"Yes, Major. I think I can."

Erich watched as the prisoner very carefully got into the vehicle. Ritter climbed in and said to the driver, "Back to headquarters, Private."

"Yes, Major."

Luke did not say a word. He felt sore and weak, but pride kept him sitting upright. He did not turn to look at Major Ritter.

Ritter did not say anything either, but he carefully studied the other pilot. He knew little about the man except that he was an American and had a reputation for being an exceptional fighter pilot, but he intended to find out more.

They reached the base and Ritter ordered the driver, "Over there at those quarters."

"You mean the officers' quarters?"

"That's right."

The driver pulled the vehicle over in front of a line of low buildings. Ritter got out and said, "Get out, Lieutenant."

Luke got out carefully and stood there breathing hard. It was all he could do.

"Come this way."

Ritter led the way into the building and called to a sergeant. "Sergeant Mueller, which one of these rooms is empty?"

"The one on the end, sir. Lieutenant Schiller has been transferred."

"I am putting this man in your charge, Sergeant Mueller. I want you to see to it that he's cleaned up. Then give him something fit to wear, some clean clothing, and then come report to me."

"Yes, sir!"

"He's a prisoner of war. He will be treated as such. Keep two guards at his door."

"Yes, Major Ritter."

"Lieutenant," Ritter said to Winslow, "I will speak with you after you've had a chance to clean yourself up."

"Yes, Major."

Ritter left the officers' quarters and went to the office of Dr. Karl Bittern, the physician of the Condor Legion.

Dr. Bittern rose when he saw Ritter in his doorway. "Well, I heard the news," the doctor said. "I thought we had lost you."

"You almost did, Doctor."

"I heard you were shot down."

"I was indeed."

"A first time for you."

"There's always a first time."

"Are you all right?"

"I'm fine, but I have a prisoner I want you to see. He's been treated rather badly."

"A pilot?"

"Yes. An American. He's been injured. I want you to give him the very best treatment."

"Why are you so interested in an enemy flier?"

"He had me under his gun, Doctor. He could have killed me, but he let me go, so I'm in his debt," Ritter explained. "You understand me? I want him to have good treatment."

Usually Ritter's expression was pleasant enough, but at

times he could look very dangerous—as he did now. Dr. Bittern cleared his throat. "Why, of course, Major. I'll give him the very best care."

"Thank you, Doctor."

Ritter left the doctor's office and went to the cookshack. The cook was a small, round man named Adolph Keller who obviously enjoyed sampling his own wares.

"Sergeant Keller, we have a prisoner. I want you to fix up a nourishing meal for him. Something tasty. Your very best."

"For a prisoner?"

"Exactly."

"Yes, sir. Where is he?"

"He's in the officers' quarters. I would appreciate it if you would take very good care of him."

"I will give him a feast indeed, Major."

★ ★ ★

The two guards who had been assigned to watch Luke Winslow's door were opposites. One was tall and lanky with a sullen-looking face, the other short and rotund with a silly grin. The tall one complained bitterly, saying, "I'll rot before I treat this American like we're told. Just give me a chance and I'll beat him to a pulp."

The shorter man laughed. "That's right. You've had a full life, I guess. Just you tell Major Ritter that you don't like the way he's doing things."

"I don't know what's wrong with the major, but I'm—"

"Shut up. Here he comes!"

The two men straightened to attention and saluted as Ritter came to stand before them. "Open the door," he ordered. He stepped inside without another word.

"Lieutenant Winslow, you're looking somewhat better."

Indeed, Winslow did look better. He'd had a bath and been given a set of German fatigues. He had a bulky bandage over his left eyebrow and he stood with more ease.

"I have to thank you, Major, for the bath and clothes—and the doctor."

"I'm sorry you were treated so badly. It was not my doing, of course."

"Yes, I understand that."

Ritter suddenly felt at a loss for words. He studied the American's face and liked what he saw. *He's the kind of man I'd like to have in my squadron,* he thought. But he said, "Please sit down, Lieutenant. I have a question."

Luke sat down. "As you well know, Major, I'm only required to give my name, rank, and serial number, which I've already done."

"It's not about things like that. This is a personal question." Ritter sat down and the two men faced each other across a wooden table. "I want to know why you didn't shoot me when you had me in your sights."

"I don't know."

Ritter grinned. "Well, that's an honest answer, I suppose. I was a dead man. All you had to do was pull the trigger. How many of our planes have you shot down since you've been in this war?"

"I've lost track."

"Some of the men you shot down no doubt died. I would be just one more."

"The others weren't helpless men in a parachute."

At a loss for words, Ritter rocked on the back legs of the chair. "I just don't understand why you're here."

"That makes us even, Major. I don't understand why you're here either."

"I'm doing my duty to the fatherland. My family is military. I was called to the service and I obeyed. But you had no call to come. Your army was not called here."

"No. We weren't."

"Then why are you here?"

"You won't like my answer, Major Ritter."

"Let me be the judge of that."

"I think Hitler is the most dangerous man on the face of

the earth. I think he must be stopped, and this seemed to be the place to do my bit to stop it."

Ritter cleared his throat. "You Americans do not understand Germany. We must have our place in the sun. *Lebensraum,* we call it."

"Living space. I understand that. The trouble is you move in on other nations, slaughter them, and then take their land from them."

"We cannot argue politics. We will never agree."

"Tell me this, then. There was a little village not far from here. There were no military targets there—no soldiers, no factories—nothing military. Just innocent civilians. You bombed it out of existence. Was that part of your duty to the fatherland?"

"It was unfortunate," he said, looking down at his hands. When Ritter had learned about the huge number of civilian deaths in the town, he had felt horrible. That had not been their intent when they had set out that day.

"The woman I was going to marry lived in that village. So did her parents, her ten-year-old sister, and her eight-year-old brother. They're all dead now, Ritter—all of them. Were they the enemy of the German Reich?"

Ritter felt his face growing warm. "I cannot answer your question except to say that in a war innocent people sometimes get killed. You know that, Lieutenant."

"They do when they're caught in a battle, but that little village wasn't in a battle. They were just going about their daily lives when all of a sudden the Condor Legion flew over, dropped bombs, and obliterated them."

When Ritter did not answer, Luke leaned forward onto the table, his eyes harsh. "Are women and children your enemies, Major?"

"War is not kind."

And then in a voice of steel, Luke said, "Neither am I, Major Ritter. If I ever get you in my sights again, I will treat you exactly as your Condor Legion treated those I loved."

Ritter got to his feet. "As I say, we cannot discuss politics.

The war is almost over. You will be treated well while you are our prisoner." He paused and sought for words. He wanted to say "Thank you for sparing my life," but the sharp planes of Winslow's face, the tightness of his mouth, the bitterness in his eyes made him understand that such a comment would not be taken well. "I will see to it that you have what you need."

The major walked out of the room and found that his hands were not entirely steady. Something about the American disturbed him greatly, and he nodded to the two soldiers and walked out of the building. The tall one grunted, "We ought to shoot the prisoner, I say."

"No need of that. The war's over."

CHAPTER SIX

AN UNEXPECTED TRIP

★ ★ ★

Luke was sitting on his bunk reading a book when the door opened. Major Erich Ritter entered and at once Luke put the book down and stood up. "Thanks for the book," Luke said. "I'm enjoying it very much."

Ritter shrugged. "I didn't know whether you would like it or not. It's the only book in English I could find."

"It's always been a favorite of mine—*Great Expectations*, a fine novel by Dickens."

"I have not read many novels," Ritter said, sitting down on one of the chairs and putting the newspaper he'd been carrying on the table. "What is it about?"

Luke sat down as well. "It's about a young boy who makes a mistake about a woman and spends his life trying to live with it."

Ritter smiled. "A common story."

"Yes."

"You like books of fiction?"

"Sometimes they're better than real life. Much easier than reality, I think."

"I prefer reality."

"I thought you might."

"Because I'm German?"

"Not at all."

"Why, then?"

"You just don't seem to be a romantic. You seem like a man who wants only what he can touch."

"I think that is right."

"I, on the other hand, am a romantic."

"Any man who fights in a war not his own is a romantic, I suppose." Ritter picked up the newspaper. "I brought a paper for you. Look at the headline."

Luke took the paper. *Republican Army Surrenders.* He looked up and said, "The war is finally over."

"Indeed it is. We're all leaving by early next week."

"Going back to Germany?"

"Of course."

Luke handed the paper back but Ritter said, "Keep it. You may want to study it."

"I don't read Spanish all that well."

Ritter shifted his weight. "I've come to say good-bye and . . . and something else." The German seemed ill at ease and had trouble finding the words he was searching for. "Thank you for sparing my life."

Luke's eyes locked with those of Ritter. "I still don't know why I did it," he said.

"For whatever reason, I'm grateful. But here's what I've come to say. You're free to go home now."

"You mean right now?"

"Anytime you choose. You can go back to your unit, or if you prefer, I can get you a berth on a ship. There's one leaving tomorrow for America."

"I have a friend I need to take with me if he's still alive."

"That will be acceptable."

"Are you sure about this?"

"Of course!"

"I was about to be shot, and now I'm free to go."

"If you wish, you can go find your friend and return here

for the night. Tomorrow I will personally see to it that you both get to the ship."

"I don't want any favors from you, Major."

"Don't be foolish, Winslow. It's all over."

"No. It's over in Spain, but the conflict is not over. Hitler will never be happy until he's conquered all of Europe. Actually, I don't think even that would make him happy."

"You're mistaken. The führer has promised that we will take no more action against our neighbors. There will be no more wars like this one."

"Do you believe that?"

"Of course I believe it."

"Then you're a fool."

Ritter flushed. "I suppose it's only natural you should think so. Come. I have a vehicle waiting. The driver will take you to find your friend, then bring you back here."

"All right."

"I hope things go well with you."

"And I suppose I need to at least thank you for this."

Ritter shrugged. "You are an honorable man, Lieutenant. We're both soldiers. We have both seen hard battle, but at least at this time we can call a truce. Come. The driver's waiting."

★ ★ ★

Streak shook his head. "I don't know how you did it. It's a miracle! You fall in a sewer and come up smelling like a rose, Luke."

"I don't understand it myself."

The two men were gathering their few belongings in Luke's room in the officers' quarters. Luke had been relieved when he had found his friend alive and well the day before, and the man had readily agreed to Luke's plan. They had spent the night in the officers' quarters, knowing the cook would feed them well. Ritter would be there momentarily to take them to the coast, about an hour's drive away.

"Ritter's a strange man," Luke said. "He's a cold-blooded killer when he's in an airplane, but he's treated me decently. More than decently, really."

"Still, he's part of the Condor Legion," Streak said as the two men made their way outside. "You know what terrible things they've done."

"I know and I told him if I ever come across him in the air again, I'll kill him. Of course, he feels the same way about me."

The two men looked up as the car rounded the corner with Ritter in the front seat beside the driver.

"This is it, old friend," Luke told Streak. "It's almost time to say good-bye to these Germans for good."

* * *

Ritter stood in front of the ship, looking up at it. "It may be a slow journey, but you'll get back to the States eventually."

"I hope so, Major."

"What will you do when you get back?"

"I have no idea."

Ritter put out his hand. "I know you don't like it, Winslow, but I will never forget how you spared my life. I believe God is in these things."

After a moment's hesitation, Luke put his hand out. The German's hand was hard, strong, and firm. "You believe in God, then."

"Why, of course! Don't you?"

"My people do." He gripped the hand of the German hard and nodded. "I'll try to think of you charitably, Erich." The major's first name was out of his mouth before he even gave it a thought.

"And I will always think of you charitably, Luke."

Ritter got back in the car, and Luke watched him go.

"Well, I'll say this for him," Streak said as he approached from a short distance away. "He went beyond the call of duty by arranging for our transportation home. He's not the kind of man I thought he'd be."

"I can't help thinking sooner or later I'll meet that man again and it won't be as pleasant as this."

Streak shrugged. "I'm going to forget it all—this whole war—and you need to do the same."

"I'll try."

But Luke was sure he could not do the same.

★ ★ ★

The two men had suitable quarters on the ship, but Luke stayed to himself for the most part. Melosa was constantly on his mind. He remembered her touch and how she had said, *"I love you, Luke."* That had been one of the last things she had said to him. He stood alone on the ship in the middle of the ocean, watching the vast spaces. Looking up at the stars, he tried to pray but found he could not. There was still bitterness in his heart against the Germans, and he feared it would destroy him.

What will I do with myself? he wondered as he turned in the direction of America. *How can I live without Melosa?*

PART TWO

April 1939–August 1940

★ ★ ★

CHAPTER SEVEN

NEW BEGINNINGS

★ ★ ★

Looking down at his plate, Streak poked at the pale contents and then glanced up at Luke. "What do you suppose this stuff is? It doesn't look like anything I ever ate."

"I have no idea," Luke said with a shrug. "After being on this ship for more than a week, you should know better than to ask."

"I'll be glad to get back to good old American cooking, believe you me!"

"So will I."

Shoving his plate back, Streak took out a bag of tobacco and a paper from his pocket and constructed a cigarette. He licked the edge and tightened the two ends before sticking it in his mouth and lighting it with a match. "I thought Spain was pretty bad, but La Vaca is worse." He drew on the cigarette and watched the smoke curl upward. "Hey, what do you suppose the name of this boat means, anyway?"

"La Vaca? You don't know?"

"Nope. Never thought to ask."

"It means 'the cow.'"

A grin spread across Streak's face. "Well, it's got the right name, I guess. It wallows like a cow every time the waves get higher than six inches. It smells like a cow barn, and the food tastes like something you might feed to a cow."

Luke shrugged and tried to put a little more of the gray mass down, but it was too much for him. He pulled an apple out of his pocket, cut it in two, and handed half to his companion.

Streak's eyes widened. "Where'd you get an apple on La Vaca?"

"I stole it when the cook wasn't looking."

Streak took a bite of the apple. "Not bad. You ever eat an apple in Washington State?"

"Never been there."

"Best apples in the world. I wish I had a bushel of them. And a good watermelon."

"Not likely to get one of those here either."

"I reckon not."

The mess hall, where the two men were seated, was grim, depressing, and unsanitary, like all the other parts of the ship. It smelled of old grease, cabbage, and other unmentionable items. Both Luke and Garrison had lost weight on the journey back to the States. The boat was transporting fruit from the Mediterranean, and black flies formed a cloud over the cargo. Nothing seemed to disperse them, and both men spent a great deal of time slapping at themselves and brushing the pesky insects away.

Their cabin was like a coffin, only big enough for a narrow bunk bed and no bathing facilities. There were no portholes, so when the door was shut it was like being buried alive. When they had come aboard they had found the sheets and blankets on the bunk were so filthy neither man would use them before washing them out in seawater. Most of the time they stayed up on deck, going below to sleep only when they could not keep their eyes open any longer.

The two men wandered up to the deck and stood at the rail watching the gray waters of the Atlantic roll. It was late in the afternoon, and huge clouds were boiling up in the west.

Luke studied them and rubbed his chin. "There could be trouble in that."

"Just what we need—a hurricane. Maybe we'll get to Charleston before it hits. After that I don't care what it does. It can rain cats and dogs for all I care."

Taking his eyes off the sky, Luke turned to face Garrison. "What are you going to do when we get to the States?"

"As little as I can."

"Sounds good to me. You know, I've been thinking about the fellows that won't be coming back." Since they'd been on the ship, fuzzy memories of all the young men Luke had seen die in combat had constantly been swirling through his head. It disturbed him that he could not remember some of them very clearly—their names or their faces. *A man should leave more behind him than that. He ought to leave a legacy of some kind.* Luke shoved the thought away with a gust of irritation. There was no point in thinking like that.

"What are you going to do, Luke?"

"Not sure."

"You could go to work for your dad in that factory of his."

"I suppose I could."

Streak grinned and punched Luke on the shoulder. "You're a caution, Luke. You'd complain if they hung you with a new rope! Why, if I had a rich daddy that owned a factory, I'd never hit a tap as long as I lived. I'd just spend the old man's money and enjoy life."

"Just become a parasite, huh?"

"You bet!" Streak's eyes were gleaming with fun. "I'd never show up to work, except when Daddy got upset and I had to."

"It doesn't sound like a very exciting life. Besides, my brother, Tim, wouldn't put up with it."

"Does he run the factory?"

"He's the vice-president."

Streak caught something in his friend's tone. "What's the matter? You and Tim don't get along?"

"Not really."

"Why not?"

"He's a straight arrow and I'm the prodigal son. Always been that way since we were in grade school, I guess. Tim's a good fellow but a little stuffy. He had a fit when I went to Spain."

"Why?"

"He wanted me to stay home and learn the business."

"Well, the door of opportunity swings wide." Garrison leaned his elbows on the railing. "I wish I had a rich daddy."

"Hey, why don't you go home with me. We'll both go to work in that factory."

He shook his head. "Nope. I'm gonna fly something or other. I don't care what it is."

"More power to you if you can find someone who needs a pilot."

Garrison stood up straight and then arched his back. "Do you have some cash you can lend me?"

"What for?"

"I'm gonna go down and teach these tamales how to roll the dice."

Luke shrugged, reached into his pocket, and pulled out some bills. "I hope they take Spanish money."

"They'll take it. Start dreaming big. I intend to strip these sailors of every dime they've got."

Luke could not help but laugh. As he watched Streak go below, he realized how close he had gotten to the man during their time together in Spain. They had played on the same football team in college, but risking death with a man and waiting when his flight was late coming back formed a relationship that was far different from a football game. Luke leaned on the rail again and stared over the monotonous gray swells of the Atlantic. "At least I'll be able to help Streak get settled," he murmured. "Dad knows lots of people. He can find us both a job flying something, even if it's crop-dusting."

As the boat continued to plow through the Atlantic, a sense of futility came over Luke. He had spent most of his life chasing some dream he could not even identify. He had thought he would find his purpose when he went to Spain to help free the Spaniards from the evil fascists, but that dream had gone down in flames, as had many of his companions. It was just as dead as they were. He tried to think of a purpose that would bring him the type of contentment his brother had possessed as long as Luke could remember, but his mind was a blank.

He pulled the remaining money from his pocket—what was left of it after his contribution to the craps game—counted it, and jammed it back into his pocket. *Sure I've got a rich daddy. Won't he be glad to see me coming home with my hand out?* he thought bitterly. Turning abruptly, he started pacing, the wind in his face, doubt in his soul.

★ ★ ★

Luke awakened in the pitch-black darkness, the same in the tiny cabin whether it was high noon or midnight. He had not taken off his clothes but simply thrown himself on the lower bunk. Groping his way to the door, he went outside and turned down the corridor to the ladder that led to the upper deck. Thoughts of Melosa filtered through his memory after having dreamed of her that night. He stepped outside on the deck and stumbled in the force of the wind. A storm was slashing at the ship with what could be the beginnings of a fury. He ducked his head and made his way to the bow. The waves were making huge troughs, and La Vaca rode them down, then was driven upward. The cold water sprayed Luke, but it was a relief to have something to think about other than his dreams.

His emotions were a mixed jumble. Part of his spirit cried out with grief over the loss of the woman he loved. The other part of him was a boiling caldron of anger. Not a good mixture—grief and anger. He stood on the deck trying to make his mind blank, but he heard a voice behind him, shouting above the wind.

"Señor—"

Luke turned and saw Ricardo, one of the hands he had come to know fairly well. "Hello, Ricardo. It looks pretty bad out there. Are we going to sink?"

"Sink? No. This is good boat. No sink." He was wearing rain gear, and his teeth made a white slash across his olive features. "Your friend, he lose all his money last night. I got most of it myself. Don't be mad with me."

"It's none of my business. How long before this old tub gets to Charleston?"

"Should be before noon today, Señor Winslow."

"If we don't sink."

Ricardo shrugged. "Don't be afraid. We no sink. This is good boat."

Luke nodded and found a smile at the thought that Ricardo did not need a lot to make him happy. If a boat like La Vaca could satisfy him, and winning a few bucks in a card game could fulfill his dream, Ricardo was a fortunate man indeed!

Luke stood in the bow for a half hour before he was joined by Garrison. Luke turned to his friend and grinned. "Have you figured out what we're going to do with all that money you won, Streak?"

Garrison draped himself across the rail. "They cheated me, Luke. I don't know how but they did. I lost all our money."

"Life is hard."

"It sure is! Here I've been killing Germans for two years now and I don't have a cent. You know, they should have paid us a bounty on those Germans. Say, a thousand dollars a kill. You'd be rich and I'd have a pretty good stash myself."

"That's what some people did back before the Revolution."

"Paid a bounty on Germans?"

"No, on Indians."

"Is that right?"

"Yep. Some of the British offered a bounty on Indian ears or scalps."

"Well, what can you expect out of a bunch of limeys!" Streak exclaimed with disgust. "How do you find out about all this useless stuff you know?"

Luke did not bother to answer, and he straightened up and pointed. "Look. I think that's land over there."

"I can't see that far, but I'm sure ready for it."

The two men tried to stay out of the way while the activity on the deck increased. Sailors were scurrying around, and Ricardo paused to wink and say, "Señor Garrison, you want to gamble a little?"

Streak glared at him and said, "Get out of here, you thief! Is that Charleston up ahead?"

Ricardo laughed. "I'm no thief, but yes, that is Charleston."

Ricardo left Luke and Streak to gaze at the approaching land. The wind died down, and as they passed by an island, Luke said, "That's Fort Sumter."

"It looks like it had a bad accident."

"Why, you ignoramus! Don't you know anything at all about Fort Sumter?"

"No. What about it?"

"That's where the Civil War started."

Streak straightened up and peered through the mist that surrounded the island. "I'll be dipped in gravy! If that isn't something. It all started right there? You know, I had grandpas and great-grandpas who fought in that war."

"So did I."

"Fought for the Yankees?"

"Some of the Winslows did. As a matter of fact, it was about fifty-fifty, I guess."

"Imagine that!" Streak exclaimed. His eyes grew thoughtful. "Just think about it, Luke. Suppose you were in a dogfight with your own brother. That'd be pretty hard to handle, wouldn't it?"

"Pretty hard. I don't know as it ever happened like that to any of my people."

"By gum, the next time we fight the Yankees we'll whip 'em."

Luke laughed. "There's not going to be any next time. That's all over."

"That's what you think. Back in Tennessee where I come from, it's not over."

The two stood talking until the ship finally glided into the docks. Luke and Streak went below and gathered their few things, then disembarked from the ship. As the two walked on the firm land, Luke commented, "I'm pretty sure this land isn't moving, but it sure feels like it is."

"It sure does. Maybe we're having an earthquake."

Luke laughed. When they got to the street, Luke spotted a taxi but quickly realized his cash supply was very low. "I don't have the money for taxi fare. We'll have to hitchhike, as much as I hate to do it." In his mind, it was similar to panhandling. He felt like a beggar, but he couldn't walk all the way to Arkansas.

"Not me. I'm gonna stay here."

"In Charleston? You don't know anybody here."

"No, but I will before I've been here too long."

Luke grinned. He knew this was true. You could put Streak Garrison in any town in the world in the morning, and by nightfall he would have made friends. He often envied this about Garrison, knowing he would never have that same ease with people.

"Well, I'm headed for Arkansas." Reaching into his pocket, Luke took out his remaining money, divided it in two, and held out half to Streak. "Here. Try not to lose it all before I get out of town."

"Aw, I can't take your money."

"Whose money would you take?"

Luke shoved the money into Streak's shirt pocket, slapped him on the chest, and said, "You've got my address. Let me know what's happening."

Garrison hesitated and then for a moment he looked thoughtful and chewed his lower lip. He was a surprisingly emotional man, considering he was able to kill so efficiently in the air. Nonetheless, he cried over movies and poems and practically anything else that was sad.

"I hate to say good-bye." Tears formed in Streak's eyes. "You saved my bacon that time that kraut was on my tail. I'da been dead meat if it wasn't for you."

"Keep the change. Next time you can save my life." Luke laughed. "Don't cry. We'll meet again." He turned and walked away quickly and knew that Streak was watching him go. *He's got a heart, old Streak has,* he thought as he left his friend, heading toward the nearest main road.

Luke didn't have any difficulty hitching a ride to get him a few miles out of town. When the driver turned onto the dirt road, Luke got out and started walking again, his thumb out. As he walked, he began to feel the emptiness returning. He felt like a man adrift in a tiny boat in the vast ocean. He knew he had a family and friends scattered about the country, but he still felt empty inside, broken only by the anger at those who had destroyed the Chavez family and the world he had wanted for Spain.

A farm truck mounded high with watermelons finally slowed and came to a stop. When Luke ran up, he found a rawboned man with a long horse face and a broad grin waiting for him. "Howdy. Need a ride?"

"Sure do."

"Folks call me Junior."

"Luke Winslow."

"Where you headed, Luke?"

"Going all the way to Liberty, Arkansas."

"Whereabouts is that? Don't know it."

"Just outside of Little Rock."

"Well, I can get you to Memphis. From there it's just a hop, skip, and a jump."

Junior put the truck in gear and pulled out on the road. He was a talkative fellow and did not seem to expect answers for the most part. He pretty well gave Luke his entire life story, including his three marriages, as they drove across

South Carolina and into Georgia. The man finally paused and cast a curious glance at his passenger. "You're all tanned. Where you been? On a vacation?"

Luke Winslow reflected on his time in Spain, dodging death in the skies while watching his friends go down, some of them burned alive as they fell, others shot to pieces by the guns of the German planes. He thought of the wreckage of the country and of the limp body of Melosa Chavez.

"Yep, Junior, that's right. I've been on a vacation."

"Whereabouts?"

"In Spain."

"Is that right? I always heard that was a nice sunny place with lots of pretty señoritas. May give her a whirl myself sometime. Always wanted to go to that place."

Luke managed a smile and then let his mind wander as the driver began describing the woman he had met at the last truck stop.

The two rode along, Junior chatting and Luke's mind wandering, all day and into the night. Finally Junior admitted to being exhausted, and he pulled over at a park in a small town. The man produced a couple of blankets for Luke and a couple for himself and they got as comfortable as they could on two park benches.

They both awoke before the sun rose and climbed into the truck again. They finally arrived in Memphis in the middle of the afternoon. Luke helped Junior unload the watermelons at a market and then thanked the man for the ride.

"You're welcome, Luke. Wish I was going all the way to Arkansas."

"I'll find a ride."

For over an hour Luke tried without success to flag down a car. Finally he gave up sticking his thumb out and simply turned and looked whenever a car came by, thinking, *They know I'm on foot, and they know I need a ride. There's no point in my begging by sticking my thumb out*. He would walk all the way to Liberty before he would stick his thumb out again.

A new Ford passed him and suddenly slowed and pulled

over to the side of the road. Luke trotted up and asked, "You going my way?"

"Get in."

Luke got in the car and saw to his surprise that the driver was wearing an army uniform and was a captain. The soldier did not speak until he got started, and then he turned and gave Luke a searching glance. "I'm Sam Ketchum."

"Glad to know you, Captain. I'm Luke Winslow."

"Where you headed, Winslow?"

"Just outside of Little Rock."

"You're in luck, then. I'm going all the way through Little Rock. I can drop you off."

"That'll be real nice. I appreciate it, sir."

Ketchum was not a big man, but he had an athletic quality in him. He looked like he could be a middleweight prize-fighter. His hands were square and brown on the wheel, and he had a blunt jaw that looked like he could take punches.

"What's your outfit, Captain?"

"Armor. Tanks mostly."

Luke shook his head. "You know, next to submarines I think tanks would be my last choice."

Ketchum turned to give Luke a hard look. "What's wrong with tanks?"

"Nothing's wrong—I just admire you fellows who can handle it. I'm pretty claustrophobic myself. But I'd take tanks over submarines. Being under the water like that would make me nervous."

Ketchum smiled briefly, which made him seem much younger. "Funny you should say that. I feel the same way myself."

As Ketchum drove, Luke, always curious about the latest military advances, asked him questions about the newest tank. Luke had studied considerably and talked to military men before he got to Spain, so he was knowledgeable. Ketchum was surprised. "You know a lot about tanks for a fellow that doesn't like 'em."

"I think we're going to need your tanks before too long."

"You mean the war in Europe?"

"That's right."

Ketchum was silent for a time. "I wish everybody could see it like that."

"I've been out of the country for a couple years, but I've been reading the papers. Don't people back here know that Hitler's gobbling up Europe a bite at a time?"

"There's a verse in the Bible somewhere. My granddad was a Church of God preacher. I can't remember where it's at, but it speaks of the Jews. Some of the Israelites were described as having eyes that didn't see and ears that couldn't hear." Ketchum snorted with disgust and dodged a dead armadillo in the road. "That about describes our country. We're sitting around with eyes shut and our fingers in our ears." He suddenly demanded, "Where have you been?"

Luke hesitated, then decided there was no harm in telling the truth. "Spain."

"You mean you've been fighting in that war?"

"Yes, Captain, I have."

"What kind of fighting?"

"I'm a pilot."

"That war sure didn't turn out the way I'd hoped," he said bitterly.

"Isn't that the truth!"

"How about the Germans? The pilots, I mean. Are they any good?"

"Plenty good. Their planes are better than ours too. They had us outgunned and outmanned. We just didn't have the equipment. We really didn't have a chance, Captain."

Ketchum cursed, then demanded, "Did you get any of them?"

"I got my share."

The man nodded and they drove several miles in silence.

"What are you going to do now?" the captain asked.

"Why, I don't know. I just got off the boat. I'm going home first."

"I know some people in the air corps."

Something stirred within Luke. "I might be interested in that. I've got to go home first, though. Get my bearings."

"We need men with experience like you. But I've gotta tell you, I feel about airplanes the same way you do about tanks. I'm scared of 'em."

Luke laughed. "I guess everybody's scared of something, Captain."

★ ★ ★

Luke went around the car and shook hands with Ketchum through the window. "I appreciate the ride, sir."

"You've got my address. I'll expect to be hearing from you, Luke. I'm also going to give your name to a friend of mine. He'll be getting in touch with you." Shaking his head, Ketchum said bleakly, "It's going to blow up pretty soon. The quicker we get ready for it, the better. Hope you'll be a part of it."

"I'll keep in touch, Captain. Good luck to you."

Ketchum nodded and drove away. He had driven Luke right through the heart of Liberty, and it had given Luke an odd feeling as he had passed the high school where he had graduated, the stadium where he had set a state record for touchdowns scored in a single game. The main street had not changed much, and Luke had looked for familiar faces as they'd made their way through town and out the other side to the more exclusive part of town. Luke thought he had detected that Ketchum had been surprised at the expansive home and grounds of the Winslow house, but the man had politely said nothing. No doubt he wondered why a son of a rich man had specifically gone to Spain to get involved in a conflict a world away.

As he walked up to the door, Luke was tempted to turn and walk away. He had not been home for more than two years, and he knew it would be hard to get involved with his family and old friends again. Still, he loved his parents and his brother and knew he had to mend some fences. He rang the doorbell and was soon greeted by his overjoyed mother. She threw herself at him as she cried his name.

"It's great to see you, Mom."

"Is it really you?" she asked. "I can hardly believe it."

"Luke Winslow in the flesh," he joked.

At the age of fifty-one, his mother still didn't have a gray hair. She had large expressive eyes and had kept her figure. Tears were in her eyes as she kissed him on the cheek and hugged him again.

"You look starved," Jolie said. "They haven't been feeding you."

"I guess I am pretty hungry."

"Come on in. There are plenty of leftovers from supper." She took his arm and dragged him down the hallway into the dining room, where his father was enjoying a cup of coffee.

"Look who I brought in," Jolie said proudly.

Peter got up at once. "Luke, I can hardly believe it. You're back!" he cried. He reached out to shake Luke's hand and then ended up hugging him.

"It's great to see you, Dad." Luke was taken aback by how good both of his parents looked. Peter Winslow, a couple of inches taller than his six-foot-tall son, had hazel eyes and auburn hair. His face expressed relief and great joy.

"Here, son. Sit yourself down and I'll get Luana to bring you something to eat. There's plenty left—as there always is."

Before Peter could leave the room, a black woman wearing an apron entered.

"Mr. Luke!"

"Luana!" Luke said with a grin. He got up and went over to hug the woman. She was heavyset, and her face was as round as the moon. Her eyes were suddenly filled with tears. "Now, don't you start squalling just because I'm home and you're going to have to take care of me again," Luke teased.

"You hush! Look at you—skinny as a bird! What them folks doin', starving you?"

"Well, pretty much, but you're going to fix that, aren't you, Luana?"

"I sure am. You sit right there."

Luke sat down and for the next hour he ate when he could and answered the questions that were fired at him. "How's Tim?" he asked when there was finally a break in his questioning.

"He's great," Jolie said. "Of course you know he and Mary have given us two grandchildren now. Gerald will be two next month, and Carolyn is ten months old."

"He's practically running the plant now," Peter put in, "which is great. I'm gradually letting him take over more of the decisions."

Peter Winslow had been a famous race car driver, but Jolie had always been fearful for him. More as a courtesy to her than anything, he had given up racing and had built a factory that made parts for automobiles. He had discovered to his surprise that he was an excellent businessman, and the factory had made him and Jolie wealthy beyond anything he could have imagined.

"Do you have any plans for your future, son?"

"I plan to be a lazy bum."

"Good!" Jolie exclaimed. "You deserve it. Now, have another slice of this cherry pie. . . ."

★ ★ ★

Going into his old room gave Luke an odd feeling. It was exactly as he had left it. He walked around the room looking at the athletic trophies he had won, the news clippings formed into a montage, the books—everything from his old life. *It would be nice if I could just go back and be eighteen years old again and move into this room and let my folks take care of me like they used to.*

Even as the thought crossed his mind, it irritated him, and when a knock came at the door he got up at once. "Come in,

Dad," he said as he opened the door.

"I just wanted to be sure you had everything you need. Since you're the same size you were when you left—or pretty close—I guess you could wear the same clothes."

"Yep. I can't think of anything that I need."

"And don't worry about going to work right away or anything like that. Just rest up. Say, maybe you and I should do some fishing while you're around."

"Sounds good."

Peter looked down at the floor and when he looked up, his voice was unsteady. "I'm glad you're home, son. Your mother and I . . . we worried about you."

A lump came to Luke's throat. "I'm okay, Dad."

"We prayed for you every day."

"I know. That's probably what got me back."

"Well, good night, son. We'll talk more tomorrow."

After his father left, Luke looked out the window. The street looked alien to him. After seeing the bomb-damaged buildings and the barren landscape of Spain, everything looked neat and tidy and untouched. *This isn't the real world,* he thought. *If something isn't done soon with that maniac Hitler, this street could be one of the next ones bombed*. He couldn't imagine how horrible it would be to worry for the safety of his own family the way he had worried for the Chavez family. And now . . .

As he turned away, an old photo caught his eye. He and Tim were shoulder to shoulder, with big grins on their faces. He wondered how long it would be before Timothy insisted that he go to work at the factory. He smiled grimly. "It won't be long if I know Tim!"

CHAPTER EIGHT

UNHEEDED WARNINGS

★ ★ ★

Pale beams of sunlight filtered through the window, striking Luke on the face. During his week at home he had simply soaked up the food, the quiet, the rest. Sleeping in a good bed with clean sheets was a luxury, and he was guessing he had already gained a pound or two.

Sleepily he rolled over and found the knob of the radio. He would listen to the radio while he decided whether to go back to sleep. A strange song was playing on the radio. The lyrics were something about three little fishies in a little bitty pool.

The inane lyrics amused Luke, and he smiled faintly. Next he heard, "Roll out the barrel; we'll have a barrel of fun." The announcer said the rousing polka was called the "Beer Barrel Polka." *A bit much for this early in the morning,* Luke thought.

"Song writers are sure covering all the bases and coming up with deep thoughts about important topics," he said to himself sarcastically. The next song was much more mellow, a sad ballad called "South of the Border Down Mexico Way." At least this one told a story. It was about a young man who had left his sweetheart but would eventually meander back to

Mexico and pick up his love life again.

The meaningless lyrics of popular songs suddenly seemed to Luke like a counterpart to what the American public was thinking. Even in the short time he had been back, it had become obvious that the people back home had little interest in and even less knowledge about what was happening in Europe. He had always felt you could sense the pulse of a nation through its popular art, and as far as he knew, the war was not mentioned in a single song on the popular radio show called *Your Hit Parade*.

"Three little fishies and a mama fishy too," he grunted with discontent and sat up on the bed abruptly. He rubbed his eyes and tried to think of a movie that dealt with the subject of the juggernaut called Germany that threatened to envelop the world. There was nothing like that. Hollywood was in a tizzy over the soon-to-be-released film called *Gone With the Wind*, based on a novel by a woman named Margaret Mitchell. Out of curiosity Luke had read the book while he had been in Spain and found it to be completely ridiculous. A step back in time glamorizing a time that was never glamorous, as far as he was concerned, and turning its back on the real war to fantasize about the clash that had taken place decades ago.

Luke got to his feet and slipped into some new clothing he had bought, including a pair of gray slacks, a dark blue polo shirt with an emblem over the pocket, and a pair of white deck shoes. He went downstairs to the kitchen, where he found Luana rolling out some dough, humming to herself. She didn't hear him come in, and he reached around her to steal a piece of dough.

She jumped and declared, "You scared me!"

"That's good dough, Luana."

"You stay out of my cooking. You hear me?"

"What are you making?"

"That's none of your business."

"Oh, come on, Luana. The poor old soldier all beat up

from the war has come home. The least you can do is be nice to me for a change."

Luana had been adamantly opposed to Luke's leaving Arkansas to go fight. She had never understood the war in Spain and for some unfathomable reason had decided that the war was over the sinking of a battleship. Luke had tried to explain that she was thinking of the Spanish-American War, but nothing convinced Luana. She was a stubborn woman, but he knew she cared for him.

"I'm hungry. What's for breakfast? Is there any of that pie left?" Luke asked as he started for the refrigerator.

"You stay out of that pie. I'm keepin' your breakfast warm in the oven. You go sit in the dining room and I'll bring it right there."

Luke ignored her and opened the refrigerator. "Ah, there it is." He pulled it out, grabbed a plate out of the cupboard, and cut a large slice of pie.

"You're gonna spoil your breakfast, and I made pancakes just for you."

Luke put a bite of the pie in his mouth. "But I might die of a heart attack on my way to the dining room," he mumbled around the pie. "Just think, for all eternity I'd be wishing I'd eaten that pie."

"You ain't supposed to be talking like that about heaven."

"Do you think there's apple pie in heaven?"

Luana glared at him but then broke out in a chuckle. "You are *bad*, Mr. Luke!"

"No I'm not. I'm good, and this is the best apple pie I've ever had in my life."

"That war didn't make you no better!"

"You're a hard woman, Luana."

"You gonna find out hard if you don't stay out of my cookin'."

Luke carried the rest of his pie to the dining room to enjoy after his breakfast. Luana brought him a plate with three large pancakes and another plate with sausage and then sat down to chat with him while he ate. For as long as he could remember she had been there for him. She must have been a teenager when she came to work for the Winslow family, and she had been as responsible for his upbringing as his parents were—sometimes even more, he thought.

"I prayed for you every day while you was gone to that old war," she told him.

"I knew you would be. Probably the reason I came back alive was your prayers."

"I ain't got no doubt about that. I had my whole church praying for you too." Luana went to a Pentecostal church and sang in the choir every Sunday. She didn't always sing exactly in tune, but she did sing loud, which seemed to be a common attribute for members of her church choir.

"Did you ever think you'd get kilt while you was over there fightin' in that war, Mr. Luke?"

"I thought about it a few times, but there wasn't much I could do about it. I just had to do my job." Luke was not entirely truthful about this but didn't want to alarm her.

"Well, I don't want you goin' off to no more of them old wars in Spain or any of them other foreign places. You stay here and you go to work with Mr. Timothy and your daddy. It's high time you find you a good woman, get married, and have some chil'uns."

"That sounds like a good plan to me."

Luke's mother came into the dining room with a smile on her face. She leaned over and kissed him. "You're having pie with your breakfast? Luana, I can't believe you let him get away with that."

"I done tried to stop him, but you know how stubborn your son can get." Luana stood up and returned to the kitchen.

"You got a telephone call while you were asleep," Jolie said as she handed him a slip of paper. "I wrote the name and number down."

Luke looked at the information thoughtfully and shook his head. "Who is she?"

"Maxine Rogers? Why, she's a reporter for the *Arkansas*

Gazette. I'm surprised you've never heard of her."

"What does she want?"

"She wants to interview you."

"Not interested."

"Yes you are. You're always talking about how people are not aware of what's going on in Europe. Well, here's your chance to let them know. Thousands of people read the *Gazette*, so you can speak to every one of them."

Luke made a face. "A woman, you say? Isn't it against the Bible for women to be reporters for newspapers?"

"I don't know where you heard that, but I certainly don't think there's anything like that in the Bible."

Luke laughed. "I think you're right. Okay. I'll call the homely old girl."

"How do you know she's homely?" Jolie demanded, interested in spite of herself.

"Good-looking girls get married and don't become reporters for the *Arkansas Gazette*. I'm surprised you don't know things like that, Mother."

"You go call her right now."

"Yes, Mother." Luke laughed. He stood up and gave his mother a bear hug, picking her up off the floor. "You're the best-looking woman I've ever seen. Whoever this reporter is, she won't be as pretty as you."

"Put me down, you fool!" Jolie protested, but actually she loved his teasing.

Luke made his way to the phone and dialed the number.

At once a woman answered, saying, "Maxine Rogers."

"Mrs. Rogers, this is Luke Winslow."

"It's not Mrs. Just Maxine will do."

"Fine. I'm Luke."

"I'd like to do an interview. I want to do a story on the war."

"Which war?"

"Why—in Spain."

"That war's over."

The woman laughed. She had a good voice, full of life, and

sounded fairly young. "Then I'll let you pick the war, Luke. Tell you what. If you'll join me for dinner tonight, I'll buy."

"Are you sure that's legal?"

"Am I sure what's legal?"

"Buying me supper. You might try to influence me by lavishing a good meal on me."

"It won't be that expensive. Do you know where Leonard's Cafeteria is?"

"Had many a meal there."

"How about if we meet there at seven o'clock?"

"How will I know you?"

"I'll wear a red hat and have a notebook in my hand."

"All right. Leonard's it is at seven o'clock."

Putting the phone down, Luke walked back into the kitchen. "I'm going to miss your supper tonight, Luana. A woman's buying me a meal at Leonard's."

"You don't need to be eating there! My cookin's much better," she protested.

"Leave him alone, Luana," Jolie said. "We need to get his story in all the newspapers."

Then his mother turned to him and said, "But don't make any appointments for tomorrow night. Timothy's coming over. And I've asked your cousins Wesley and Patrick and their families to come over too."

"Sounds like the gathering of the Winslow clan. What's Wesley doing now?"

"You don't know? Why, he's become one of the most famous photographers in America."

"Good for Wes. I knew he'd make it. I suppose those kids of his are about grown."

"Yes. They're all in high school here. The twins are fifteen and Leslie is fourteen."

"Makes me feel old." Luke grinned, then left the room.

"I wish he'd find hisself a wife. She'd keep him home and outta trouble," Luana said. "Don't want him runnin' off to no more of them old wars!"

★ ★ ★

"How much am I allowed to spend?" Luke asked. He held his tray as they got in line, and mischief danced in his eyes as he turned to the woman. She was actually a pleasant surprise, being somewhere in her late twenties, he was guessing, an attractive redhead with green eyes. He had expected a dowdy woman.

"A dollar fifty ought to fill you up."

"A dollar fifty? Why, I might *spill* that much."

Luke turned and moved down the line. He chose a salad, catfish with slaw, collard greens, and corn bread. He watched Maxine choose a salad and one piece of chicken. "You must be broke if that's all you can afford to eat."

"I'm trying to lose weight."

"Lose weight where?"

Maxine stared at him. "All over," she said. "Now, let's grab that table over there."

Leonard's was crowded, as it usually was. The two sat down and transferred their plates to the table.

"Do you ask a blessing before you eat?" Maxine asked.

"No. Do you?"

"Just a silent one."

"I was hoping you'd pray good and loud so people would know how religious we are."

Maxine could not keep the smile off her face. "You're awful. I'm going to tell your parents on you. I'm positive that they don't know how badly you behave."

"Oh, I'm afraid they do."

Luke began to eat the fish while Maxine bowed her head.

"You know my parents?" Luke asked when she was done.

"I met your dad once at a meeting. As a matter of fact, you look a lot like him."

"I'm much better looking than he is! Everybody says that, and I'm sure you'll agree."

"No you're not. Your father is one of the most handsome men I've ever seen."

"Well, I used to be better looking than him before I got all beat up in the war."

"Speaking of the war, can I interview you while we eat?"

"That depends. This interview may not go the way you imagined it would."

"What do you mean?" She was picking at the lettuce, eating one small bite at a time.

"If I'm honest with you, you're not going to like my comments."

"Suppose we just do it and then you let *me* decide whether or not I like it."

"All right. Fire away with your questions."

"You were risking your life in Spain. Do you think it was a waste of time?"

"That's coming right down to it. No, I don't think it was a waste of time."

"But the Republicans lost the war."

"They wouldn't have if we'd had more help from our government."

"What do you think our government could have done?" Maxine asked. "We're not at war with anyone. We couldn't have sent our troops over officially."

"Germany did. Who do you think I was fighting over there? The Condor Legion was made up of Nazis, pure and simple."

"That's different."

"Sure is," Luke said. He poured pepper sauce all over the collards and put a forkful in his mouth. "You ever wonder why collards taste so much better than other greens?"

"I guess I thought they all tasted pretty similar."

"Oh no. Not at all. They all have a different taste. Now, collards are—"

"I'm not interested in collards. I'm interested in your thoughts about the war in Europe."

"What war?" Luke asked innocently.

"What war! You know what I'm talking about."

"I thought it was over. I've been home a week and you're the first person I've heard mention it. Although there was an article in *Life* magazine, I believe, about some shooting going on over there by some fellow called Hitler, but it doesn't seem to have disturbed anybody all that much."

"You're pretty cynical about our country, then."

"I heard a song on the radio this morning. It was about three little fish in a pool, and it says, 'They swam and they swam all over the dam.' Kind of gets your ear, doesn't it?"

Maxine stared at him with a pained expression. "I'm afraid you're right, Luke. Actually, I was hoping this interview might help wake some people up."

Luke was surprised. He had assumed she just wanted a fluff story. "If you really mean that, we can get down to business, but it'll ruffle some feathers."

"Ruffle away. Tell me about the atrocities the Germans committed over in Spain."

He couldn't speak for a moment as he remembered the charred remains of the family he had come to think of as his own.

"I'm sorry," she said. "That wasn't right of me to speak of it so lightly. I know you saw some terrible things when you were in Spain."

Luke pushed the fish around with his fork. "I'll tell it just like it was and you can put it in your paper, but it won't do any good."

"It might."

"The only thing that would wake America up would be bombs falling on their own houses," Luke said flatly. He took a deep breath. "All right. Go ahead and ask anything you like."

Maxine began to fire questions at him, and Luke answered her, his face set in angular planes and his eyes angry.

★ ★ ★

The next evening the Winslow clan gathered at Peter and Jolie's home, and as Luke looked around the huge dining table, he thought about how odd it was that these three branches of the Winslow family had all settled in the same area.

Luke's cousin Patrick pushed his plate away and said, "That was a delicious meal, Luana."

"Why thank you, Patrick," she said as she gathered an armload of dirty plates. "I's glad you liked it."

Patrick and his wife, Seana, were seated across from Luke. Patrick was the pastor of the First Baptist Church of Liberty, and his three children—twins Chad and Casey, along with Keir—had been corralled and brought to the dinner. They were all watching him with obvious admiration.

Wesley Winslow and his wife, Leah, had brought their three children as well—Clive and Brandon, fifteen-year-old twins, and Leslie, a year younger. Although Patrick and Wesley were distant cousins, their families were so similar that the two men felt almost like brothers. Their twins were just a year apart in age, and among the six kids, there was only a two-year age spread.

Throughout the meal, the kids had kept Luke busy telling war stories. He had softened them enough to make them acceptable to the family, especially during a meal, and finally Chad Winslow, son of the Baptist preacher, said, "Luke, when you shot down all those planes, did all the men die?"

"No. Some of them parachuted out."

"How many did you kill?"

"I didn't keep count, Chad. As a matter of fact, you don't think about the men so much. You just think about their plane. Just getting it out of the air." Even as Luke spoke, he knew this was not true. The battle between himself and Erich Ritter had certainly been man against man, not machine against machine.

Leslie, blond with green eyes and pretty enough to be on a magazine cover, said, "Maybe sometime you could come to the high school and we could have an assembly, Luke."

"I don't think that would be the best idea."

"I think it would be a great idea," Wesley said, "and I'd like to photograph it." Wesley Winslow, at the age of thirty-five, did not have the good looks of most of the Winslow breed. He was more of a plain-looking individual.

"What for?"

"Why, I might be able to get Luke's story in some of the big city papers."

"That'd be a good idea," Leah said. Looking at her, one knew where all three of the children had got their golden blond hair and emerald green eyes.

"That's not a bad idea," Patrick said. He was a big man, getting a little heavy now, who had played fullback during his college years at the University of Arkansas.

"I think that's a good idea," Luke's brother said. "It'll be good for you to get your story out." Timothy's family had not come. Mary and the kids were visiting Mary's sister in Hot Springs. Tim had already talked to Luke once about coming to work at the factory and had been put off in a rather gentle fashion.

"I'm not sure anybody wants to hear my story, Tim," Luke said.

"Why, of course they do!" Tim said with surprise. "It's big-time news."

"I think Tim's right," Peter put in. "Why don't you do it, Luke?"

He shrugged. "I'll be glad to go, but I can't guarantee the results."

All of the young people were excited about the prospect of their famous relative speaking at their school.

"I'll go talk to Mr. Franks at school tomorrow," Leslie offered.

"Who's he?" Luke asked.

"Donald Franks—he's the principal."

"Okay, Leslie. You set it up and I'll come."

After the meal Patrick's wife, Seana, who had said little,

pulled Luke off to one side. "Why don't you want to go, Luke?"

"You really want to know?"

"Yes."

"The reason I don't want to go is because of those young men I'll be talking to. They're so young, but by the time they get out of high school, maybe even before, I'm afraid young men like that will be dying all over Europe and maybe even elsewhere in the world."

"You can't know that, Luke."

"See? You're related to me and you don't believe me. Why should they? They're interested in three little fishies in a little pond and *Gone With the Wind*."

★ ★ ★

By the time Luke had spoken for five minutes with the principal of Liberty High School, Luke knew his initial instinct was correct. His stories about the war in Spain would not be appreciated.

"I'd appreciate it if you didn't dwell too much on your . . . uh . . . service in Spain," Donald Franks was saying.

"Why is that, sir?"

"Oh, we don't want to get the students upset."

"Don't you believe that my service in Spain was necessary, Mr. Franks?"

"Certainly not. You see what it came to, Mr. Winslow. Our country doesn't have any business getting involved in a foreign war like that."

Luke knew it was useless to try to change the man's mind. Instead he agreed to share a few remarks with the students about life in Spain and leave it at that.

★ ★ ★

A week later, when Luke stood up to speak in the auditorium, he told the students about some of the food he had eaten while in Spain, he told them about trying to communicate in a foreign language, and he told them about the magnificent old castles and cathedrals he had seen. All the while he kept thinking about friends he had lost in the war in Spain.

"Let me tell you about Barney Carter," he finally said. "He was born in a little town in North Carolina, went to a school about like yours here, and decided to try to do something to make the world a better place." He hesitated before continuing. "The last time I saw Barney he had been torn to pieces by machine-gun fire from a German airplane. The bullets struck him in the head and almost cut him in two. He was dead when his plane crashed into a field in Spain."

Total silence fell over the auditorium, and one glance at Donald Franks revealed a man who was outraged.

"Barney died for a cause. He knew what was going on in the world. He knew that a man called Adolf Hitler is determined to rule the entire world. If someone doesn't stop him, some of you young men out there will die like Barney did."

Again the silence was almost thunderous. "I know my opinion is not popular, but let me just tell you what has happened. In 1935 Adolf Hitler violated the Treaty of Versailles by introducing military training for Germans. In September of that same year all German Jews were stripped of their citizenship and all of their rights by the Nuremberg Laws, and in March 1936 German troops occupied the Rhineland." Luke went on remorselessly. "He sent military aid of all kinds to help a ruthless dictator called Franco in Spain. In March of '38 he took over Austria, doubling the size of the German nation, and in October of that year the German troops occupied the Sudetenland.

"And now it's 1939. Hitler has threatened the Jews in every way a man can, and in March the Nazis took over the rest of Czechoslovakia. In May Hitler signed an alliance with Italy, and he's ready to make his next move. And I can tell you what it will be. He will set his sights on some small nation in

Europe, and he will invade it. The world will protest and he will promise never to do it again, but he will. He will never be stopped except by force."

Luke finished his speech and received a smattering of applause.

After the students had filed out of the auditorium, Donald Franks approached Luke, his face red. "That was terrible!" he said furiously. "You have alarmed these young people and caused them undue anxiety."

"No I haven't. They're not alarmed. They're bored and so are you, Mr. Franks."

Luke abruptly left the building and found Maxine Rogers waiting for him just outside the door. "I didn't know you were here," he said.

"Your mother called me and told me you'd be speaking today. I wanted to hear you."

"What did you think of their reaction?" Luke asked grimly. "I was underwhelming, wasn't I?"

"They don't understand it."

"That's right, they don't, but they will when these same young men go out to face Hitler's soldiers."

★ ★ ★

After the speech at the high school, Luke went into a self-imposed seclusion. During the next two months, he spent most of his time at home, by himself. He began to drink more than he should. He did see Maxine Rogers a few times during this period, although he had no interest in pursuing a relationship. He was consumed with the relationship that had died in a senseless war in Spain.

Finally one day Tim came to the house and found Luke reading a book in the living room. Tim greeted Luke and then sat down and laid his cards on the table.

"Luke, you're breaking Dad's heart and Mom's too. It's not just the drinking, but you're doing nothing with your life."

Luke had been out late the night before, and he knew his eyes were bloodshot. He laid the book down. "What do you suggest I do?"

"You're my big brother, Luke, and I love you. You could have a satisfying career."

"At the factory?"

"Well, of course at the factory. It's going to be your company one day—yours and mine. It's already doing well. You could help make it even better—and bigger—but you don't seem to care."

"And you think if I throw myself into a career I'll be all right?"

"Of course I do. It's just what you need. You need a focus for your future."

Luke took a deep breath. He knew his parents were disappointed in his behavior and his lack of direction. "All right, Tim," he said with a shrug. "I'll give it a try."

"Great! Will you come in tomorrow?"

Luke nodded, although his heart wasn't in it.

"I'll meet you at the factory at eight o'clock. You're going to love it!"

Luke smiled but knew that Tim was wrong.

CHAPTER NINE

TURNING A BLIND EYE

★ ★ ★

September brought cooler breezes, and the leaves had turned to red and gold on the hardwoods down the streets of Liberty. Luke left the house and drove the old pickup truck that his father had helped him buy to the factory, his mind blank. The two months he had put in at the Winslow plant had been a waste of time. He had tried to become interested in the business and thrown himself into the work, but he simply didn't have whatever it is that makes a man a successful businessman. Maybe Tim had received the allotment for the family.

He approached the factory thinking, *Here it is. The biggest business in Liberty, a thriving auto parts factory, and it will all belong to me and Tim one day.* He tried to work up some excitement about that but could not. Part of this, he knew, was the fact that his mind was still in Spain, and he seldom went through a day without painful memories of Melosa and her family. Even as he drove along now, he remembered playing ball with Isadora and Victor. He remembered how their white teeth had flashed and how their laughter had floated on the air.

Then almost immediately the harsh, terrible memory of their crushed and broken bodies as he had dug them out of the rubble seared his mind. Luke gritted his teeth and tried to wrench his mind away, but it was becoming more and more difficult to ignore the images.

As he pulled into the parking lot, into the space with his name on it, his mouth twisted with a wry expression. Tim had introduced him to a woman named Loretta Maddox. Loretta's father, Thomas, was an influential member of the United States House of Representatives. He had been instrumental in bringing contracts to many Arkansas businesses, and Tim was desperate for his brother to make the alliance.

"Look, it's time for you to get married, Luke," Tim had said only a week earlier, "and Loretta's a beautiful woman—smart too."

"And her father is a representative who can throw business our way," Luke had sneered.

"That's a rotten thing to say!"

"Don't tell me it isn't true."

"It's just business, Luke."

"If I get married, it won't be for business."

"Everything I say is wrong," Tim said. He had been disappointed in his brother's behavior ever since he had returned from overseas. He just couldn't understand what had happened to him. Squaring his shoulders, he said, "You ought to be thankful for a chance like this."

"I'm just not cut out for this kind of life—getting up every day and working at a desk in an office."

"If you'd stop drinking so much and put your heart into this business, you might find out you *are* cut out for it. I know you love airplanes and airplane engines—I thought this would be the perfect environment for you."

"I do love airplanes and airplane parts. But pushing papers around on a desk and telling other people what to do in a car parts factory is a far cry from tinkering with an airplane engine until it purrs like a kitten and then taking that same machine up above the clouds . . . They're worlds apart," he said with frustration.

Tim had glared at him and walked away.

Now as Luke got out of his car, he thought of the three dates he had had with Loretta Maddox. They had gone to a football game at Liberty High School, and that had brought back old memories. They had gone to a performance of the Arkansas Symphony Orchestra, which thrilled Loretta but did little for Luke. And they had gone to a movie that neither of them liked. Even though Loretta had other men pursuing her, Luke knew that if he was willing to throw himself into the courtship, he could interest her. But he had little interest and no energy for it. By the time he had put in a day at the factory, he had little energy left to do anything else. Nonetheless, he has asked her on another date for that evening, more to keep Tim off his back than anything.

As he entered the building, he was greeted by many of the workers. He returned the smiles and greetings and headed toward his office, but before he could enter, he heard his name. Turning, he saw Tim, who was coming to him with a frown on his face. "It's nearly ten o'clock. Where have you been?"

"I overslept."

Tim glared at him. "Come into my office. We've got to talk."

The talk amounted to a lecture on how Luke would never amount to anything or be of any help to the company until he made some changes—in his lifestyle and in his attitude. Luke accepted what his brother said, knowing it was all true. When Tim finished, Luke promised him he would try to do better.

"I don't know what's wrong with you, Luke. Everything you've ever done you've succeeded at, except that war thing, and that wasn't your fault. You've always had enough drive for ten men. Why can't you put that same drive into our business? Can't you see what this could mean for your future?"

"It would mean security, a lot of money, and success in the world of business," Luke said flatly. "I'm sorry, and I know this is hard for you to understand, but I'm not terribly interested in those things."

Tim read the cynicism in Luke's tone. "And what's wrong with wanting a good life?"

"I'm not convinced it's all that good."

"Is what you've got any better? What did Spain get you? Nothing but a bunch of bad memories."

Luke straightened up and had to bite back the hot reply that rose to his lips. He hated these sessions with Tim! He had not told anyone about Melosa, but he knew that his family was aware that Spain had done something terrible to him. It had made him different, and he could not even tell his parents about it, much less Tim, who thought the whole thing had been a fiasco.

Tim shook his head. "Are you and Loretta still going out tonight?"

"Yes, we are."

Tim started to give him some advice, but the look on Luke's face made him change his mind. "Well, I hope you have a good time. Now, let's go over these invoices I mentioned yesterday. I'll show you what I was talking about. . . ."

* * *

Luke took Loretta Maddox to the Robinson Auditorium in Little Rock for a performance of the Ballet Russes. Loretta had studied ballet herself and was thrilled by the performance by the Russians. She turned in the middle of the production to say, "Isn't it wonderful?"

Trying to joke about it, Luke said, "I wonder why they don't just find taller girls—then they wouldn't have to stand on their toes." At once he saw that this offended her, and he said in a softer tone, "I suppose it is good, but I think you have to know more about it than I do to appreciate how difficult it is."

Loretta said no more, but after they left and were on their

way home, she said, "What's the matter with you, Luke? Nothing suits you. You're always in a foul mood."

"Didn't you listen to the radio today?"

"No, I didn't. I didn't have time."

"Hitler invaded Poland today."

"Luke, all you can think about is that war over there. There's nothing you can do about it."

"Somebody had better do something. I don't know why England's not jumping in. They'll have to fight Hitler sooner or later. Even they can see that now."

"Of course they won't. They're on an island. Hitler can't get at them there."

"Did you ever hear of airplanes, Loretta?" Luke asked grimly. "That little island isn't all that far from France. If Hitler takes France, all they'll have to do is send his bombers across the English Channel. Bombs will be falling within months."

"He can't conquer France. That's a big country—a powerful country. That could never happen, not in a million years!"

Luke did not argue with her, for he had found it to be futile. He spent the rest of the evening wishing he were anyplace but Little Rock and out with anyone except Loretta.

★ ★ ★

During the next couple of weeks he went out twice more with Loretta, but it was not until October that Luke made a mistake that was to change his life. He had gone to have dinner at the home of the Maddoxes, and Loretta had pleaded with him not to talk about the war. "Daddy's sensitive about it. He's a sweet man, but he doesn't like to be crossed."

"I'll try to behave."

"Good! I know he likes you."

Thomas Maddox was a good representative. He was loved throughout the state and had been returned to office three times. His eye was on a senate seat, and his supporters were ready to rally around him. He had ambitions for higher things and made no secret of his goals.

It was just the four of them at dinner—Luke and Loretta and Loretta's parents. Loretta had two older brothers who no longer lived at home. During dinner Maddox talked with favor about the chances of getting a government contract for the Winslow plant. "I think it's just a matter of time, my boy. I've already discussed the matter with your father and your brother. You do good work, and I don't think it'll be any problem to swing some business your way."

"That would be most helpful, sir."

"Of course, that war in Europe will be over soon now, so I doubt if we'll be getting any military contracts."

"What do you mean the war in Europe will be over, Mr. Maddox?"

"Why, now that Hitler's conquered Poland, he's promised to go no farther."

"He promised to go no farther after he went into the Sudetenland. Don't you remember?"

Maddox's face started to grow red. "I don't think he actually said that."

"Yes, sir, he did. He actually said that. He also promised not to take Czechoslovakia, but you'll notice that he did. He's going to take it all—all of Europe."

"Oh, you've become a fanatic about this thing! Your experience in Spain has colored your views. Hitler knows he could never go any farther. He wouldn't dare attack France."

"That's what everyone says. They all agreed that Hitler would never attack France because he would be afraid of the Russians at his back. Well, Mr. Maddox, you know what happened in August. The Nazis signed a non-aggression treaty with Russia, so now Hitler doesn't have to worry about Russia at his back. There's nothing to stop him from attacking wherever he wants to."

"He'll never attack France. Poland will be his last conquest. He promised."

"If you believe that, sir, you are a fool."

A silence reigned over the table, and Maddox stood up. "You may leave my house and never come back! You are the fool! I'm sorry your father will have to hear about this."

Luke got to his feet as well. "Well, Loretta," he said as he pushed his chair in, "I suspect this is the end of our little courtship."

"It certainly is!"

Luke left the house and went at once to a bar. He drank until he was so drunk he could hardly drive. He was pulled over by a highway patrolman, failed the sobriety test, and was jailed and charged with driving while intoxicated.

As drunk as he was, Luke knew he could not continue living the way he was. By the time his father came to the police station to get him, Luke had sobered up somewhat. But as soon as they were outside, Luke said, "Dad, I need to move on."

"We can beat this thing, son," Peter said. "You just had a bad night."

"No. It's more than that. I'm leaving tomorrow."

"What are you going to do? Where are you going?"

"I have no idea, Dad."

That night Luke packed his clothes, and the next morning he said good-bye to his parents. His mother begged him to stay, to try to make things work at the factory, but he knew he would never be happy there. When he left it seemed symbolic of his life that he was driving a wreck of a truck away from a house that was fit for a prince. He did not even look back. He knew he was leaving a life to which he could never return.

CHAPTER TEN

LAST CHANCE

★ ★ ★

As Luke came out of a fitful sleep, which had been swept by dreadful dreams, he reluctantly opened his eyes. He had to struggle for a time to remember where he was, for he had been in so many small dreary towns during the past months it was impossible for him to keep them all straight. They were all the same somehow, and one of the dreams was that he was living the same day over and over again—one of drunkenness and failure.

Slowly the present came drifting back, and he struggled to sit up in the bed. As he looked around, he remembered that he was in a boardinghouse in Broken Bow, Oklahoma. Broken Bow seemed no different from the other towns where he had drunk himself into a stupor and lost his job. Now the gray light of day had begun to filter through the single window beside his bed, and as he threw his legs over the side, a terrible pain shot through his head. It was as if someone had driven a red-hot ice pick through one temple and straight through his brain. He muttered a cry of pain and sat there, waiting until the pain ebbed. When it was finally bearable, he rubbed his eyes and glanced over at the clock beside the bed.

He saw that he had forgotten to wind it and it was stopped at three o'clock. Hurriedly he grabbed his pocket watch from the bedside stand. It took an effort to focus, but he saw with a shock that it was almost ten o'clock.

Ignoring the pain, he got up and had to hold on to the wall for a moment until the nausea and dizziness had passed. Finally, with trembling hands, he pulled on his clothes and then picked up the pint bottle he had left beside the bed. He stared at the inch or so of amber liquid remaining, and then without another thought, tilted the bottle to his lips and finished it. A shiver ran through him, and with an angry gesture, he tossed the bottle toward the wastebasket. The bottle missed the basket and shattered on the floor. *Won't hurt the decor much,* he thought.

He started for the door, but when he put his hand on the knob, he looked around at the room and thought of his family and the home he'd grown up in—neat and clean and wholesome. The furniture he was looking at now was old and mismatched. The sheets were dirty. Remnants of past meals were scattered throughout the room, and three empty whiskey bottles sat on the dresser.

"I'm glad my parents can't see me like this," he muttered. He left the room and made his way downstairs, relieved to see that his landlord wasn't in the living room or kitchen. As he drove toward the airfield, where he worked as a mechanic, his head was splitting and his mouth had a foul taste.

It was a sunny, bright day in May, and it occurred to Luke that he had been back from Spain for more than a year now. He didn't notice the flowers or the trees or the fleecy clouds overhead, but rather he was tormented by thinking of the jobs he'd had and lost in the last year. His stint at the family factory was not something he ever wanted to try again. The next one after that hadn't been bad, but he had spent too many evenings drinking, and he was soon fired.

Each subsequent job had been a step down, and as he hurried toward the airfield he remembered being in jail in Missouri. His cell mate, Walter, had once been a member of the state legislature and a successful businessman, but he was nothing more than skin and bones at this stage of his life. Luke remembered how one night, when everyone else was asleep, Walter had begun telling his woes, how he had lost everything—money, family, and position. His voice had been scratchy like an old record as he had said, "I had honor once but I lost it. You know how you lose honor, Winslow? The rats take it, a little bit at a time. They don't take it all at once, just a tiny nibble and then another. And finally it's all gone." Then he had begun to cry. "And you never know you're losing it until everything is gone," he said when he had pulled himself together enough to speak. "Why does a man act like a beast?"

Luke knew he was in the same sorry state Walter had been in, with nothing to live for but the next drink. Luke struggled on until he reached the field and parked outside the hangar. He had not been flying for months. No one would hire a drunk for a pilot, but he had managed to get on the maintenance crew for a small transport company that had six airplanes. He was a good mechanic and, despite drinking constantly, was able to hang on to his job because of his skill.

"Hey, Winslow, Brooks wants to see you." One of the mechanics was looking at him with what seemed to be pity. He gestured toward the office and shook his head as a warning. "Watch out for him. He's mad as a bear with a sore tail."

"Thanks, Mack."

"Watch yourself!"

Luke stepped into the office where Tal Brooks, the owner of the company, was sitting behind the desk. Luke gave the man a cautious look and mumbled, "Sorry to be late, Mr. Brooks."

Brooks was a tall, lanky man with a shock of black hair. He looked up from his desk, removed the cigarette from the corner of his mouth, and eyed Luke with displeasure. "Well, you finally decided to show up. Sorry you had to have your beauty sleep troubled by such a thing as work. Don't guess you've got that down—hard work."

"Sorry. I overslept."

"You're drunk."

"No, just a bad hangover. I'll be all right."

Brooks reached into the desk drawer in front of him, pulled out a box, and opened it. He counted out some bills and tossed them with contempt on the desk. "There's your pay up to today. You're fired, Winslow."

For an instant Luke tried to regain at least a remnant of his pride. He wanted to take the money and shove it into the man's face, but he did not. He remembered the empty whiskey bottle and knew he had to have a drink. If he hated anything in the world it was begging, but he forced himself to say, "Just give me one more chance. I won't let you down."

"That's what you said last time. Take your money and get out. I told you when I hired you I've never hired a drunk that lasted more than a month, and I guess I never will."

"Look, Mr. Brooks, just give me one more chance. I know I drink too much, but—"

"You don't *drink too much*," Brooks said hoarsely. "You're a drunk. One drink would be too much. Now get out and don't ever give my name as a reference."

Luke picked up the money and stuffed it into his trouser pocket. He made his way to the locker where he had a few tools and packed them into a paper bag. As he started toward his truck, he saw the other mechanics glancing at him furtively. He was used to their pity—or their disgust—but he'd reached the point where he had no pride left.

He stood uncertainly and tried to decide which way to go. He was so befuddled he could not think straight.

"Gotta find another job," he muttered. But no ideas came to him. He finally said, "I'll get something to drink first. Then I'll decide."

He tossed his bag into the truck and drove to the liquor store, but even as he did, he knew he was kidding himself. He remembered something that Streak had told him once. *"Kill other people if you want to, Luke, but don't ever kill yourself."*

He entered the liquor store and bought two pints of the cheapest vodka available.

"Have a good day," the clerk called as he started to leave.

Luke turned and curses rose to his lips. Couldn't the man see that he wasn't going to have a good day? Luke wanted to shout at the top of his lungs, *Don't you know you're selling poison to people, man, that you're murdering folks right and left and then you tell them to have a good day?*

But he whirled and left the store, and instead of going to look for a job, he went back to his room. He sat down on the bed, opened one of the bottles, and drank straight from it. The liquor hit him hard, and he sat there staring at the picture on the wall. It depicted two children about to step into an enormous cavity in the ground, but behind them was a bright, mighty angel with outstretched wings who was coming to their rescue. Luke had seen the picture many times, but now it angered him. "Where's my angel?" he muttered and drank again, bitterness rising in him like a flood.

He sat there getting drunk as quickly as possible, and at one point he picked up the last letter he had received from his mother. *God is waiting for you, son,* he read, *and one day you'll find Him.* Luke wadded up the letter and threw it across the room. "Well, God," he muttered drunkenly, "where are you? Did you lose me? Here I am!" His voice rose. "You see what a fine man I've become?" He took another drink, then flung himself on his back as the room began to swim and the bed moved underneath him. His last thought before he passed into a drunken stupor was of Melosa as she had been the last time he'd seen her alive.

* * *

A rousing knock on the door brought Luke out of his chair. He had been sitting there in his underwear trying to get up enough energy to go out and look for a job. It had been almost a week since he had been fired, and he had halfheartedly tried on a couple of occasions, but there was not much work available in Broken Bow, Oklahoma. He had sold his truck, gambled away most of what he'd gotten for it, and spent most of his remaining cash on a bottle of whiskey.

The knock rattled the door again, and Luke shouted, "All right, I'm coming." He opened the door and found his landlord standing there. Ethan Krowder was a burly man with tattoos on his arms left over from his navy days. He was beetle-browed and always surly, and now the anger flared in his eyes. "Get out of here, Winslow! I ain't runnin' a charity here."

"Wait a minute, Krowder. I'll get the money. Just give me a few more days."

"You're a week behind already. I need the room. You need help to leave?"

Luke stared at the ex-sailor hard and shook his head. "No, I'll get out."

"See to it you do. You've got fifteen minutes. You're nothing but a bum, Winslow."

Luke understood that Krowder wouldn't need much of an excuse to pound him with his massive fists. Instead of replying, Luke began throwing his few belongings into a suitcase. It didn't take long. As he passed Krowder in the doorway, Luke said, "I'll send you the rent I owe you."

Krowder laughed harshly. "Yeah, sure you will. Now get out of here and go bum off somebody else." He slammed the door with a curse and warned him not to come back.

Luke left the boardinghouse and, as usual, needed a drink, but he had less than a dollar in change in his pocket. A thought came to him, and he turned to go to the post office. His mother had sent him money on several occasions, and he hurried down in hopes of finding a letter from her. But when he asked for his mail, there was only one postcard.

"Is that all there is?"

"That's all," the clerk said.

Bitterly Luke turned and walked outside before he even looked at the card. He needed a drink badly, and he knew he would wind up drinking cheap wine. He stopped and read the postcard. He saw the signature was from Streak Garrison, and he scanned the lines: *Got a transport business going on here, partner. Could use another pilot. Not much money in it, but you'd be flying again. Be like old times.*

The return address was in Galveston, Texas. Galveston might as well have been on the moon. Luke had no money for bus fare or food. He stood there uncertainly for a moment until a dim glimmer of an idea occurred to him.

He traced his way through the rougher part of town until he came to a storefront with a hand-painted sign: *Rescue Mission.* Luke had been there before when he had depleted his funds, for the mission offered a meal every night—mostly soup and sandwiches—although you had to listen to a sermon in order to get it. Taking a deep breath, he entered and was greeted by the director.

"Hello, Brother Lindsey."

"Well, Luke, come on in. How about a cup of coffee?"

"That would be good."

The small, neat man led Luke back into the kitchen. "Nobody here just now, but I think we've got some pie left. You hungry?"

"I am, Brother Lindsey, but I've got a bigger problem." He felt like a hypocrite calling the man "Brother Lindsey." That implied they were both Christians, and Luke knew he was anything in the world but that.

"What's the problem?" Lindsey scurried around getting a cup of coffee and a big slice of apple pie. "Haven't seen much of you lately, Luke."

"Well, I've had tough luck. I know you hear that story a lot," he said with an effort.

"Quite a bit. What's the matter?"

"I've got a job, but it's in Galveston. I don't have any way to get there. I'm totally broke."

"What kind of a job is it?" the man asked. He had a pair of steady gray eyes, and Luke had the uncomfortable feeling he was looking deep into his soul. He mentioned Streak Garrison, how they had flown together in Spain, and how he had offered him a job flying.

"Well, Luke, I think you know you're not fit to fly. You're not fit to drive."

"I know it, but this is my chance. I'm going to quit drinking and pull my life together."

Lindsey did not even smile. He leaned forward and said, "Do you believe in God at all?"

"Of course I do."

"Have you ever given your life to Christ?"

"No. Most of my family are Christians, though," Luke said slowly. "Pretty much all of them except me."

"But you believe in God, you say?"

Luke took a deep breath. "Preacher, I just don't know what I believe anymore."

"All right. God believes in you. I'll ask you to do one thing and then I'll help you."

"What is it?"

"I want you to let me pray for you."

Luke had expected this, for Lindsey prayed with everyone. "Sure, Preacher. You go right ahead. I need all the prayer I can get."

The two made their way to a table and Luke closed his eyes and listened while the man prayed. He had long ago lost his faith in prayer—if indeed he had ever had such faith.

When Lindsey finally said amen, Luke dug into his pie.

"I can't give you much cash, but I'll give you a little eating money." Lindsey put his hand in his pocket and pulled out three dollars. "You wait right here. I think I can help you with a ride to Galveston."

Luke sat there looking down at the money in his hand. At one time, he had been a man of pride, but now he had been reduced to begging. Bitterness seeped through him, and he lowered his head, suddenly uninterested even in the pie.

"Well, you're in luck, Luke. One of our sponsors owns a truck line. He drives a route down to Galveston. He said you could ride with him. They got one leaving in the morning at seven o'clock. You got any place to stay tonight?"

"No."

"Well, better stay here, then. I'll get you up early and give you a good breakfast and take you over to the truck line."

Luke forced himself to look up into the steady gray eyes. "I never thought I'd grow up to be a beggar, Preacher."

Lindsey shook his head. "We're all beggars in one way or another, Luke. Remember that thief on the cross? He was a beggar too, but he made it to heaven." He leaned forward and put his hand on Luke's shoulder, his face filled with compassion. "I know you will too, sooner or later, Luke."

★ ★ ★

Charlie Dickson told stories during the entire drive from Broken Bow to Galveston. For the first hundred miles Luke had tried to listen and make appropriate comments when the man paused, but after that he had simply collapsed back against the seat of the semi and let the man go on and on, wondering if he would ever stop. They had driven straight through, and Luke's nerves were crying for a drink.

Charlie finally slowed the truck and came to a stop. Luke roused himself and looked around bleary-eyed.

"This is the airfield. Good luck to you, Luke."

"I appreciate the ride, Charlie."

"No problem. Take care of yourself, you hear?"

Luke practically fell out of the truck. He was weak and sick, but he forced himself to move forward. He approached a man gassing up a twin-engine plane. "You know where I can find Garrison Air Transport?"

"Right down that road," he said, pointing. "You know Streak?"

"Sure."

"Well, he's set up in one of the old hangars about a quarter mile down there. Hey, you don't look so good."

"I'm okay," Luke said. He turned and began walking. With every step he took he doubted he would make it all the way. The quarter mile seemed more like five. His legs were trembling with weakness, he was nauseated, and he couldn't wait to get his hands on a bottle. Finally he approached the old hangar and saw a plane outside with *Garrison Air Transport* painted on the side.

"Well, I made it, but Streak may shoot me." He went into the building and immediately heard his name called.

"Hey, Luke, you no-account rascal!" Streak Garrison came over, a broad smile on his face. But Luke saw something change in Streak's eyes at the sight of his old friend.

"Don't tell me, Streak. I look like a bum, which is what I am."

"You look terrible, Luke."

"Well, I'm not in my prime."

"I can see that. Come on." Streak couldn't conceal the disappointment in his expression. But he shrugged his shoulders and came up with a smile. "Are you hungry? Let's get something to eat. I'll tell you all about my business!"

★ ★ ★

Luke ate a hamburger and fries as Streak told him about his attempt to get started in business. Streak had bought his first plane when he was living in Charleston soon after he returned from Spain. But business was sporadic and he soon realized he would get more flights if he had a more central location. Whenever he got a flight to anywhere in the middle of the country, he took some time to scout out the local airfields and try to get a feel for what it would be like to live there.

Before long he decided to move to Galveston and within a few months had located a small house to rent. Streak was able to buy a second plane with the additional business he was getting flying to the west coast.

Luke was impressed with what his friend had accomplished. "You've done better than I have, Streak." He hesitated and then said, "You offered me a job, but now that you've seen me, I'll understand if you don't want me. I wouldn't blame you if you didn't."

Streak leaned back and sipped at the coffee in his thick mug. "How much are you drinking, Luke?"

"Up until now, all I could get. If you hire me, Streak, not a drop when I'm flying."

"Most guys who are used to drinking don't do so well when they try to cut it back. You know that as well as I do."

Luke had a vision of himself hanging on by the tips of his fingers. If he didn't make it here, he would fall into an endless chasm of horrors. "I can handle it. I've got to. You're my last chance, Streak."

Streak made up his mind. "We'll give it a shot. One slip and you're out, though. No second chances, Luke. I'll be smelling your breath ten times a day."

"I don't envy you that, but I won't touch a drop when I'm flying or when I'm due to."

"That's good enough for now." Streak reached over and punched Luke in the arm. "Well, it won't be as dangerous as flying against the Condor Legion, but the way these old planes are rattling, there's not much difference. Come on and I'll show you the ships."

CHAPTER ELEVEN

A Promised Meeting

★ ★ ★

As Luke lined the plane up for a landing, he felt like he had flown around the world. He had christened the two-engine plane *The Old Devil,* for it had proved to be such on every flight he had made in her. He spotted the field below, glad there was still enough daylight to land by. The sun was dropping down in the west, and the shadows were long. He wrestled the plane down, muttering, "Well, I'm glad I got you back in one piece, you old devil. Now, just don't fall apart on this landing."

A sudden lurch of the plane pulled it over to the right, and Luke had to physically wrestle it back. The wheels hit, and the entire plane shuddered as he bounced along the airfield with excessive force. It was a struggle to hold the plane steady, but he managed to keep it going fairly straight until he slowed down to a crawl. Taking a deep breath, he turned the plane and taxied up to the hangar. He saw Streak waiting to greet him, an anxious look on his face, with Herbert, the mechanic.

Herb guided him into the hangar; then with a sigh of relief, Luke cut the engines. The one engine exploded with a loud backfire, and Luke shook his head with disgust. Groaning, he got out of the seat and stepped out of the plane.

"How was it, Luke?" Streak asked. He was covered with grease.

"It's like flying a cement mixer, Streak. We've gotta do some work on it. That port engine cut out three times. She went absolutely dead. I thought I'd never make it."

Lines made their way across Streak's broad forehead, and he chewed his lower lip thoughtfully. "We'll have to overhaul it."

"I know what that means," Herb said. "Lots of overtime." He was a small man with a wealth of dark blond hair and light blue eyes. In the three months Luke had been working there, he had learned that Herb always liked to touch people as he talked to them. Now the man came over to Luke and began nudging him with his elbow. "Where'd it cut out, huh? Did you think you were going to lose it?" He peppered Luke with questions, punctuating each with a nudge, and finally Luke shoved him away.

"Herb, you heard what Streak said. We're going to have to overhaul it. Now I've got to go get some sleep." Luke had started his day at five o'clock that morning and was exhausted after the long day.

"All right," Streak said. "Herb and I'll start on the overhaul first thing in the morning. I can't afford to have one of my planes out of commission. Let's call it a night, everyone."

Luke made his way wearily to the small room that Streak had provided for him in the hangar. It had been a storage room once, and there was only one small window. It was unbearably hot—not that he'd expected anything else from Texas in August—but Luke had used his first paycheck to buy a small fan, which he had set in the window. It wasn't perfect, but it helped. As he stepped inside the room, he turned on the fan, then grabbed a towel. Streak had even installed a shower in the hangar's bathroom for him.

Stripping down, he stepped under the cool water, letting it sluice down his body as he felt his fatigue press at him like a giant fist. He had worked hard and kept his word to Streak about his drinking. He drank when he had time off on his own but never when he was flying or when he was due to fly. He gave his hair a final rinse and tore himself away from the cool shower. He dried off and put on clean clothes before plodding wearily back to his small room.

He noticed two envelopes on the small table by his bedside. Streak must have put his mail there when he'd been flying. Luke sat down on the bed and picked them up. One was from his mother and one was from Tim. He opened the one from his mother first. She had written a rather long letter, which he read slowly. It was filled with news from home as well as her concern for his well-being. His dad had included a smaller note, which simply said, *I know things get tight sometimes, Luke. If you need help, let me know. I'm always here for you. We love you and think about you every day.*

He had enclosed a ten-dollar bill, as he did in almost every letter he sent. A warmth came over Luke as he realized how fortunate he was to have parents like this.

The letter from Tim urged him to return to Arkansas. *There's a place for you here, and I know you can do well if you put your mind to it, Luke. This is going to be your business someday, yours and mine, and I'm praying that you'll come home and we can pick up where we left off.*

Luke shook his head and muttered, "You never give up, do you, Tim?" He put the letter down and lay down flat on the bed, which was merely a cot with a thin pad for a mattress. He sighed and let the fatigue seep out of him, and as he drifted off to sleep, he realized he had come a long way since he had started working for Streak. He still craved drink almost constantly, but he had cut back enough so that he had recovered some of his physical vitality.

Sleep came to him finally like a warm darkness. At some time during the night he had a dream about Melosa. They were in Spain, walking down a corridor between two lines of fruit trees that were blossoming in brilliant colors. In the dream she looked up at him and smiled, and he smiled back at her and then they started talking about what life would be like after they were married and moved to the United States.

Then she began to fade. He cried out to her, but she disappeared into a swirl of mist, crying out his name. "Luke—Luke!"

He woke up abruptly, as he always did after such dreams. He did not feel rested, but he knew he wouldn't be able to get back to sleep again that night. He looked at his pocket watch and saw that it was almost six o'clock. He got up quickly and dressed.

Herb was already bent over one of the engines, and Streak was coming in at the same time Luke was.

"Morning," Streak greeted. "What say we go get some breakfast, Luke?"

"Sounds good to me."

The two of them left Herbert to work on the engine alone, and when they stepped outside, dawn had begun to light up the east. They got in Streak's car and drove to a nearby café. As they went in, they were greeted by Lettie Simms, the waitress, who always flirted with both of them.

"Well, the first and second best looking guys in Texas." She came up and pushed herself against Luke, winking at him. "You've been hiding yourself, Luke. I've been lonesome."

Luke liked Lettie. She was a little heavy but still a good-looking woman in her late twenties. She had been married twice and was now looking for a third victim, as Streak put it. "You don't need an old man like me, Lettie. Find yourself a young guy." Ever since Luke had turned thirty-one he'd been thinking of himself as old.

"Hey, you got lots of life left in you, big guy!"

The two sat down and Streak ordered pancakes while Luke ordered sausage, eggs, and biscuits. While they ate, Lettie hovered over Luke, occasionally putting her hand on his shoulder.

Streak grinned when Lettie finally turned her attention to some other customers. "That woman's after you, Luke."

"I'm too old and tired for chasing after waitresses."

"Wouldn't hurt you to relax a little bit, start dating again. You've been doing good, Luke. You got the drinking under control."

Luke dipped his biscuit in the redeye gravy and took a bite. He chewed slowly and then took a sip of his coffee. "No I haven't," he finally said, shaking his head doubtfully. "It's a battle every day. You know, Streak, I've been in some pretty tight spots, but for the first time in my life I'm scared."

Streak stared across the table at him. "Scared of what? If Erich Ritter didn't scare you, I'd think nothing would."

"I'm afraid one of these days I'm gonna lose my battle with the bottle. I'm afraid I'll become one of those helpless drunks you see in an alley."

"You won't do that. God's going to take care of you like He has me. You just need to give your heart to the Lord."

Luke did not answer, for he had no answer to give. He knew Streak was right, as he knew his own family was right, but the bitterness over losing Melosa had built a wall between him and God. He knew it was foolish to blame God for anything, but still he found himself doing it. He ate slowly, aware that Streak was watching him.

"Do you ever think about Spain?" Streak asked, leaning forward and fixing his eyes on Luke.

"Sure I do."

"Yeah, you lost a good woman there."

"Yes, I did." Luke knew he wasn't being very good company for his old friend. Streak had often tried to get Luke to talk about what he went through in Spain, but Luke resisted revisiting the worst days of his life.

"I haven't told you much about my family, have I?"

"Just that they farm in Tennessee."

"Yeah. I grew up near Chattanooga. My parents had a small place. A hundred twenty acres, but most of it's not much good for crops. It's good for cattle, though."

"You have brothers and sisters?"

"Just one sister. Her name is Joelle. She's a nurse at the hospital in Chattanooga. Hey, I've got a picture of her here."

Streak pulled his wallet from his pocket, extracted a small photo, and handed it to Luke. Luke took it and studied the young woman in the picture. She was wearing a white nurse's uniform and cap. "She's very attractive."

"Yep. She's pretty and strong too." Streak took the picture back from Luke and gazed at it, fondness written across his broad features. "She always wanted to be a missionary, but when Dad got sick she had to stay home and take care of him." Slipping the photograph back into his billfold, he added, "She wanted to be a missionary even when she was a little girl, dreaming about going to Africa or China—somewhere exotic like that. But she hasn't made it yet."

"You told me your dad died. So it's just you and your mother now?"

"Well, not even that now. We lost Mom six months ago. She had a heart attack and then she was gone."

"I'm sorry to hear that, Streak." Luke continued to eat slowly and asked thoughtfully, "Well, why can't Joelle go and be a missionary now?"

"Well, it's like this, Luke. She feels like God is using her there on the farm. After Mom died, Joelle took in a girl who was in trouble with the law, and before long another one came. People started hearing about Joelle and how she had a soft spot in her heart for girls who needed a place to stay, and before long, she had a regular ministry started. It's not all girls who are having trouble with the law, though." He took a bite of his pancake. "Some don't have parents or have parents who are in jail. One girl came when she got pregnant and her parents wouldn't let her stay at home."

"Sounds like quite a place."

"I'll tell you what," Streak said. "As soon as we get a couple days off, we'll fly up there and you can meet Joelle. You'd like her, I think. Of course, we'll have to get on our feet first—get this place in the black."

Luke grinned. "Well, it doesn't look like that'll happen any time soon, but I'd like to meet your sister."

As the two finished their breakfast, Lettie came up and

leaned her hip against Luke's shoulder. "What about it, Luke? I get off at six."

"I'll be in the air at six, Lettie. Maybe next time."

* * *

The engine overhaul took longer than any of them had predicted. Luke helped Herb on the overhaul whenever he could squeeze some time in between flights, and Streak helped whenever he could spare the time.

As he tightened the last bolt, Herb said woefully, "I hope we don't have any more overhauls for a long time. I'm plumb tired out." He put his hand on Luke's shoulder. "You've got to make that early flight tomorrow. You better go get some rest."

"I guess you're right, but I'm going to get something to eat first." He cleaned up, went to the nearby café, and as usual, found Lettie there. Since there was no one else in the café, she hovered over him while he ate.

"What about going out tonight, Luke?"

"I'm pretty tired, Lettie."

She leaned against him and ran her fingers down his cheekbone. "I can take care of that. Come on. You deserve a little relaxation every now and then."

"I've got to take an early flight out tomorrow."

Lettie laughed. "I'll see to it that you're a good boy."

Luke was tired, but suddenly the idea of going back to the small, hot room in the hangar had no appeal. "All right, Lettie, but I have to be in early."

* * *

Luke woke with a start and looked around wildly. His head was splitting, and he realized that he had gotten drunk again. Lettie had egged him on, and now he remembered with self-disgust that he was in her bedroom. He looked over at the pillow that was marked with the imprint of her head, and he got out of bed feeling terrible. He listened, but hearing nothing, he assumed Lettie was already at work.

He quickly pulled his shirt and slacks on and then spotted the bottle of whiskey on Lettie's dresser. He tried to ignore it as he put on his socks and shoes. He stood up, gave the bottle one more look, then started for the door.

He turned the doorknob and then quickly changed his mind. He strode back to the dresser and took a big swig of the whiskey. He examined the bottle and saw that there was only a dribble left. He finished it with one more swig and then quickly left. He walked down the street until he found a cab and directed the driver to the airfield.

When the cab pulled up by the hangar, he paid the cabby. Luke's heart sank when he saw Herb gassing up the plane and Streak getting ready to climb aboard. Luke took a deep breath and looked down. His clothes were wrinkled, and he needed a shave. He knew there would be no sense trying to hide the fact from Streak that he had been drinking. He walked up reluctantly and muttered, "I'm sorry to be late."

Streak stared at Luke and came closer. "You're drunk, Luke," he said, shaking his head.

"I was drunk, but now I'm fine. I can fly."

"I told you I wouldn't let you fly when you'd been drinking. I can smell the alcohol from here. I'll take this flight."

"Let me take it. I'm okay."

"I'm taking the flight. You sober up today. Later in the day when you're feeling more like yourself, you can give Herb a hand."

Luke felt awful, in more ways than one.

"Tell you what," Streak continued, "as soon as I come back, we'll fly to Tennessee for some of Joelle's good home cooking."

Luke saw it was a lost cause. Finally he stood on the airfield as Streak got ready to take off. He felt a hand on his shoulder.

"Come on, Luke," Herb said. "I've got plenty to keep us

both busy all morning at least."

Luke could not even answer, he was so filled with disgust at his behavior. He walked away from Herb, wishing he had never met Lettie Simms, but it was too late for that. *It's too late for most things*, he thought, and he turned and watched Streak's plane growing smaller until it became a mere dot and then disappeared from his sight.

CHAPTER TWELVE

DOWNED IN GEORGIA

★ ★ ★

Luke turned as he heard Herb call his name. One look at the small mechanic's face alerted him. Herb had just hung up the phone, and his face had bad news written all over it.

"What's wrong, Herb?" A cold chill swept over Luke as the mechanic tried to speak.

"It's . . . it's . . . Streak!"

Fear touched Luke's nerves in a way he'd not felt since fighting in Spain. No one knew better than he did the dangers of flying, and Herbert would not be so tense unless it was really bad news. "What is it?" he demanded almost harshly.

"It's horrible, Luke. His plane has gone down in northern Georgia."

"Is he all right?" Luke managed to ask, his voice hoarse. "How'd you hear about it?"

"The hospital just called. He's alive. I know that much. Here's the number. You gotta talk to a Dr. Sanderson there. He said to call him right away."

Luke took the wrinkled fragment of paper that the small mechanic handed him and went at once to the phone. He dialed the number and heard the operator say, "Baptist

Hospital, Dalton. How may I direct your call?"

"I need to speak with Dr. Sanderson."

"Hold on, please."

Luke had been through similar situations many times in Spain when the men in his squadron had not come in when they should have. The familiar sensations of anguished fear came rushing back to him. His hands were sweaty, and he sat down abruptly to conceal the weakness in his knees from Herb, who hovered over him.

"This is Dr. Sanderson."

"My name is Luke Winslow, Doctor. I'm calling about Roscoe Garrison."

"Are you family?"

"No. Just a good friend. How is he, Doctor?"

There was an ominous pause, and Sanderson's voice came reluctantly. "He's not in good shape. We're trying to get in touch with his family. Do you know them, and do you have a number where we can reach them?"

"He has one sister is all I know about. She lives just outside of Chattanooga. Her name is Joelle Garrison. I don't have a number, but it should be in the book."

"I'll have the office get in touch with her." Again the small hesitation that told Luke more than he wanted to know. "If I were you, Mr. Winslow, I'd get here as quick as you can. If you want to see your friend again, don't waste any time. It's very serious."

"I'll fly in right away."

Luke put the phone in the cradle and said, "Is the ship gassed up?"

"Yes. It's all ready. You want me to go with you?"

"No. You'd better stay here."

"Well, call me as soon as you hear anything. I'll stay close to the phone."

"Okay, Herb."

Ten minutes later Luke was taxiing the plane out onto the field. As he took off, a sense of fatal doubt began to grasp him. He gained his altitude and headed toward Georgia. He tried to concentrate on flying the plane as fast as the old engines would take it, but he couldn't stop wondering if he would arrive in time.

★ ★ ★

"I'm here to see Roscoe Garrison."

The woman in the white uniform looked up from behind the desk. "Roscoe Garrison? Let me see, please." She looked at the records in front of her and then something changed in her expression. "He's in intensive care."

"How is he?"

"You'll have to ask the doctor."

"Thanks."

"Are you family?"

"No, I'm just a friend. How do I get there?"

"Take the elevator up to the third floor and then turn right. Anyone you see can direct you from there."

"Thank you. I need to see Dr. Sanderson."

"I'll leave word with his office that you're waiting. I don't think he's in the hospital right now, but he'll be here in about an hour for his regular rounds."

"Thanks." Luke's head seemed to be in another world that had no connection with this hospital and the mission on which he'd come. He had had to do this in order to keep the fear from controlling him. All during the flight all he could think of was how it was his fault that Streak had crashed. *I should have been in that plane.* The thought ran through his brain over and over again. Now he pushed the button of the elevator and rode it to the third floor. He stepped outside and approached the nurses' station on his right.

A thin young woman in a white uniform looked up and said, "Hello. Can I help you?"

"I'm here to see Roscoe Garrison."

"Are you a family member?"

"Not exactly."

"You'll have to wait. He can only have visitors every four hours and then only for fifteen minutes. The waiting room is right down there."

"Can you tell me how he is?"

"You'll have to ask his doctor about that, I'm afraid."

"I talked with a Dr. Sanderson. Can you get him on the phone?"

"Dr. Sanderson is due to make his rounds in another hour. I'll make sure he sees you then."

Luke walked down to the waiting room and sat in one of the chrome chairs covered with pale green Leatherette fabric. Several other people were in the room as well, reading magazines or dozing. A very fat man had fallen asleep, his head tipped to one side, his mouth open. A young woman was reading a story to two young children. She glanced up at Luke and nodded. Luke nodded back and then looked through the magazines on the table. He didn't find much of interest in the old issues of *Good Housekeeping* and *Ladies' Home Journal*.

He leaned back against the wall, staring blankly at the pictures on the opposite wall. He felt numb, his mind fragmented. He kept thinking that if he had stayed away from Lettie, refrained from drinking, and made the flight as he was supposed to, Streak wouldn't be lying in a hospital bed.

The hour seemed to drag by. From time to time Luke would glance at the clock high on the wall, and it seemed at times not to have moved at all. When the fat man woke up, he stood up and stretched.

"Hello," he said to Luke. "My name's Aldridge."

"Winslow."

"You got folks here?"

"Friend."

"My daughter-in-law's here. She had a bad accident."

"Hope she'll be all right."

"She's not going to make it. My son's in the army. He's trying to get back, but the doc says she's not going to last until he gets here."

PART THREE

November 1940–June 1941

★ ★ ★

Luke had no idea how to respond to this. "I'm very sorry," he said finally.

"It was just bad luck. Just plain bad luck." He shook his head and wiped his eyes with his handkerchief. "There's coffee over there. Do you want some?"

"Yeah. Coffee would be good."

Luke got up, and Aldridge poured two cups of coffee and handed him one. "It ain't the best coffee in the world, but it's hot and it's black. Sugar's there if you want some."

"Black is fine." He stood there sipping at his coffee while Aldridge told him all about his daughter-in-law. Luke was sorry for the man but could listen with only half of his mind. When Aldridge paused, Luke left the waiting room. He found the rest room and washed his face. When he straightened up, he saw that his hands were trembling. He needed a drink badly, but he knew that would not do. He did not want to go back into the waiting room, but there was no place else to go.

When he left the rest room, he saw a tall, sandy-haired man wearing a white coat talking with one of the nurses at the nurses' station.

The nurse saw Luke and said, "Mr. Winslow . . ."

He went over to the desk.

"This is Dr. Sanderson," she told him.

The two stepped away from the desk and Luke asked, "How is Roscoe Garrison, Dr. Sanderson? Is he going to make it?"

"I wish I had better news."

"What is it exactly?"

"Too many internal injuries, and he's lost far too much blood. By the time the crew got him here, he was almost gone. We're keeping him alive as best we can. I spoke with his sister over the phone. She'll be coming in. You know any more relatives we could get in touch with?"

"No. I don't know of any others. Can I see him?"

Sanderson shrugged. "You can sit by him. The rules say you can stay only fifteen minutes, but I'm leveling with you, Mr. Winslow. He probably won't wake up, and he's not going to make it through the night. I'm sorry."

Luke stood there numbly, wanting to beg the doctor to do something, but he saw the finality in Sanderson's dim face and couldn't say a word. He followed Sanderson down the hall, and they entered another nursing area. Sanderson led Luke to one of the beds and then turned and said, "I'll be around for a while if you have any questions, but there's really nothing I can do." He started to say something else, but he only shook his head, quickly turned, and left the room.

Luke simply stood there unable to move. Streak lay on the bed with tubes running from his body to various pieces of equipment and bags full of colorless liquids. Luke finally made himself speak to his friend. He leaned close and whispered, "Streak, can you hear me?" He saw that his words made no impression at all and knew that death lurked in the room just as it had in Spain. It struck him as ironic that Streak could survive aerial combat and come home to the safety of this country only to go down in a pointless accident.

Luke sat down in the chair by Streak's bed and tried to pray, but it was hopeless. *Why should God hear me?* he thought bitterly. A slow movement caught Luke's attention. Streak's head was turning slightly from one side to the other.

Luke cleared his throat. It was so dry he wasn't sure he'd be able to make a sound. "Streak . . . can you hear me?"

Slowly the man's eyes opened, and when recognition came, his lips moved slightly. Luke had to lean over to hear him.

"Hey . . . Luke."

"How are you, Streak?"

"Not . . . so good."

A long silence, and Luke said, "Don't try to talk."

"I think . . . I better," Streak whispered. He struggled to lift his arm, but it was covered with bandages. "I'm not . . . gonna make it."

"Sure you will."

"Come closer," he whispered. Luke bent over, and Streak's voice was a thin, reedy sound in the quietness of the room. It made a counterpoint to the humming of the machines that surrounded him. "Don't let this . . . get you down, buddy. Not . . . your fault."

"Yes it is," Luke said, his voice harsh and brittle.

"I'm ready . . . to meet the Lord. . . . It's my time."

Luke reached out and put his hand on his friend's shoulder. "Hang on, Streak."

But Streak was fading. Luke took the man's hand in his own. He squeezed it and Streak returned the pressure. "Got . . . a favor to ask."

"What is it, Streak? Anything."

"I can't . . . help Joelle. She's gonna lose the place. Didn't tell you that." His eyes closed for a moment before reopening. "Took everything . . . to pay for Dad's medical expenses." The words came slowly and with great effort. "I won't be around to help . . . so I need you . . . to take my place. Will ya, old buddy?"

Luke's eyes filled with tears. It was the first thing Streak Garrison had ever asked of him, and he owed this man his life. "I'll take care of her, Streak. I promise."

Streak's eyes began to close again, but he was smiling. "I feel better. . . . It'll be all right. . . . Thanks, partner."

Those were the last words Roscoe Garrison ever spoke. His life slowly drained away, and Luke knew as the battered body relaxed that he had lost the best friend he'd ever had.

★ ★ ★

Luke was walking the streets of Dalton, Georgia, soaked to the skin from the warm rain, agonized with grief and guilt. He had never felt so helpless in all of his life.

I've got to meet his sister. I've got to help her, but how am I going to do that? He didn't want to go back to the hospital and face the reality that Streak was never going to take another breath. He paced down street after street and finally convinced himself to go back and begin to do what he could to keep his promise to a dead man. He passed a couple of liquor stores, and they drew him like a magnet. In desperation he broke into the fastest walk he could bear, simply to get off the street and away from temptation. He returned to the hospital, his nerves crying out for a drink.

He tried to brace himself for meeting Streak's sister as he rode the elevator. He was at a loss as to how he could help the woman. He thought of trying to keep the business going, but one plane was gone and he knew it had not been insured. There was only one plane left, and he saw no way to make a go of the business with one plane.

He stepped off the elevator and saw a tall woman speaking with Dr. Sanderson. He could see her face clearly, and he recognized her as Joelle Garrison. She looked a little older than she had in the picture, but she was unmistakably Streak's sister. Her features were drawn and filled with grief.

Time seemed to stand still, and Luke struggled with weakness. He had known nothing but failure for such a long time, and now the weight of responsibility, his promise to Streak, and the impossibility in his mind of doing anything to help the woman who stood there kept him immobile.

I've got to keep my promise to Streak!

Luke tried to move forward but found that he could not face the woman.

He abruptly whirled and walked swiftly back toward the elevator. *I'll just get one drink,* he told himself. *That'll steady my nerves and give me time to think.* He rode the elevator down and stepped outside into the rain once more. He retraced his steps until he was standing in front of the liquor store he had so quickly passed not fifteen minutes earlier.

CHAPTER THIRTEEN

THE HAVEN

★ ★ ★

Opening the door to the wood stove, Joelle checked on the fire burning cheerily there, added a chunk of white oak firewood, then slammed the door shut. Straightening up, she smiled at the five girls who were gathered around watching her. "If you're going to cook, you've got to have a fire, I always say."

"When did you learn to cook, Joelle?" The speaker was the smallest of the five girls. Sunny was twelve and had a mop of blond hair and a pair of blue-gray eyes. She looked angelic but was known to throw temper tantrums from time to time. She was in a good humor now, however, and waited for Joelle's answer.

"When I was younger than you, my mama taught me how to cook, and I'm going to teach all of you."

"I don't wanna learn how to cook." The speaker was Phyllis, who at age fifteen was the oldest of the girls who were currently living with Joelle. She had hair as black as the darkest thing in nature and large dark eyes, and there was a sensuous and bold air about her. She had developed a womanly figure and had a sultry look of rebellion on her face.

"What do I want to learn to cook for? I'm gonna hire somebody to do all my cooking," Phyllis declared, tossing her head.

Fourteen-year-old Shirley ran her hand through her mop of auburn hair. She had large blue eyes and was in an argumentative mood, as usual. "You're never gonna be rich enough to hire a cook," she said. "You'll have to learn just like the rest of us."

Phyllis snapped back, "You'll have to learn to cook, Shirley, 'cause you're gonna be in prison. You steal things all the time, and sooner or later you're gonna be put in jail for it. You're lucky they let you off the hook this time, but one of these times they're gonna send you to jail instead of lettin' you come here."

"I'm never gonna go to jail!" Shirley answered and would have flown at the older girl, except Gladys, her best friend, also age fourteen, put her hand on Shirley's shoulder. She had a wealth of brown hair, brown eyes, and was usually quite withdrawn.

"Don't fight," Gladys said. "You two fight all the time." She was the mildest of all the girls, a peacemaker and a delight to Joelle.

"It's her fault," Shirley said.

June leaned over and whispered something in Phyllis's ear. She was one year younger than Phyllis, and the two girls were much alike in temperament. June had flaming red hair and blue eyes, and it was she and Phyllis who gave Joelle the most problems.

"What are you whispering, June?" Joelle asked.

"Nothing," June answered sharply. "Can't I whisper a little bit, for cryin' out loud?"

"It's usually better for everyone if no one whispers when they're with a group," Joelle said. "Everybody pay attention now. I'm going to teach you how to make corn-bread dressing. If we make it today, it's one less thing we have to do tomorrow. We'll have enough to do on Thanksgiving to keep all of us busy."

The girls gathered around the island in the middle of the large old-fashioned kitchen. Joelle's father had made the walnut island, as well as a lot of the other furniture in the house.

Sunny moved closer. "I want to help."

"All right, Sunny. We start with some day-old corn bread."

"Why does it have to be a day old?" Sunny demanded.

"Because that's the way Mama made it, and we're using her secret recipe . . . only it won't be too secret anymore because I'm going to share it with all of you."

"What if the corn bread's three days old?"

"That would probably be fine too, but since we have this corn bread I made yesterday, we'll use it." Joelle went through the process of making corn-bread dressing, having the girls take turns measuring and stirring, and got fairly good cooperation from everyone except Shirley.

Joelle hoped to give the five girls who had been entrusted into her care skills such as cooking and keeping a house. It was a difficult task where Phyllis and June were concerned, but Joelle was optimistic and never gave up with any of her girls.

The Haven was the name Joelle had given to her home for wayward girls. Right now the group was very manageable, with only five girls in residence, although as many as twelve had been a part of the household at one time. Some had managed to turn their lives around, becoming confident, happy Christian women, and some had not. Those who did were a joy, and those who left were a tragedy to Joelle.

As they worked, Phyllis leaned over and turned up the radio. The music that blasted out nearly took the wallpaper off the walls!

"What in the world is that?" Joelle asked.

"That's Woody Herman on the clarinet. He's playing 'The Woodchoppers' Ball.' Don't you ever listen to good stuff?"

"Turn it down a bit, will you?"

June leaned over and changed the station. The strains of a man singing "You Are My Sunshine" filled the kitchen.

"That's better," Joelle said.

Phyllis gave the radio a disgusted look. "It's corny. Why can't we listen to decent music around here?"

The argument continued from there but stopped when they heard a car pull up out front.

Sunny ran and looked out the front window. "It's the preacher," she cried.

Phyllis gave Joelle an arch look. "The preacher's sweet on you, Joelle. You two oughta go out dancing some night."

"Oh, Brother Prince would never do that," Joelle said. "I don't think he knows how to dance."

"No," June laughed. "He's too holy to dance. I think he's so holy he wouldn't eat an egg laid on a Sunday."

"You hush, now. Be nice," Joelle warned. She turned as Asa Prince entered with Sunny. He was a lanky man, over six feet, with coarse brown hair and warm brown eyes. He was not handsome at all but reminded Joelle of the picture she had seen of a rather youthful Abraham Lincoln. He was homely with sunken cheeks and deep-set eyes that were mournful a great deal of the time but now were bright as he entered the kitchen.

"Hello, ladies," he said cheerfully. "Getting ready for Thanksgiving?"

"Yep," Sunny said. "Joelle's teaching us how to make cornbread dressing."

"I don't see why we can't go out to a restaurant," Phyllis complained. "I like restaurants. You don't have to cook and wash dishes."

"Just where do you think you'd find a restaurant that's open on Thanksgiving?" Shirley asked.

"Even if you could find a restaurant that was open," Asa said, "you wouldn't get anything as good as what you can get around here." He straightened up and rubbed his belly. "I can't think of anything that smells better than Thanksgiving dinner in the oven. Turkey and dressing and sweet potato pie . . . pecan pie. Are you going to have all that, Joelle?"

"Yes, we are, and we're expecting you to come and help us eat it."

"Well," he said with a smile, "I suppose I could force myself."

"Here. You can try this. Taste this stuffing and see if there's enough sage in it."

Joelle held out a spoonful and fed it to Asa. He chewed thoughtfully and nodded. "Maybe could use a little more."

"All right. More sage it is." While Joelle added sage, she said, "I'm planning to cook two turkeys tomorrow. Can you think of someone in the church who might need a turkey?"

"I'm sure the Williamsons would appreciate some help. Since she lost her husband, Mrs. Williamson has had a hard time. With six children to feed, a turkey would come in handy."

"I'll make enough stuffing so you can take a big bowl of that over too."

"Bless you, Sister Joelle. That's like you."

"All right, girls, let's put it in the oven," Joelle said.

"I'll do it," Shirley said as she opened the oven door.

"Sit down and have some coffee and tell me about the sermon you're going to preach next Sunday," Joelle suggested.

"I don't want to hear it twice!" Phyllis exclaimed, even as she followed the man to the dining room and sat at the table beside the preacher. "Once is enough for any sermon."

Asa was not offended. He was accustomed to Phyllis and June, who were constantly resisting anything to do with church. "That's all right," he said. "We'll just wait until Sunday for that. Let me tell you about my hunting expedition. Tom Miller and I went out looking for a deer last week. . . ."

As Asa spoke he eyed the five girls. He'd had his doubts about Joelle's calling to open a home for wayward girls, but he had admitted his error since then. *She's done a fine job. These girls would be out on the street or worse if it weren't for her.* He studied the five and then his eyes went to Joelle. She had the most expressive eyes he had ever seen, and at the age of twenty-eight, she had a girlish figure. He had been drawn to her for years now and was surprised she hadn't married yet. As a poor preacher he knew he had little hope of marrying her, but still there flickered in him, even after all this time, the dream that one day she would become his wife.

The girls all laughed as Asa told them about the last in a line of little things that had gone wrong on his hunting expedition.

"Needless to say, we didn't bring home a deer that day!" he exclaimed.

"I guess things don't always go as we expect, do they," Joelle said. "Okay, girls. It's time to get started on your chores." She stood up and retrieved the job chart from the kitchen counter.

The girls moaned in unison.

"June, you get started on the laundry. I'll help you with it after I get the kitchen cleaned up. Phyllis, your job is sweeping the floors. Shirley and Gladys, you change the sheets on all the beds. Sunny, I want you to go out and collect the eggs and feed the chickens, and then feed Marshall." The old horse wasn't good for much these days, although Joelle had discovered that he seemed to have a calming effect on the girls.

She put the chart down. "And make sure all the jobs are done correctly. We don't want anyone to have to go back and do it again."

They all left, chattering like a group of magpies.

When they were gone Asa turned back to Joelle. "You look tired," he remarked.

She laughed and reached up to tuck some hair back in place. "I used to think a double shift at the hospital was hard, but keeping five girls out of trouble—now, that's really tiring." She moved over to the stove, picked up the big coffeepot, and refilled his cup. She poured a cup for herself, sat down, and added a spoonful of sugar. "But I don't mind it. I have no doubt it's what God has called me to do."

"It's a wonderful ministry, Joelle, but I know it's very demanding."

The two sat there talking, mostly about the affairs of the church, but also about their plans for Thanksgiving and Christmas. Finally Joelle looked up and smiled. She had a beautiful smile that lighted her whole face. "I'm going to make pies later on. Pumpkin and pecan. Which do you like best?"

"Pumpkin, but pecan's good too."

"If you like both, you might just have to have a slice of each. We'll plan to eat around two o'clock, by the way."

"I'm looking forward to it. You're the best cook in the county." He watched as she sat there silently. She was the one woman he knew who could sit quietly without it feeling awkward. Sometimes they would sit together on the porch not speaking for as long as fifteen minutes, yet without any sense of discomfort. Most people felt they had to keep a conversation going, but Joelle had the gift of silence. Finally he broke the silence by saying, "You've taken on a lot, Joelle. Too much, I think. You look pretty well worn out."

"It's what God has given me to do," she said simply. "I'm thankful that I'm able to do it."

"Do you ever think about your first dream to be a missionary?"

"I think I was so anxious to serve the Lord that I ran ahead of Him. Missionaries have to be sent by God, don't they? They don't just decide to go."

Asa grinned and took a sip of his coffee. "I know what they say about missionaries and their calling. Some got called and sent—others just up and went. Those that just up and went usually don't last very long. The work's too hard."

"I probably wouldn't have lasted long either. This is what God wants me to do. The Haven is more than just a desire. It's what God has put on me, and I'm glad of it. I love it, Asa, but I must admit there are times when I'm just not sure how to handle the girls."

"You haven't had an easy time of it—getting a nursing degree and then taking care of your father when he was sick and then your mother. Now the Haven."

"Well, as you know, the Haven started with just one girl after Mom passed away. I took in the McClellan girl when nobody else would. I had no plans for the whole thing to take off from there."

"I remember everybody thought she'd go straight to the devil, but somehow you were able to win her to the Lord." Asa shook his head doubtfully. "I still don't see how you did it. That was a miracle."

"It was the Lord who did it, of course, and after she left other girls just kept on coming."

Asa suddenly felt a freedom and a boldness he had seldom felt. He cleared his throat and blurted, "If you would marry me, we could do it together."

She had been lifting her cup to her lips. She stopped dead still and slowly turned to him. "You've been thinking about that for a long time, haven't you, Asa?"

"I have thought about it for a long time. It's probably not even fair to ask you, because you know I'll never have a lot of money. It's a poor church, and if I left for another one, it would probably be no larger. I'll never be a big-time preacher."

"That doesn't bother me."

Hope sprang up in Asa. "Then, you mean—"

"I don't know as I'll ever marry, Asa. I don't feel led in that direction right now. All I can think of is the Haven."

Asa's head dropped and he was silent for a moment. When he looked up he managed a grin. "I'm not going to stop asking you." He changed the subject, for he was slightly embarrassed and was not going to push it. "What about the loan on the place here?" He was well aware that Joelle was not very secure financially.

"I've got to go talk to Mr. Damon at the bank right after Thanksgiving."

"Would you like me to go with you? Maybe I can be of some help—provide a character reference if nothing else."

"No, but thanks, Asa. I tell you what you can do, though. You can bring in some wood. It's going to take lots of wood to cook all this food for my brood—and for you."

★ ★ ★

The house was full of the aroma of freshly baked bread and turkey cooking in the oven, all mixed with the faint odor of woodsmoke. The girls were scurrying around helping Joelle finish the cooking and get the table set. Joelle had been hard put to keep up with all the girls, and she suddenly realized that she had not seen Phyllis for thirty minutes. She moved out of the kitchen searching for her, and when she didn't find the girl in the house, a sudden thought came to her. She went out to the barn. There over in the shadows she saw Phyllis. The girl had her arms around a young man, a neighbor.

"Phyllis, get in the house!"

Phyllis turned but was not frightened. There seemed to be no fear in the girl, and no threats would make her act any differently. "I don't have to mind you. You're not my mama."

Joelle ignored the girl. It never paid to get into an argument with her. She said, "Ralph, you leave right now."

"Oh, look, Miss Joelle, we didn't do nothin' wrong."

"I'm not going to argue with you, Ralph. If you want me to have the sheriff tell you to stay away, I can do that." Joelle had no intention of carrying out such a threat, but she faced the young man squarely and saw that he was uncomfortable.

He released Phyllis and started for the door.

"You don't have to leave just because she says so," Phyllis called out.

"I guess I do, Phyllis. This is her place."

"You come back sometime when she's asleep," Phyllis said defiantly.

"I wouldn't do that. Look, I'm sorry, Miss Joelle. I didn't mean no harm."

"Just leave, Ralph."

As soon as he was out the door, Joelle said, "Phyllis, you can't—"

"Don't you tell me what to do!" Phyllis held herself up

straight, and her eyes glinted with a fierce anger. "You ain't no kin to me."

"Phyllis," Joelle said patiently, "I don't want anything bad for you. I only want good things—a good life!"

"I don't want to hear any of your preaching. Throw me out if you want to. I'm not going to stay here anyhow. I'm getting out as soon as I can."

Joelle watched as Phyllis ran out of the barn, and a heaviness came over her. This was the hardest part of trying to work with these girls who had been, for the most part, abandoned by their families. Most of them had developed a hard shell and would not listen to anything remotely like criticism. Gladys and Sunny were the exceptions, but most of the girls who came through here had hardened themselves. Phyllis was perhaps the worst. Slowly Joelle moved out of the barn and went toward the house. "I can't let this spoil Thanksgiving," she said, and she lifted her head and began to pray that God would give them a good time together.

★ ★ ★

The table was laden with food, including an enormous turkey, corn-bread dressing, mashed potatoes, giblet gravy, English peas, cranberry sauce, celery stuffed with cheese and pimentos, and plenty of fresh-baked bread.

There were seven at the table: the five girls plus Asa Prince and Joelle. The girls were chattering as usual, and Joelle interrupted them by saying, "Brother Prince, would you ask the blessing?"

"Make it a short one," Sunny said, her eyes sparkling with mischief. "I'm starving to death."

Asa didn't quite manage to hide his grin. "All right, Sunny. I'll do my best." They all bowed their heads, and Asa asked a brief and fervent blessing. As soon as he said amen, Sunny said, "I want one of the legs."

"A leg it is." Asa had been elected to do the carving, and

he sliced off one of the huge legs and handed it to Sunny. "What will you have, Phyllis?"

"I want white meat."

"Fine. Let me slice off some of this breast." Rather awkwardly Asa cut the turkey up, handing out portions of white or dark meat as each person directed, and finally he served himself.

"I'm surprised you didn't eat the parson's nose," June said, her bold eyes filled with mischief.

"What's the parson's nose?" Gladys asked shyly. She had been abused by her stepfather and had not said a word to anyone for the first two weeks she was at the Haven.

"It's the tail." June laughed. "We always called it that at home."

Asa found June amusing. "When I was growing up, we were lucky to get the parson's nose or anything else. Eleven of us in the family, and even this huge turkey wouldn't last more than a few minutes. We could strip a bird quicker than you could blink."

Everybody was in a festive mood and all of the girls contributed to the polite conversation, many of them sharing some of their own Thanksgiving traditions. When the girls were clearing the table, getting ready to serve dessert, Asa said, "I want to ask your girls to take part in the Christmas pageant at church."

Phyllis and June both shook their heads as he had expected, but to Joelle's pleasure, the other three agreed.

"I'll let Mrs. Anderson know she can expect you when rehearsals start next week."

Joelle cut the pies and Shirley asked everyone which kind they wanted. When everyone had a piece, June said suddenly, "Wait a minute. I don't think any of us are gonna be here for Christmas."

"What are you talking about?" Joelle asked, a puzzled expression on her face.

"I heard you talking to that banker man on the phone.

People are saying the bank's gonna foreclose on this place. We'll all have to leave here."

"Is that right, Joelle?" Phyllis asked, giving her a hard look. "Are we going to be thrown out of here?"

Joelle covered herself well. She simply smiled and said, "You all know that things are tight all over the whole country. It's no different here, but God is going to provide. I don't want any of you to worry."

Phyllis and June gave each other cynical looks. "I don't think so," Phyllis said darkly. "I think we're all gonna be booted out. Bankers never give anyone a break."

"I'm going to see Mr. Damon at the bank tomorrow," Joelle said. "And I want you all to pray that God will give us favor again so the bank will give us more time to make the mortgage payment. If he'll just give us the extra time, we should have the money soon."

"What I heard about old man Damon is he ain't giving nobody nothin'," June said.

"That's right." Phyllis nodded. "He threw the Samuels family off of their farm when they couldn't make their payments. He'll do the same thing to us."

Joelle changed the subject, but afterward, when the dishes had been put away and the girls had gathered around the dining table to play Monopoly, Asa and Joelle were sitting alone in the parlor.

"Is the financial situation really as bad as it seems?" Asa asked.

"It's going to take the grace of God to get us through, but if God has called me to keep this farm for these girls, then He'll provide a way. But I'd appreciate your prayers, Asa."

"I'll have the whole church pray. We all want the Haven to keep on going."

* * *

The sun was hidden behind threatening clouds. It was a cold day, even though it was noon, and Joelle shivered as she stood outside the old First National Bank building. There was a forbidding look to it, with bars on the windows as if it were a prison. *It's like they're keeping the money inside and not letting any of it get out,* she thought.

Joelle tried to will herself forward, but although she had prayed much for courage to face the banker with a plea for an extension, Leon Damon's reputation was known throughout the county. He was not a cruel man, but he was strict in his handling of the bank's money. Very rarely did he show any mercy. His excuse was always, "It's not my money. I'm responsible for the people who entrust us with their savings, so we can't take any chances."

As Joelle stood there, she tried to compose a speech that would impress the banker, but absolutely nothing came to her. Finally she knew there was nothing to do but simply go in and talk to the man. Forcing herself to move forward, she went through the doors of the bank and found the office of the president, which was closed. She moved reluctantly over to the silver-haired woman who sat behind a desk and said, "Miss Lucille, I need to see Mr. Damon if I can."

"Let me see if he's busy, Joelle."

Joelle stood there while the woman knocked on the door. "Do you have time to see Joelle Garrison, sir?"

"Certainly. Send her in."

Coming back, the secretary said, "You can go on in, Joelle."

"Thank you." She moved with such difficulty it was like wading through water. She prayed as she walked. *God, you haven't given us a spirit of fear, so help me not to be afraid but to have faith in you.*

Leon Damon stood up as she entered. He was a short, rotund man with a pair of steady gray eyes. He was balding with only a fringe of hair around his crown, but he smiled at her slightly—as much of a smile as he ever allowed himself.

"Hello, Joelle. Sit down, won't you?" He indicated a chair

and waited until she was seated.

"Thank you."

"I suppose you've come in to talk about your loan." Damon seated himself in his leather chair, leaned forward, and locked his fingers together, resting them on the desk.

"Yes, sir. I need to ask you for a little more time to make the mortgage payment."

Damon did not answer at once, but there was something disturbing in his gaze. "Joelle, everybody admires you for what you've tried to do for those girls, but you know some things are better done by well-established organizations. There are bigger organizations that will take these girls in."

"I know that, sir, but God has put it on my heart to help those who are in trouble. I don't think they would last long in some of those bigger places. They need love and personal attention and someone to show them compassion. All they need is a chance."

Leon Damon listened as Joelle spoke, but when she was finished, he said, "I've been thinking a lot about your place there. You don't have much income. I know you work part-time at the hospital and you're doing your very best for those girls. But sooner or later the money just isn't going to be there and that will leave me no choice. I hope you don't think me a hard man, but I'm responsible to our depositors. I can't gamble with their money. Surely you can understand that."

"But, Mr. Damon—"

"Let me finish, Joelle. As I say, I've been thinking about this, and I've come up with what I think may be the best answer. I'm going to go out on a limb and make you a personal offer. I'm going to offer to buy your place. You have enough equity that you'll be able to pay off the loan and have some money left over. Then you can look into buying or renting a smaller place. You won't have that mortgage payment hanging over you."

"Thank you for the offer, Mr. Damon, but that's not exactly the plan I was hoping for. Besides having sentimental value, my parents' farm provides good teaching opportunities. If we lived somewhere in town, my girls would never have the opportunity to learn some of the skills that come with living on a farm." She sighed. "Could you please give me another month to come up with the money I owe?"

Leon Damon hesitated, then shrugged his beefy shoulders. "All right, Joelle. Because I believe you're going to figure out a way to get your hands on that money, I'm going to let you skip your payment this month. We'll just look for the double payment next month. You do understand this is because we have to protect our depositors."

"Thank you for your consideration, Mr. Damon," she said as she rose. She couldn't have hoped for a better outcome.

"Meanwhile, give some more thought to my offer to buy your place. It's really the only way I see that the Haven will survive."

"Yes, of course. I'll think about it."

As Joelle left, Thad Sears, the vice-president of the First National Bank, entered. "Did she take the offer, Leon?"

"No, she didn't."

"Unfortunate." Sears shook his head with regret. "Well, how much time did you give her?"

"Just another month."

"She'll never make it. She's going to lose that place. I hope you made that clear to her."

"Of course I did," Damon said sharply.

Sears walked over to a map of the area on the wall and placed a bony forefinger on it. "This property of hers is in the ideal spot for a housing development. We could put up some cheap houses there, rent them out, and clean up."

Damon studied the vice-president, then said cautiously, "We've got to be careful, Thad. We can't be the villains in this case."

"What are you talking about? It's a business arrangement."

"The people might see it differently. Some of them will see this nice Christian girl trying to do a good thing while the big bad bankers are trying to take her place away from her."

"Hmm . . . I suppose you may be right about that."

Leon Damon was silent for a moment. "It's too bad, Thad. You know, I really admire that woman. She's got grit, and I like that in anybody—man or woman. She took care of her parents, gave up marriage, but she's bitten off more than she can chew."

"Too bad," Thad Sears said with a shrug. "But business is business."

CHAPTER FOURTEEN

END OF THE ROAD

★ ★ ★

By mid-December the cold weather arrived in earnest. The first half of the month was the coldest December people could remember. Those who lived in the South would thereafter refer to the winter of 1940 as the "bad winter," and all events would be reckoned by it: "That was before the bad winter of '40," or "That happened just after the bad winter."

Luke had endured the cold as stoically as he could, and now he shivered as the biting wind cut through the lightweight fabric of the only jacket he had with him. While he was thinking longingly of the warm jackets he knew were in his closet at home, something cold bit his cheek. He looked up to see by the glow of the streetlights tiny flakes of snow swirling in the hard northeast wind. He wished fervently he were back in Spain with its heavenly warm sunshine. Lexington, Kentucky, however, was no Spain, and the winter was bringing nothing but misery to Luke.

He finally reached the mission where he had been staying for three days, having drunk up all of his earnings. The only job he could hold down was being a dishwasher at a greasy café. He had left his room in the mission to buy some whiskey, and now the pint was hidden in his pocket. Entering the mission, he avoided everyone, for he could not bear the thought of being preached to. He couldn't understand why people insisted on sharing their faith with him and wanted to shout at them, "I know the truth! I've been preached to all my life. Just leave me alone."

He stumbled up the stairs, entered his small room, and kept his jacket on. Eagerly he took the bottle out, removed the cap, and downed three swallows. He sank down on the bed as the liquor bit at him and the warmth spread throughout his body. He had not eaten since the noon meal, and the alcohol hit him hard. Awkwardly he removed his shoes, still holding the bottle, then lay down on the narrow bed and pulled the blanket up over him, shivering from the cold and the alcohol.

He kept sipping at the bottle, longing for oblivion, but his mind would not shut down. For some reason he began thinking of the sermon he had heard the day before. If you stayed in the mission, you were required to listen to the sermons. Usually Luke managed to ignore them, but this time the preacher's words kept drilling at his mind. The young man had preached from Psalm 15, beginning with the words "Who shall dwell in thy holy hill?" But that was not the verse that suddenly came back to Luke. He remembered the preacher saying, *"This psalm tells us who a righteous man really is, and in verse four it says a righteous man is 'he that sweareth to his own hurt, and changeth not.'"*

The verse came clearly to Luke, even though his mind was foggy from the alcohol, and he wondered vaguely, *What does that mean? A man that sweareth to his own hurt and changeth not?* For a long time he lay there trying to make sense of it, and then somehow it came to him. *Why, that means when a man swears something, he has to do it, even if it means he gets hurt keeping his word. Like if he told a fellow he'd sell him a car for five hundred dollars and somebody else offered him six, he couldn't change his mind and take the higher offer. He had promised to sell it for five, so he has to keep his word and take his lumps.*

Through his alcoholic haze, Luke again heard the words of the preacher, who had finally summed it up by saying, *"A man keeps his word, brethren, even if it hurts him."*

Those words burned into Luke's mind. He managed to put the cap back on the bottle and set it on the floor beside his bed. He pulled the blanket over his face and tried to clear his mind, but the preacher's voice kept repeating in his mind, *"A man keeps his word even if it hurts him."*

★ ★ ★

Each day Luke struggled to stay sober enough to do an adequate job washing dishes, then each night he used liquor to try to forget how useless his life was. But even as he drank himself senseless, he kept remembering Streak Garrison and how the man had saved his life by making that flight that was supposed to be Luke's. He relived that scene in the hospital over and over again, thinking of the promise he had made to help Streak's sister. He felt bad that he had done nothing about it. He had reneged on his promise just like he had given up on everything else meaningful in life.

That evening as Luke got off work, he hurried past the liquor store, even though his nerves were crawling with desire for the drink. But he gritted his teeth and went straight to the rescue mission. He found Jim Edmonds, the director, standing beside a wood stove. "It's pretty cold out there, isn't it, Luke?"

"Brother Edmonds, I've got to leave here."

Edmonds was a well-built man with thick shoulders and a firm neck. He had played football for a while for the Green Bay Packers and was able to handle any trouble. "And go where, Luke?"

"I've got to go to Tennessee."

"Maybe we ought to talk about it. Come on into the kitchen. We'll have a cup of coffee and you can tell me about your plan."

Luke followed Edmonds into the kitchen, and for the next half hour he sat there drinking coffee, his hands trembling with the need for drink. He told the whole story to Edmonds and finally said, "So you see I've got to go try to help Streak's sister."

"I think it's a good thing for you to do," Edmonds said quickly, "but this may not be the best time. The radio says there's a snowstorm coming up. Maybe a blizzard."

"I've got to quit making excuses. Whether there's a blizzard coming or not, I've got to do it, but I didn't want to leave without telling you why."

"How are you going to get there? Train?"

"I haven't thought about that yet." Actually Luke did not have enough money even for bus fare.

Edmonds reached into his pocket and pulled out several ones. "This'll help a little bit. I wish it was more. But I really do think you should wait until this weather clears up."

"I don't think I can do that, but I want to thank you for all you've done for me."

"Well, I'll be praying for you, as I always have, along with all the other fellows here. When will you leave?"

"Right after breakfast tomorrow morning."

"I'll see you at breakfast, then."

★ ★ ★

The snow had stopped, but the air was crisp with cold. As Luke trudged along the country road, his feet were numb. They broke through the crust of snow that had fallen the night before, and the wind bit at his face. He'd had a series of short rides that got him through Kentucky and most of Tennessee.

He had spent the night in a barn, but the hacking cough that had started the day before was worse. A coughing fit suddenly doubled him over. This was no ordinary cough. It was like being torn in two.

When he straightened up, his face felt tight against the cold. He heard a vehicle approaching from behind him and looked back to see an old Chevrolet truck. He wearily stuck his thumb out and the truck stopped.

"Hop in," the driver said.

"Appreciate it," Luke said. He got in, happy to get out of the wind. He didn't know if his numb feet would ever recover.

"How far you going?"

"I'm looking for the Garrison place, near Chattanooga. Have you heard of Joelle Garrison?"

"Oh sure. I can get you almost there. I only live five miles from the Haven. Have you come far?"

"Pretty far." Luke leaned back and closed his eyes. He was racked with the cough several times as they made their bumpy progress down the highway.

"Well, this is as far as I go," the driver said after a time.

Luke opened his eyes. "I appreciate the ride."

"I wish I could take you the rest of the way, but I'm low on gas."

"Just tell me where it is. I'll make it from here."

"Straight on down this road five miles. When you see a big silo on the left, you turn on the road to the right, and the Garrison place is just a quarter of a mile farther on."

"Thanks again for the ride."

Luke barely heard the man's good-bye. As he stepped out of the warmth of the truck, the cold swept back into his bones, and it was all he could do to trudge along. He had to stop often when his hacking cough would cut off his breath. Finally he saw the silo that the man had mentioned and stiffly turned down the road to the right. He kept walking until he saw a house. He had almost reached it when he stumbled and did not have the strength to get up. It was growing dark, and he knew he would freeze to death if he stayed there. Still, the strength had left his body. He tried to get up, began coughing, and then he knew he would never make it to the house. He whispered, "Streak, I did my best. . . . I just couldn't make it."

As Luke lay there, he knew he was dying. His body grew numb, but strangely enough, he felt his mind growing clearer. He thought of a Sunday morning when he'd sat beside his parents in church—a rare morning when he had listened to the sermon instead of dozing. He had been only fourteen at the time, but as he lay in the freezing snow, he realized that he could still remember the sermon—at least part of it. *Come unto me.* Those were the words the pastor had repeated over and over that morning.

Now as his life was leaving him, Luke knew a regret that went through him like a sword. Dying—and no God!

Come unto me.

Luke heard those words repeat in his mind but he knew it was too late to repent now. There was no room in the kingdom for a drunk who had ignored God his entire life.

Come unto me was his last thought. . . .

CHAPTER FIFTEEN

RESCUED!

★ ★ ★

Picking up the hammer with her right hand, Joelle reached into a paper sack and pulled out a fat pecan. Placing it carefully on the flatiron she held upside down between her knees, she struck it with a sharp blow. She hit it twice more, then put the hammer down and stripped the thin shell away from the nut on the inside.

"I don't see how you get these pecans out whole, Joelle." Gladys, sitting on a stool at the island across from Joelle, was picking the nuts out of her broken shells. "I have to pick all the little bitty pieces out," she added with a look of disgust.

"I guess it's something you learn over time, Gladys. I wasn't good at it when I was your age either."

The two were enjoying the waves of heat coming from the wood-burning stove. The radio on the countertop was turned down low, but they could hear Kate Smith singing "Silent Night." Gladys, using a pick, extracted a fragment of nut and dropped it into a bowl. Throwing the hull into a paper sack at her feet, she said, "I saw a picture of Kate Smith. She's fat."

"Yes. She is pretty heavy," Joelle agreed.

"I thought movie stars and singers had to have good shapes."

"I don't guess so, at least not singers. Kate Smith is everybody's favorite. My favorite song of hers is 'When the Moon Comes Over the Mountain.'"

"I like that one too." Gladys sat quietly then, continuing to pick the pecan meat out. From far off came the sound of a dog howling, and she looked out the window. "It's getting dark."

"I should get supper started pretty soon, but we're having leftovers tonight. That always makes it easy."

Gladys sat back down and watched Joelle work. "Joelle," she said quietly, "I . . . I don't know what I would've done if you hadn't taken me in."

Joelle looked up with surprise and saw the pain on the girl's face. It was exactly the sort of attitude that had touched her heart and caused her to want to help girls like Gladys. She knew that the girl had been abused by her stepfather, and she also was keenly aware that the girl had never really accepted the fact that her stepfather's actions weren't her fault.

Gladys looked down at the floor for a time, then whispered, "I never told anybody, but . . . I was thinking of killing myself. I was so ashamed, Joelle!"

Joelle put everything on the work surface and gathered the girl in her arms. "You did nothing wrong, Gladys, and now that you're a Christian, you can put all that behind you."

"I just can't seem to forget it. It keeps coming back."

Joelle sat down next to the girl. "Gladys, you know God says that when He saves us by the blood of Jesus, He takes all of our sins and scatters them as far as the east is from the west. I heard one evangelist say that He takes all of our old sins and buries them in the deepest part of the sea. Then He puts up a sign that says *No Fishing!* That's what I want you to think of. Don't go back into your past and think of the bad things that happened to you. Jesus took all of our sins. You start out fresh, brand-new.

"When Jesus was here on this earth, He met some pretty

bad sinners, but He forgave *all* of their sins—everything—not just the small sins."

"I sure would like to be able to forget everything, but those thoughts keep coming back."

"I think that's the devil doing that. The Bible calls him the accuser. When we do something wrong, we ask God to forgive us through the blood of Jesus, and He always does. But then later on, especially when we're quiet, maybe trying to get to sleep, the devil comes and points to our old sins and says, 'Look at *that*. You call yourself a Christian? Look what you did!' Don't listen to him, Gladys. You just say, 'Devil, you'll have to take that up with Jesus.'" Joelle laughed then and squeezed the girl's shoulder. "It's good to have friends like that."

Gladys smiled. "I'm so glad I came here, Joelle."

At that moment Joelle experienced a warmth and a certainty that was not always with her. At times she had many doubts. Trying to help these troubled girls was very hard, and the threat of having the property taken by the bank was a constant concern. She had to struggle with her doubts and fears, but moments like this, seeing the light and hope in Gladys's eyes, made it all worthwhile.

"Say, isn't it almost time for Lum and Abner?"

"I'll get the station," Gladys said, jumping up to tune the radio. Soon the familiar words of the announcer crackled to life: "And now let's see what's going on down in Pine Ridge." The two sat there listening to the captivating antics of Lum and Abner. Two crusty old bachelors getting themselves involved in ludicrous situations made the country laugh and forget their problems. Although things were not as bad as they had been in the thirties, the financial downturn was still holding the country tight in its grasp.

Suddenly Gladys lifted her head. "Listen. Somebody's running down the hall."

The door burst open, and Sunny and Shirley came running in. "There's a dead man out in the road!" Sunny cried.

"What?!" Joelle couldn't believe they were serious.

"There *is*!" Shirley insisted, nodding vehemently. "He's laying there not moving."

Joelle rose and quickly followed the two girls outside. *I should have worn a coat,* she thought. *It's bitter cold out here.*

"There he is!" Sunny cried. "You see?"

Indeed, there was a still form that was partially covered with snow. Joelle immediately put her fingers on the man's neck. She detected a very weak but unmistakable pulse.

"We've got to get him in the house. Go get the other girls."

She tried to wake the man as the rest of the girls gathered around. "Sunny, you support his head. The rest of you each take a leg or a shoulder."

She could see that the girls were frightened to touch him, but she said, "He'll be all right. He's not dead." With great difficulty they managed to pick up the still form of the tall man and get him to the house. Getting him up the porch steps was more of a problem. "Hold his head carefully, Sunny. He might hurt his neck if you don't support his head."

They managed to get up the steps, and Shirley opened the door for them. They moved into the house, and Joelle said, "Let's put him in my bedroom. I don't think we could get him up the stairs." Her bedroom was downstairs, while the girls stayed upstairs.

They maneuvered the still form onto the bed. "Gladys, you go call Dr. Brennen."

To their surprise the man suddenly began coughing—a retching, tearing cough.

"He's sick," Phyllis said. "He'll give us whatever he's got. Maybe it's cholera."

"Nonsense. He might have the flu or maybe pneumonia. Run now, Gladys. Tell Dr. Brennen to get here as quick as he can."

Gladys ran into the kitchen, and they soon heard her speaking excitedly over the phone. Joelle leaned over and looked into the man's face. He was so thin and cold it was impossible to guess his age. She brushed the snow out of his hair, and as she did so, Sunny leaned forward and pressed against her. "He's going to die, ain't he, Joelle?"

"No. I hope not. We'll pray that God will heal him."

June Littleton shook her head, cynicism in her voice. "Yeah, the preacher come and prayed when my ma was sick, but she died anyway."

"Well, we're going to pray that this man will live. Now, let's get some blankets over him." She stood there beside the sick man as the girls brought blankets, and she studied his face, wondering who he was. From the look of his clothes, he was obviously a tramp. She remembered when she was but a little girl how the hobos would come to the house and her mother would always feed them, even though they had little themselves. She placed her hand on the man's forehead. "Lord Jesus, you're able to do all things. Please heal this man."

★ ★ ★

Luke was vaguely aware of music and of hands touching him. Some of the hands seemed gentle and others seemed rough. With the hands came voices, and through the deep blackness there was one voice in particular that he learned to trust, for the hands that accompanied that voice were sure and quick. Despite the helping hands, the fever tortured him. He felt at times as if he were being roasted over a fire, and other times he shook and trembled with cold.

Time had no meaning for him. Bad dreams troubled him. Sometimes he could escape them, other times not. He was just coming out of one of these dreams, fleeing a scene he did not want to remember. He heard a creaking sound he could not identify, and he realized he was lying on something soft. Slowly Luke opened his eyes and found himself looking up at a ceiling that was made of boards—tongue and groove. He knew that much. He was puzzled and could not think, and finally he turned his head to one side and saw a woman sitting beside him. She was rocking back and forth, and her eyes were fixed on a book she held in her lap. She looked vaguely familiar, but he was too weary to take a closer look. Suddenly he coughed, and his chest felt as if it were tearing him in two.

"Ah, you're awake."

As Luke struggled to control the cough, the woman leaned over him and put her cool hand on his head. He stared at her, trying to put it all together. "Where is this?"

"This is my house," the woman said. "You've been very sick."

Luke licked his lips. His mouth seemed as dry as paper. "Can I have . . . some water?"

"Yes. You must be very thirsty." Luke watched, still confused and somewhat afraid as the woman poured water into a glass from a pitcher. She came back and put her arm under his shoulders and helped him sit up. "Here. Drink this. Slowly, now." Luke drank small sips, pausing occasionally to breathe. Some of the water ran down his chin onto his chest.

As the water cooled his throat, his mind cleared, and when she put him back on the pillow, his memory came flooding back. *I was headed for Streak's sister's place. This is Joelle.* He recognized her from the picture. She was older, no doubt, but looked the same.

"Can you tell me your name?"

Luke blinked his eyes and licked his lips. The memory was clearer now, especially of how Streak had died because Luke had been drinking. He was suddenly afraid that if the woman found that out, their meeting would be tragic. "My name's Luke . . . Williams," he said.

"Well, Luke Williams, you're going to be all right. I was a little afraid you weren't for a while there. I'll tell you what. I'm going to heat up some broth for you."

Luke watched her go, and as soon as she was out of the room, his mind swirled. *I came here to help her, and here I am nearly dying. She's having to take care of me instead.* A black depression touched him then, and he lay there, wondering bitterly if he would ever do anything right.

When the woman came back, she set her tray on a small

table and helped him sit up in bed, pushing a couple of pillows behind his back. She seemed quite strong and had had no trouble supporting his weight.

"I want you to eat every bit of this," she said as she took a spoonful of the broth. "It's warm, not hot, so we don't have to worry about burning your tongue."

He opened his mouth and swallowed it.

"I feel like a baby," he whispered.

"You just go right on feeling like that." Joelle smiled. "God got you here just in time."

Luke looked into the woman's clear eyes. He could see a resemblance to Streak, and he thought about what she had said but did not speak. He ate all of the broth, and then she helped him lie down again. "Now, all you need to worry about is sleeping and eating. If you do that, your body will do the rest of the work to get you back to health."

Luke wanted to thank her, but sleep overcame him before he could form the words. This time the darkness was not ominous but warm and comforting.

★ ★ ★

When Luke woke up, he found one of the young girls looking down at him. He had been here four days and every day he was feeling a little stronger. He could not yet get the names of the girls completely straight. "I've forgotten your name," he said.

"I'm Phyllis. Joelle's at work at the hospital, and she asked me to take care of you. Are you hungry?"

"Yes." It seemed that Luke was always hungry. Phyllis whirled and left, soon returning with a plateful of vegetables, including mashed potatoes, boiled carrots, and green beans. Luke sat up and she put the tray across his lap and set a glass of frothy milk on the bedside table. She sat down and watched him as he devoured the food.

"You eat like a starved wolf," she said, not trying to hide her laugh.

"I guess I've missed a few meals."

"I guess you did. Joelle said you would have died if we hadn't found you when we did." She tilted her head to one side and stared at him. "Where did you come from, anyway, Luke?"

"Nowhere in particular, I guess," he said, spearing some green beans. "I've been traveling around for a while."

"Are you running from the law?"

"From the law? No. What makes you ask that?"

"Lots of guys that wander around like you did something wrong." She laughed. "I don't know what you've done, but some of us here have prob'ly done worse."

"How long have you been here, Phyllis?"

"Almost five months now. It's a real drag." Phyllis reached up and ran her fingers through her hair. "I'm getting out of here pretty soon. This is a bunch of losers."

"They've been real good to me."

"Oh, Joelle's good to people, but I need to get out. I'm going to Hollywood. I'm prettier than some of them movie stars, don't you think?"

Luke could not help but grin. "I think so."

"Yeah, I'm going to be in motion pictures with Clark Gable."

Luke did not mention that there were probably several million other girls who would like to do exactly that.

As he finished his food, Phyllis told him about some of her other favorite actors. "But Clark Gable . . . he's the best," she concluded. She picked up his tray and started toward the door just as Sunny was coming in.

"Now, don't you pester Luke with questions!" Phyllis told Sunny sternly. "He needs to rest."

"I won't," Sunny said. She plopped down on the chair beside Luke's bed. "How old are you?" she asked.

"I'm thirty-one, Sunny. How old are you?"

"I'm twelve. Are you married?"

"No. Not married."

"Ever been married?"

"Never have."

"How come?"

Luke could not help but smile at the interrogation. "Just never met a woman that would have me, I guess."

"You're not ugly," she said. "Your face is all shrunk up here." She touched her own cheeks. "And you got whiskers. But if you were shaved and fatted up a little bit, you'd look okay."

"Well, that's good to hear."

Sunny continued to pepper Luke with questions, but rather than being an annoyance, he found he actually enjoyed the girl's company. It was a nice change from hanging out with other drunks. Soon Luke started asking his own questions and found out that she had no parents and no relatives that she was aware of. She had landed at the Haven after she'd been caught stealing food from a grocery store.

"I like it here. Joelle's good to us all. Phyllis and June, they don't like it. They're gonna run away."

"I think this is a pretty nice place here. What are you going to be when you grow up?"

"I'm gonna be a nurse like Joelle."

"That sounds like a good idea."

The two were still chatting twenty minutes later when Joelle came in. She had been working the overnight shift at the hospital. Her cheeks were red with the exercise and cold. "Sunny, you scoot now."

"I'm not through asking questions."

"Yes you are. You leave Luke alone."

Joelle edged the girl out, shut the door, then proceeded to take Luke's temperature and pulse with the professional air of a nurse. She took the thermometer out and studied it, then said, "Ninety-eight point two. That's good—and your pulse is good."

"Must be all the good care I've been getting here."

"I think you're over the worst of it. Where were you

headed when you passed out in our front yard?"

Luke had been wondering how long it would take her to ask that question. Now he gave her the answer he had rehearsed. "I was thinking about heading south. The cold weather has pretty much done me in."

"It's done a lot of people in."

"I'd like to help around here for a while, though, to pay for my keep."

Joelle laughed. She had a good laugh, a deep laugh for a woman. "You're not going to be doing much for a while. You need to eat and rest. I've got to go fix breakfast now. I'll send one of the girls up with a tray for you in a little bit. You want to sit up for a while in the chair?"

"That would be good."

Joelle helped him into the chair and pulled a blanket over him. "I'll move the radio closer so you can listen to whatever you want." She positioned the radio.

"Thank you, Miss Garrison."

"You might as well call me by my first name like everybody else does."

Luke smiled up at her. "Okay, Joelle."

★ ★ ★

Luke put on his freshly ironed shirt, tucked it into his pants, and tightened his belt. It felt wonderful to finally get out of his pajamas. He made his way into the kitchen, noting on the calendar on the kitchen wall that it was Friday, December 22. "Almost Christmas," he declared.

Joelle turned from the stove, startled. She cautioned him, "Now, Luke, you don't need to do too much."

"I won't. I'll just sit here and watch you cook. That doesn't take much energy."

"I'll tell you what." She took a large lard can from the corner of the counter and said, "You can work on our Christmas decorations."

"What is this?"

"Red berries. See, we're stringing them." She handed him a needle and thread that was partly filled with berries. "You just stick the needle into the berry and shove it down to the end. We can't afford any store-bought decorations, but we'll have a big turkey and all the trimmings."

Luke picked up the needle and pierced one of the berries, then pushed it down to the end of the thread. "I haven't had much experience with needles and thread."

He kept threading the red berries while Joelle moved around the kitchen. He noted her efficiency and strength as she worked. It reminded him of his own mother. "Where are all the girls?"

"Brother Prince loaded them all into the pickup truck and took them out to get a tree. I don't know how they're going to fit all the girls plus a tree in the back!"

"That should be quite a sight."

"He's going to put the tree up in the living room, and we're going to decorate it."

"I hear you're engaged to the reverend."

"Where'd you hear that? Oh, Sunny, I suppose."

"Yeah, she told me that."

"You can't believe everything Sunny says. Asa's just a good friend. I don't know what we would have done without his help and the help of our church. It's a small church," she said, "not much money, but they've pitched in with all kinds of help. They furnish clothes for the girls, and they always see that we have plenty to eat."

They worked quietly for a few minutes and then Joelle switched on the radio. "Time for the news," she said.

> President Roosevelt, the only American president ever elected for a third term, accompanied by the vice-president, addressed a crowd at Hyde Park today, promising to be the same Franklin Roosevelt you've always known. . . .
>
> Novelist F. Scott Fitzgerald died yesterday at the age of forty-four. . . .
>
> German troops continue to herd Warsaw's Jewish

population behind an eight-foot wall, enclosing the city's ghetto district. . . .

"That's bad news," Luke said grimly.

"Why are they doing it?" Joelle wondered.

"Hitler and his crowd hate Jews. They think they're an inferior race."

Finally the newscast ended, and Luke shook his head. "It looks like the whole world's gone crazy. I don't see any hope."

"There's always hope. Hitler is evil, but God will eventually bring him down."

Luke went back to stringing his berries, but as he did so, he watched Joelle go about her work. At first Luke had been impressed by Joelle's spiritual strength; now he also saw that she was an attractive woman. She was tall, slim, and had an air about her that he liked but could not identify. It wasn't exactly joy, but that was certainly part of it. He had figured out that she was having a tough time holding this place together, but he could also see that she kept that fact carefully hidden from strangers.

He was thinking about how he could possibly help this strong woman when he himself was as weak as a kitten.

The door slammed, and Joelle said, "They're back."

Asa Prince came in, his cheeks ruddy. "We've got a fine tree, Joelle," he said. "I'll have to make a stand for it, but we can decorate it tonight."

"That's great, Asa."

"What are you doing there, Luke?" Asa asked.

Luke held up a string of red berries. "Doing my part to make decorations."

"That'll look good on the tree."

Luke was aware that the preacher was staring at him, and finally Asa asked, "What are your plans, Luke?"

"Well, first of all to get a hundred percent healthy. Then when I'm healthy, I thought I could stay here a while and do some work around the place to try to thank Joelle and the girls for saving my life. There's plenty to do, I imagine."

Asa hesitated, concern evident on his face. "I can find you a place to stay."

"Why, Asa," Joelle said, "we've got plenty of room here."

Prince started to speak and then changed his mind. "I guess I'll go build a stand for the tree now."

As soon as Asa left, Luke turned and grinned. "The preacher's jealous."

"Don't be silly!"

"I don't blame him. He's in love with you, and he doesn't want another fellow hanging around."

"That's nonsense. I told you we're just friends."

★ ★ ★

On Sunday night, Luke went to the Christmas pageant at Asa and Joelle's church and sat with her and Phyllis and June. The other three girls had parts in the production.

"What did you think?" Sunny asked as she ran up to Luke after the pageant.

"I think you were born an actress," he said, much to her delight, putting his hand on her blond head.

He complimented Shirley and Gladys on their performances too when they joined the group.

As they returned from the pageant, Luke felt worn out. The trip to church had taken all his strength. He collapsed onto a kitchen stool and watched as Joelle began preparing for breakfast. She always did that the last thing at night to save time in the morning.

Luke cleared his throat. "Sunny showed me that room out in the barn yesterday. I'm moving out there."

"Don't be ridiculous. It's freezing cold out there."

"I'll use the little wood stove that's out there, and the old cot I found up in the attic."

"You can't sleep in that barn."

"I've had your bed long enough. You need your room back. I'll stay there tonight and tomorrow, but after Christmas

Sunny will help me get settled out there. I'm not good for much yet, but I do want to stay and work for a while to pay you back for what you've done."

"You don't have to do that." Despite her words, Joelle was secretly pleased. Phyllis had said from the time Luke came, "He'll just be another mouth to feed." But Joelle had not believed this. She saw something in Luke Williams that puzzled her. There was strength in him but also weakness. Now she smiled at him and said, "We'll all help. We'll fix you up a nice room out there. Now, you'd better go to bed. You've had a long day."

"I think I will. I'm pretty tired."

Luke got up and started to leave, then turned and said, "I don't know if I've thanked you yet for saving my life, but if I haven't, I want to thank you now."

"Why, anybody would have done it."

"But you did it." Luke turned and made his way to the bedroom. He quickly undressed and got under the covers. He thought for a while how much he admired Joelle Garrison. He saw a lot of her brother in the woman, and he went to sleep thinking, *I've got to help her out of this financial trouble somehow.*

CHAPTER SIXTEEN

SURPRISES FOR LUKE

★ ★ ★

Luke straightened up, leaning the ax against the stump. The sky was a hard blue stretching from horizon to horizon with only a few clouds drifting in from the west. It seemed to him that the sky was hard enough to scratch a match on. The girls had all left for school a half hour earlier, laughing and giggling as they walked to the bus stop. Joelle was working in the kitchen, and Luke had come outside to split some firewood.

Taking his eyes from the sky, he looked at his palms with a grimace. Washing dishes at a small café had certainly not prepared his hands for this. He looked at the small pile of wood he had split. Asa had sawed the trees down, and most of them were about a foot to a foot and a half in diameter, just the right size for firewood when they were split into quarters. Luke took a deep breath, picked up one of the two-foot lengths, and balanced it on the stump that served for a chopping block. After examining the log for any natural splits, he took a deep breath and swung hard, but he just nicked the edge of the log.

"Good one!" Luke exclaimed sarcastically. He righted the

length of log again. "You might as well get ready. You're going to be split." He laughed. "I'm talking to myself. I guess my next stop's the lunatic asylum." He had always liked to split wood, and this was good white ash, the easiest of all woods to split. He grasped the ax again and swung it over his head. This time it struck right where he wanted it to, and the wood fell to each side as splinterless as a cloven rock. With a grunt of satisfaction, Luke picked up one half, split it, and was just preparing to split the other when a voice behind him said, "Luke, you shouldn't be splitting all that wood. You're not strong enough yet."

He turned and saw Joelle standing behind him. She was wearing a blue house dress with an old sweater buttoned up over it. He couldn't help noticing how the sweater outlined the contours of her figure.

"It won't hurt me to split wood," he said. "I've always liked it, and this is easy wood to split. One time I went out and cut wood for my folks and I cut down sweet gum. I don't guess you've ever tried to split a sweet gum log, have you?"

"No, I never have."

"Can't be done. Just won't split. I'm afraid I said some bad words that day."

Joelle laughed. "Well, don't let me hear you say any of them now. Now, come on in. I've been keeping some pancakes hot for you."

"That sounds good to me." All the chatter from the girls in the morning was sometimes more than he could handle, so he sometimes waited until they were at school to have his breakfast. Leaning the ax up against the stump, he followed her into the house. As always, the kitchen was filled with wonderful odors of cooking. Luke sat down at the island and ran his hand over the wood. "I always wanted to be able to make things like this, but I was never much good at it."

"It's beautiful, isn't it? Did I tell you my father made it? He was a wonderful carpenter and cabinetmaker before he got sick."

"He did good work."

"Where did you grow up, Luke? You never said."

He hesitated. "Mostly around Little Rock, Arkansas. Or rather in a small town near there."

"I've never been to Arkansas."

"Pretty country there," he said. "Especially up in the north in the Ozarks."

"What does your father do?"

"He's a businessman."

"I bet you went to college, didn't you?"

"I did, but I quit after a couple of years. How'd you know that?"

"You're better educated than most—" She broke off and looked embarrassed.

"Most hobos? I've had more chances than I deserve."

"I didn't mean to say that."

"Nothing wrong with it. That's pretty much what I've become—a tramp."

Joelle shook her head, and her hair shimmered under the light of the sun that filtered in through the east window. "Don't say that. Here. You can get started on this pancake." She put a dinner plate down in front of him with a pancake that covered the entire surface.

"That's as big as they come," he said.

"There's another one just like it staying warm in the oven."

Luke began to cut the pancake, and then he picked up the pint jar of syrup. "What kind of syrup is this?"

"It's maple syrup. I make it myself."

"How do you make maple syrup?"

"You cook water, sugar, and maple flavoring together. There's not much to it. It's not as good as the real thing, though."

Luke poured the syrup over the pancake and speared a morsel with his fork. Putting it in his mouth, he chewed it and at once shook his head. "This is the best pancake I've ever had."

"That's quite a compliment. Here—I almost forgot to give

you some sausage. We make it ourselves. It's a secret family recipe. I hope you like it."

Luke tried the sausage and pronounced it excellent. Before he finished his first pancake, she took the other one out of the oven. "I don't know if I can handle two," he said.

"If you're sure you don't want the whole thing, I'll eat half. That'll be plenty for me."

As they ate, Luke asked Joelle about various aspects of the work at the Haven. She did not mention finances, but he knew she was troubled about them. It was a pleasure to sit there in the warm kitchen after being out in the cold weather. He glanced over at the calendar on the wall, which featured a big green John Deere tractor. "Can you believe it's 1941 already?"

"It is a little hard to believe. Christmas seemed to zip by, and now it's already January sixth. Do you make New Year's resolutions?"

"Not for myself," Luke replied with a grin. "I don't need them. I'm perfect in every way. I'll make some for you if you'd like."

Joelle laughed. "No thank you. I'll make my own. I always made them even when I was a little girl. Of course I don't always keep them, but I think it's good to set goals for yourself at the beginning of every year. Robert Browning said something about goals once."

"The poet Browning?"

"Yes. He said, 'Man's reach should exceed his grasp, or what's a heaven for?'" Joelle paused to think about what she had just said. She had a way of thinking things over that was both attractive and unusual. It was as if she tasted things with her mind as she would taste a bit of food. "I like that. A man's reach should exceed his grasp." She laughed. "Well, I guess I know something about reaching beyond my grasp. I'm always tackling things that are too big for me."

"You've done a wonderful job here with these girls."

"It seems so little. Others do so much more than I do."

"It's not a little thing. It's hard work, I know, but it means so much to these girls. I've been talking to Sunny and to Gladys. They pretty much think you hung the moon."

"Oh, those two. They'd love anybody who showed them any attention."

The two talked about the various personalities represented in the group of girls as they finished their breakfast. Luke got up and carried the dishes to the sink.

"Just leave them. I'll do those, Luke," Joelle said as he started to wash them.

"All right, then I'll go back out and split some more of that wood."

"Wait a minute. You need some warmer clothes. Come with me."

Puzzled, he followed her. She went into one of the upstairs bedrooms and began to pull some garments out of the closet. "These belonged to my brother, Roscoe."

Luke stood absolutely still, for a sudden rush of memories came to him as he watched her handle his friend's clothing. He recognized the heavy mackinaw shirt in the bright red-and-white plaid that Streak had worn in Spain. Evidently he had brought it home and left it here on one of his visits.

"Let me see. These ought to do you, although you're smaller than my brother was." Joelle held the shirt up to Luke's shoulder, and there was a sadness in her eyes.

"You were fond of your brother, weren't you?"

"We were very close. When we were growing up, we were inseparable," she said, her eyes growing misty. "Most boys would run off and leave their sisters when they went places, but Roscoe always took me with him." She quickly turned back to the closet and continued picking out some more clothes. She found a pair of heavy wool trousers, a hunting cap with padded flaps to come down over the ears, and a pair of heavy-duty boots. "Try these on," she said. "See if the size is close enough."

Luke took the clothes out to his room in the barn. He had a queer feeling as he put on the heavy clothes she had given him. He had felt closer to Streak than he ever had to any other man, and a sadness swept through him. Finally he went back to the house and found Joelle in the kitchen. She was sitting at the table looking at a photo album.

"Look," she said in a voice tight with emotion. "Here's my brother when he was in Spain."

Luke stepped forward, and his heart gave a little lurch. There was a snapshot of Roscoe Garrison—and beside him was Luke himself! The two of them were standing in front of a fighter plane and both were wearing helmets. He feared that she would recognize him, but she was evidently looking only at her brother.

"See the plane that he flew?" she asked.

"Yes." Luke could not speak for a time and then cleared his throat. "I know he must have been a good man."

"Yes, he was. He had his faults, as we all do, but I loved him dearly. He's only been gone a few months, but I keep expecting him to come through the door or for a letter to arrive from him. It's just hard to believe he's gone."

Luke could not think of a single remark to make. Regret was working in him like a razor. *It should be Streak standing here beside Joelle. Not me. If I had taken that flight, that's the way it would have been. I don't know why God didn't take me instead.*

"I guess I'll go out and split some more wood," he finally said.

"There's one thing you could do that would help me more than splitting wood," she said, "although we'll need more wood split before too long."

"What's that?"

"The old truck needs some work, and I'm a little worried about getting an estimate. I really can't afford any expensive repairs."

"Well, I'm pretty good with things like that. I'll have a look at it. Can you show me where the tools are?"

Joelle put on her heavy coat, and the two walked outside. The truck was parked beside the house, but she took him out toward a second barn he hadn't been in yet. When she opened the door, Luke stopped in his tracks.

"Look at that!" he cried.

"That was Roscoe's pride and joy," Joelle said. "It was wrecked. The man that owned it crashed it, and Roscoe put it back together."

Sunlight was flooding the barn with the doors open and threw its gleams on the beautifully restored biplane. Luke slowly walked around it. "It looks brand-new."

"When Roscoe was visiting at home, he spent as much time as he could out here working on it. This plane hasn't been flown in a long time now."

"It's a beauty," Luke breathed. He ran his hands along the side of the plane, which was painted a light silver.

"You like airplanes?"

"I guess I do."

"He used to take me up in it. We had so much fun together." She hesitated, then said, "The tools are over here."

Luke tore his eyes away from the biplane and followed her to a workbench and cabinets. He opened some of the cabinets and exclaimed, "You've got enough tools here to start a mechanic's shop."

"I know. Roscoe used to say the same thing. I hope you can fix the truck. The brakes are making a funny noise. Kind of a grinding sound."

"Probably the drums will have to be turned."

"Does that cost a lot?"

"Not much if I can talk somebody into giving us a bargain."

"The engine is coughing too."

"Probably needs a tune-up. I'll see what I can do."

Joelle leaned back against the garage wall, her arms crossed. She didn't speak, but there was a faraway look in her eyes.

"Lots of good memories there," Luke said.

"Yes. I guess we all have good memories and bad memories too."

"I've got some memories I could do without."

Joelle turned to look at him, an earnest look on her face. "I've learned to handle bad memories."

"How do you do that?"

"The Lord has shown me how to put all my memories in boxes."

"What do you mean by that?"

"Well, I have two boxes—imaginary, of course. One of them has a big sign on it that says *Good Memories*, and the other has a sign that says *Bad Memories*. When something bad happens, I just mentally open that bad memories box, put the thing in there, slam the lid, and lock it. When I'm feeling sad, I open up the good memories box and take out something that was really good. A fun holiday when the rest of my family was alive . . . or a beautiful sunrise . . . or a real turnaround in one of the girls here at the Haven. I take those good memories out pretty often."

She smiled at Luke, and he found himself envying her. Not knowing what to say, he blurted, "At least I can fix the truck," and went at once to work gathering the tools he would need.

★ ★ ★

Fixing the truck turned out to be a rather simple matter. He found out that the drums would not have to be turned, that they just needed new linings, and the engine actually was in good shape. It just needed new plugs and points and some fine-tuning. Going into the house, he found Joelle and said, "I think I can get the truck running pretty good for maybe ten dollars."

"Ten dollars!" Joelle's face brightened up. "Wonderful!" She left and came back with a small purse. "Are you sure ten dollars will be enough?"

"Well, you can give me twelve, but I doubt if it'll take that much." She handed him the money and he smiled at her. "How do you know I won't run off with the money and the truck?"

Joelle smiled, and he noticed a small dimple in her right cheek. "You wouldn't get far on twelve dollars. Besides, Luke, I'm a good judge of character. You've got an honest face. You'd never deceive anyone."

Luke, who was mired in deceit up to his neck, felt a surge of guilt. The smile disappeared and he said gruffly, "I'll be back soon." He turned and left the room quickly.

Joelle stared after him. "That was odd. He acted like I insulted him."

★ ★ ★

Luke had finished the work on the truck and now was checking it to be sure he hadn't missed anything.

"What's going on, Luke?"

Luke turned to find Phyllis standing before him. She was wearing a brown skirt and a lime green sweater that revealed the outlines of her figure all too plainly. "Just getting this truck ready to run."

"Are you a mechanic?"

"I've had to be."

"Maybe you can take me to town," she said as she moved to stand very close to him. "We could take in a movie or something."

There was a sensuous quality in this girl that was as blatant as if she had a sign around her neck. She was headed for trouble, but Luke was not tempted to go down that road again. "Don't go in much for movies, Phyllis."

She put her arms around his neck but he immediately pried them off.

Anger flared in her eyes, and she asked, "What's the matter with you? You got religion like Joelle?"

"No. I wish I did, though."

"Most religion ain't worth nothing. You'd be surprised how many men come after me, church members and all."

"I guess that's true enough. Not everybody in the church is perfect."

"I'll say they're not!"

"You know, I still remember a sermon from when I was just a kid. The preacher said the kingdom of God is like a net that swings down through the ocean. It comes up with fish. Some are good fish and some are bad fish. I remember the preacher said the angels separate the good fish from the bad fish in the last day."

"I don't believe any of that stuff," Phyllis said.

"Phyllis, do you think Joelle's a phony?"

Something changed in Phyllis's face. "No. She's okay, but there ain't many like her."

Joelle stepped out onto the porch and headed toward them. Phyllis, without another word, whirled and left.

Joelle caught the rebellious, sullen look on Phyllis's face, and when she came up to stand beside Luke, she said, "What's the matter with Phyllis?"

Luke did not want to tell stories on anyone so he just shrugged. "She's just having a bad day."

Joelle met his eyes. "She's going to run into trouble with men. She doesn't have good judgment."

"I think you're right."

"Did she try to get you to kiss her?"

Luke shuffled his feet and shrugged. "She's just a kid."

"No, she's not just a kid. She's headed for real trouble."

"She respects you, Joelle. She told me that much, although she doesn't have much use for most religion."

"She's had a real tough life. Much harder than I had, so I can't judge her." Joelle shifted her attention to the truck. "I didn't come out here to talk about Phyllis. I actually just wanted to check on your progress with the truck."

"Oh, it's in good shape. The brakes are fine now. The motor's running like a watch." He was still thinking, however, of Phyllis and glanced toward the house. "What will happen to her, Joelle?"

"She'll have to choose."

"Choose what?"

"She's going to have to choose which way she wants to go. It'll be up to her. That's the way it is with all of us, isn't it?"

"I guess so."

"Most of the girls who come here only know one way, and I feel like God put me here to show them there's another way," Joelle explained. "That they don't have to go the way of the world, that following Jesus is another option."

"Well, you're doing a good job of it."

She flushed at the compliment. "It's only by God's grace. I certainly couldn't do it without His help."

★ ★ ★

Phyllis had come to help Joelle in the kitchen voluntarily, which was not like her. Joelle knew there was something on the girl's mind, and she waited patiently for Phyllis to let a hint out.

"That guy Luke is funny, Joelle," Phyllis blurted after a time.

"What do you mean, funny?"

"For one, he's never been married. And I decided to make a pass at him." She stared at Joelle, waiting for the older woman to protest. When she did not, Phyllis laughed. "I figured you'd bawl me out for doing that."

"How did it go?"

"Didn't go at all. I was surprised. Usually I have to fight guys off. Luke gave me a complete brush-off. What's the matter? Am I getting ugly?"

"Of course not. Luke's just got the right idea. You don't need to be so free with men."

"Don't preach at me, Joelle."

"I can't help it. That's my job!" she said teasingly.

"I s'pose it is." Phyllis was staring out the window over the sink. "I'm guessing he's not really all that holy. One of these days I'll catch him at a weak moment. Prove he's just like all other men."

"Leave him alone, Phyllis. He's had some hard breaks, I think."

"And who hasn't?" she snapped on her way out of the kitchen.

CHAPTER SEVENTEEN

TIME RUNS OUT

★ ★ ★

Joelle sat stiffly in the chair facing the president of the First National Bank. She had come in early and had had to wait in the outer office for some time. This seemed to be a bad sign for her, although she could not have said why. Her hands were clenched together tightly, and she had dreaded this meeting ever since it had become inevitable. With the help of her church, she had managed to make the mortgage payments on the Haven for the past few months, but now once again she did not have all the money on time. She watched as Leon Damon shuffled her loan papers, peering at first one and then another.

He looked up and shook his head. "Well, I've warned you what was going to happen, Joelle, and it looks like it has."

"I'm sure I can make the March payment, Mr. Damon, if you would just give me another week."

"I don't want to be hard on you, but don't you see, Joelle, that this is impossible? Month after month you struggle to get enough funds together. I truly don't see how you've held on to it as long as you have. Not that I'm unsympathetic, for I know you're a good woman and you're trying to make this world a better place, but it's time to face up to reality."

The room seemed to shrink in on Joelle. She wanted to simply get up and run away, but she knew that wouldn't solve anything. "The church is working on raising the money right now. Look. I've got half of it right here."

Damon looked at the bills Joelle pulled out of her purse. "I'm sure I'll have the rest in another week. Brother Asa says one of the church members may be able to come up with the money."

Damon shook his head. "I've explained to you before, Joelle. I'm responsible to the depositors. It's not my money, so you'll have to make your payment next week or I'll have to take action."

"You mean we'd have to leave my home?"

"Well, that's about what it amounts to. Look, I've been thinking about the offer I made you back in November and I've decided to raise it." He named a figure that was somewhat higher than the last offer. "I think you'd better take it, Joelle. That'll give you enough money to find a smaller place to take care of your girls."

Joelle was tempted. It would be so easy simply to let him take over her problems, but something prevented her from doing this. "I'll . . . I'll think about it, Mr. Damon. I appreciate your offer." She got to her feet and said her good-byes.

As she stepped out onto the street, the wind was whipping the trees back and forth in the stiff breeze. Overhead the sky was a colorless gray that seemed to reflect her own spirit. Getting into the truck, she leaned forward and put her forehead against the steering wheel. "What am I going to do, Lord? You'll have to help me!"

★ ★ ★

Gladys had been gathering eggs, and leaving the yard where the hens were penned up, she saw Luke mending a fence that kept the goats from getting out. Going over to him, she said, "That fence keeps falling down."

"It's like me. Getting old and decrepit."

Luke had become very fond of Gladys. She was fifteen now with a wealth of brown hair and a pair of trusting brown eyes. Joelle had told him the girl had been abused by a worthless stepfather, and Luke had gone out of his way to make a friend out of the girl.

Gladys put the eggs down and came over to stand closer to Luke as he worked. "Do you know if Joelle's heard anything more about Phyllis since she ran away?"

"I don't think so. I just know the sheriff found out that she left town with that carnival that came through."

"That's what Joelle told me. At least she'll have a good time in the carnival."

"What makes you think that, Gladys?"

She looked at him with some confusion. "Why, it's fun at a carnival. There are rides to go on and there's popcorn and hot dogs."

"It's not as good as it looks. I thought when I was a kid I'd want to join a carnival. One came to town and I worked for a week helping them. It's a pretty rough life."

She pulled her coat tighter about her shoulders.

"I'm glad you don't want to run away, Gladys. You're doing the right thing to stay here. This is a good place for you."

"I don't know what I'm going to do. I'll have to leave here someday."

"You don't have anything to worry about."

"What are you talking about?"

"Well, you're a smart girl. You're pretty. You're healthy. You've got people who care for you."

"I don't even have a family."

Luke put down the hammer and turned to face her. He saw the troubled expression in her eyes. "Why, sure you have. You've got Joelle. You've got the other girls here. You've got the people at church—and you've got me."

"Do you mean that?"

"Sure. Look, Gladys, I've known girls who would give anything to have your breaks. There was one girl in our hometown. She took a dive into a pond, hit bottom, and was completely paralyzed. Had to live the rest of her life in a wheelchair. That's not like you. You've got your whole life in front of you."

Gladys stood before him thinking hard, and finally they turned at the sound of a truck approaching. They watched as Joelle got out, and Gladys said, "She doesn't have good news, Luke. Look at her face."

Joelle greeted Luke and Phyllis with a wave but didn't come over to speak to them.

★ ★ ★

For the rest of the day Joelle kept herself as isolated as possible. She had taken on two new girls in the last month and usually spent a great deal of time with them, but it was obvious she wanted to be by herself today.

When the girls were doing dishes after supper, Luke saw her put on her coat and quietly slip outside. He followed her and found her standing underneath a large pecan tree, staring off at the sky.

"You didn't get good news at the bank, did you?" he asked as he came up beside her.

"How did you know that?"

"You're not very hard to read. Your feelings are right there on your face most of the time."

"I'd make a sorry card player, wouldn't I?"

"You've been running on nerves, Joelle. You can do that for a while, but sooner or later it catches up with you. Most of the time, if you stretch your nerves too far, they snap." He looked up at the sky and murmured, "I know something about that."

She shook her head slowly back and forth and wandered over to a nearby bench. "I can't understand it at all, Luke."

"Understand what?"

"Why I failed."

"You haven't failed. You've done a great job with these girls."

But Joelle continued to shake her head. Luke had never seen her so discouraged. "I've tried to do what I thought God told me to do, but it's not working."

"Yes it is. It *is* working."

"What about Phyllis?" She turned on the bench and faced him, her eyes full of pain. The moon was bright and its silver light washed over her face. "I did my best, but she's lost."

"You can't know that."

"She ran away with a carnival, of all things. You know what that means."

"But while she was here with you she saw a lot of truth. She heard some good things, and she saw some good people. Mostly you. It soaked in, Joelle. She won't be able to get away from it. That's the way it is with me. I know my life's been a mess, but even when things are the darkest, I look back to some times when good people impressed themselves upon me. I'm sure you've read the parable in the Bible about a man who went out to sow seed. He sowed a lot of it that didn't come up, but some of it fell on good ground. I think that's going to happen to Phyllis."

He continued to try to encourage and comfort her, but finally he was aware that tears were running down her face. It shocked him, for he had never seen her cry before. He put his arm around her and pulled her close. "Maybe I can help," he said gently.

He held her as she gave in completely to her grief. She cried openly, her body wracked with sobs. Finally she seemed to calm down and eventually became quiet. She looked up at him and he gently wiped away her tears from each cheek.

"You're going to be all right," he whispered. He leaned forward and kissed her on the lips.

When he pulled away, she asked, "Why did you do that?"

"Why? Why is a man drawn to a woman?"

"For a lot of bad reasons."

"Sure. But there's one good one. A man finds beauty in a woman." He dabbed at a tear he had missed. "And I find it in you."

Joelle could not answer. She was so stricken she could do nothing but cling to him. Finally she whispered, "I'm too tired to go on, Luke. I just can't make it like this." She stood and went into the house.

Luke sat on the bench for a long time. He looked up into the stars, almost expecting to see God among them, but he saw only the brilliance of their beams. With a sigh, he finally got up and went to his room in the barn.

★ ★ ★

Everybody at the Haven had been on pins and needles to see if the people at church would manage to raise enough money to help Joelle make the March mortgage payment. They all relaxed—temporarily—when she made her trip to the bank, money in hand. Of course, now that it was April, the tension and drama would begin again. Luke knew that the financial pressure was still crushing Joelle, and it troubled him that he was able to do no more to help her than the few chores he had assumed.

Sunny had persuaded him to take her fishing at the creek that bordered the property. It was full of plump sun perch, none of them huge but delicious when they were fried. So the two of them had made their way there, and now Luke sat on the grass with the warm sunshine on his face, listening as Sunny chattered on.

"I'm worried about Joelle, Luke. She don't look good."

"She's worried about losing this place," he said.

"Why, that can't happen. Where would us girls go?"

"I don't know, Sunny, but that's what she's worried about."

"But she don't have to worry. We can pray about it."

Luke was amused by the girl. She had become a Christian

only a short time ago, and now she wove God into her conversation as much as she did fishing or the popular songs that she liked from the radio. "You think it's that easy, do you?"

"Sure it is. We'll just pray right now." Without preamble, Sunny started talking as if God were sitting right on the creek bank beside them. "God, you've gotta do somethin' about this problem Joelle's got. You know she's only a woman and she can't handle everything, so I'm telling you, you gotta come down and do somethin' to pay this place off. And you gotta do it right away."

Luke almost laughed out loud as Sunny bombarded heaven.

The girl concluded with, "Take care of it right away, God. Amen."

"Don't you think you're pushing God a bit too hard?"

"Oh no. He likes it," Sunny said, a serious look on her face.

"He likes to be told what to do?"

"He said if we want anything, we have to ask for it. Don't you ever read your Bible, Luke?"

"Not much anymore. I used to."

"Well, you need to read it again. Joelle read that verse to us last Sunday. Don't you remember? If you ask anything in my name, I'll do it. That's what Jesus said, and He's God, isn't He?"

"Yes, He is."

"So that settles it." Sunny gave a cry and pulled a plump red-eared sunfish out of the water. "Look at that. I'm gonna eat him all by myself." She grabbed the fish and carefully pulled the hook out of its mouth. She glanced at Luke. "Don't you worry. We prayed and God's gonna take care of it."

"Okay, Sunny, if you say so."

★ ★ ★

All night long Luke was restless. He finally got up and got dressed, although it was still dark and probably an hour until dawn. He left his room in the barn, smelling the rich, loamy aroma of fresh-broken soil. The air was sweet with the coming of spring, and he walked for some time down the path that led to the stream. He stopped at the point where he had gone fishing with Sunny and sat down, listening to the sibilant whisper of the water as the creek bubbled over stones.

Luke thought, as he often had, about the turns his life had taken. He thought of his family and how he had disappointed them. He thought of Melosa, and he was aware that the keen grief that had practically torn him apart immediately after her death was no longer the same. Time had eased it a bit. He knew he would always remember her, but now it was easier to remember the good times they had shared.

"Maybe God's doing something in me. Taking away that bitter memory," he mused. He thought of Streak then, and the memory was more bitter. "I'm trying, Streak," he murmured. "I'm trying as hard as I can, but I don't see any way." He missed the man more than he had ever thought he could miss a friend and knew that until the end of his life, Streak Garrison would be part of him.

Gradually Luke began to feel he was not alone as he sat beside the stream. He knew no one else was nearby, but even so, he felt that another person was there. He had had this feeling before—mostly when he was very young. He actually felt the presence of the Lord. "I wish I could come to you with a clean record," he prayed, "but you know I can't do that. I feel like I'm past hope, but I've heard my folks say so many times that no one is past hope. So I'm asking you right here tonight to change my life. . . ."

Luke continued to pray, and as he did, he felt a peace begin to enter his spirit. He laid his whole heart out before God, confessing the mess he had made of his life, naming his sins one by one as he called on God. "I know that Jesus died for me, and I know, God, you don't want me to live like this. So I'm asking you to come into my life, take away this bondage I'm under with alcohol, and I'm asking you to let me be the man who can help Joelle carry the load that's too heavy for her. I promised her brother I'd help her, but you know I'm not able to do anything with my own power."

Luke continued to pray until a gray crack of light began to appear in the east. By the time it was dawn, Luke Winslow knew he had come to a fork in the road and that he had chosen a different way. "I can't do anything myself, God," he continued with tears in his eyes, "but I'm going to do everything you tell me. I'll join the church. I'll be baptized. I'll go anywhere you tell me to, so just use me in a way that will be pleasing to you."

He said amen and heard the rooster crow as he made his way slowly to the house. "Well, Judas," he said, smiling at the ridiculous name Sunny had given the bird, "you made the sun come up, or at least you think you did."

He suddenly stopped in his tracks as if he had run into a wall. A thought had come to him so strangely and abruptly he knew it could not be of his own thinking. Uttering a short cry, he whirled and ran to the barn where Joelle kept Streak's plane and yanked the door open. He went inside and began to laugh. "Thank you, Jesus!" he yelled, his arms lifted. Then he turned and ran full speed toward the house.

★ ★ ★

Joelle heard the knock on her bedroom door and awoke with a start. Usually she woke up at about dawn anyway, but that morning she had overslept. "Who is it?" she asked, thinking it was one of the girls.

"It's me, Luke. Open the door, Joelle."

Joelle jumped out of bed and grabbed a robe. Fearful that one of the girls was hurt or perhaps had run off like Phyllis, she yanked open the door and stared at Luke. "What is it? What's happened?"

"I was out by the creek this morning—"

"Shh . . . you'll wake the girls up."

"Time for them to get up anyhow."

"Come in and tell me what the trouble is." She pulled him inside and shut the door. "What's wrong?"

"Nothing's wrong. Everything's just right! Joelle, I know you've been praying for me to find Jesus and I have this morning out by the creek. . . ." Words tumbled through Luke's lips, and Joelle stood there transfixed. "So I'm saved and I know it."

"I'm so happy for you, Luke," Joelle said with tears in her eyes.

"But that's not all. Put some clothes on. I've got something to show you. God's going into business here at the Haven."

When she just stood staring at him, he said, "Hurry up. I'll wait for you."

As soon as the door closed, Joelle changed her clothes and ran downstairs. She found Luke standing on the porch. "What is it? What are you so excited about?"

"Come on. I'll show you." He took her arm and practically flew across the yard to the barn where the plane was kept. When he got there, he flung the doors open and then turned to face her, his eyes dancing with excitement. "Sunny prayed for God to send help, and I'm the one He sent."

"What do you mean, Luke?"

"You see that airplane? We're going to start a crop-dusting service. We're going to make enough money to pay this place off. All the bills will be paid."

"But it hasn't been flown in nearly a year. I don't know what kind of shape it's in."

"I'll check it over real good. There isn't anything I can't fix on an airplane."

"But who will fly it?"

"Joelle, you're looking at one of the best pilots you'll ever see in this world! I'm almost as good as your brother, I'll bet."

She stood there listening as Luke waved his arms with enthusiasm. He would pause from time to time and pat the plane as if it were a favorite pet or a young child. Finally she said, "You really think we can do it, Luke?"

"Yes! I think God sent me here. I came in a mighty roundabout way, but I know we're on the right track now." He suddenly gave her a hug that took her breath away. "You know something? I've always heard that there's gold at the end of a rainbow, but right here at this place I found my reward. I've found the gold I've been looking for." He kissed her and said, "Here's my gold right here in my arms."

Joelle leaned against Luke, her heart beating rapidly. He held her tightly, and she felt safe and secure for the first time in many years.

CHAPTER EIGHTEEN

The Silver Eagle

★ ★ ★

Every member of the household had gathered outside around the silver biplane, watching with excitement as Luke went around checking the various components of the ship. It was the middle of May, and Luke had spent endless hours tuning it up and getting it in first-class condition. He had spoken with such enthusiasm about his plan that he had inspired one of the wealthier members of Asa and Joelle's church to donate the money to add tanks for the insecticides. They had been able to buy the insecticide on credit, which, of course, was a concern for Joelle. Luke had simply laughed and said, "Don't you worry. We'll have that loan paid off before you can even turn around."

Luke pulled his helmet on and grinned at the group. "We're going to launch this thing right and give all the glory to God."

Joelle could not have been happier with this new Luke—he was completely different from the man she had nursed back to health. Since he had found God beside the creek, he had been filled with joy and happiness, and his health had returned almost with a bound. He looked strong and healthy as he stood there before them with the morning sun coming over his shoulder.

"I'll tell you what we're going to do," Luke said. "How many of you know how Joshua took Jericho?"

"I know," Sunny yelled. "He marched around it seven times."

"That's right, and that's what we're going to do. A Jericho march around this airplane."

"Are you sure it'll fly?" Gladys asked doubtfully. "You haven't taken it up yet."

"God doesn't sponsor any failures, girls. Of course it will fly. Now, let's do a Jericho march."

Joelle laughed and said, "Follow me, girls." She started marching around the airplane, and the girls fell in line behind her, with Luke at the end. When they had marched around seven times, Luke said, "Now, let's all give a holler for God." They all cried out aloud, and Joelle said, "Good luck, Luke."

"Wish yourself good luck. You're going with me!"

"What!"

"Yes. You're going to have the first ride in the Silver Eagle here. That's what I've decided to call it. The Silver Eagle. Eagles are mentioned in the Bible and this one's silver, and I'm convinced this is how God plans to save the Haven."

When she didn't respond immediately, he said, "Don't you believe it, Joelle?"

Suddenly she smiled brilliantly. "Yes. I do believe it, but I was just thinking back to the last ride I had in this plane with my brother. He would be thrilled if he knew somebody had gotten it back into shape."

Luke handed her a helmet and they both climbed into the plane, with the girls calling encouraging words as they did.

The engine roared, and soon the plane begin to move, bumping over the uneven ground. They picked up speed, and before she knew it, they were off the ground. The earth seemed to fall away beneath her, and she felt the same thrill she had always felt when she had flown with Roscoe.

Luke banked the plane and did a complete circle around

the farm. "There's the Haven," he said. "See. The girls are looking at us. You want me to do a loop?"

"No, I don't!" she yelled back over the noisy engine.

Luke laughed and then began to test the plane. He flew low over a field, keeping the plane steady as he went the length of it, and then pulled up just before encountering a group of tall walnut trees at the end. Luke was a great pilot, Joelle could see, for he timed it exactly right. He made a loop and came back over the same field, again pulling up just in time to avoid the trees. It was exciting and she enjoyed every second of it.

Finally Luke brought the plane in for a landing and got out. He looked the other way as Joelle struggled to keep her skirt tight against her legs, and then he reached up and lifted her to the ground. All the girls came rushing up, demanding a ride.

"I've got a job to do this morning, but I'll give every one of you a ride sometime this week. That is, if you're keeping up with your chores and your schoolwork . . . and if you bring me coffee whenever I want it and—"

"Okay, okay, we get the point," Sunny said.

"I'm just teasing," Luke said. "I'll see that you all get a ride, but right now I've got to be sure this spray works."

Joelle and the girls watched as Luke filled up the tanks and checked them to see that they fed, and all the time she was thinking about how much he had changed. Luke had already managed to get three crop-dusting jobs lined up. When he had made the deal on the third one, he had told Joelle, *"If I do a good job on these, we'll soon have more work than I can handle. We're closer to these fields than anybody else, and besides, it's tough flying here in these hills. A lot of pilots wouldn't want to tackle it."*

Now she asked, "Aren't you worried about the danger, Luke?"

He put his hand on her shoulder and squeezed it. "Don't you worry about me. God sent me. Like I said, He doesn't sponsor any failures." He suddenly pulled her into an embrace. "Don't worry," he whispered in her ear. "It'll be fine." He laughed then and walked away.

She watched him climb into the plane and take off. As he banked the plane and she watched it disappear, Joelle wondered, *He never says anything about what he feels for me, but he's kissed me and he's hugged me. I wonder why he never tells me how he feels?* She was mildly disappointed, for she had grown quite fond of him. He was a hard worker, he always acted like a gentleman, and now he was growing into a man who loved his Lord. Deep down inside, Joelle's deepest desire was to have a godly husband and a house full of children.

★ ★ ★

Luke had put in a long day in the cockpit, and when he landed early in the evening a month later, Joelle came running out to meet him. "Look at this, Luke." He stopped, pulled his helmet off, and ran his hand through his hair. "What is it?"

"It's our account book. Look!"

He peered over her shoulder. "What about it?"

"All the bills are paid, Luke!" Her eyes were dancing with joy. "Everything's paid and Mr. McCollum called. He wants you to work all of his fields from now on."

"Why, that's great, Joelle. That means a steady income."

"It's so wonderful, Luke. It really is."

Luke started to put his arms around her and then something stopped him. Joelle looked up at him and finally spoke her heart. "Luke, I thought you were beginning to care for me." Words would not come to Luke—at least not the words he wanted to say. He looked down at the ground and then shook his head. "You deserve a better man than I am, Joelle." He turned and walked away before she could answer.

He doesn't love me, she thought. *He's made it more than obvious.*

As Luke walked toward the barn, he felt as bad as he had felt in a long time. It had been so exciting getting the plane ready to fly and finding crop-dusting jobs and then actually flying again, but none of these accomplishments were as important to him as was the woman he had come to care for so deeply. His deepest desire was that Joelle would love him in return . . . but that would never happen if she knew the truth about who he was.

If she knew that I was responsible for her brother's death, she'd hate me. With that thought came the temptation to have a drink, but he shook his head and said, "No. That's not the answer. I don't think I'll ever have Joelle as a wife, but at least I can help her keep her head above water financially."

PART FOUR

September 1941–December 1942

★ ★ ★

CHAPTER NINETEEN

MELOSA . . . JOELLE

★ ★ ★

"Oh, Luke, it's so exciting!" Joelle had come out to the plane where Luke was replenishing the supply of insecticides. When he rose to face her, her eyes were dancing with excitement, and without even knowing she did so, she pulled on his shirt sleeve. "You've done so well, Luke. You ought to be very proud of yourself."

"It's a little soon to be claiming any victories," Luke remarked. He studied her clean-running physical lines and noted again, as he had many times before, that her face was a mirror that changed often. She was a beautiful and robust woman with soft depths and a woman's spirit, and despite the curtain of reserve she kept at times, at this moment she had a provocative challenge in her eyes.

"Why, Luke, I don't know why you're not jumping up and down. You've done a wonderful job of pulling us out of the hole we were in."

"We're not out of it yet," Luke warned. "Most of the dusting is over for the season now. In this business you have to make your money for a few months and then wait for the next season."

"But we have done that. It was a stroke of genius buying that old plane and hiring another pilot to help you."

Indeed, it had taken luck and hard work to expand the operation. Luke had located another old biplane that had no engine and had managed to find an engine that had no body. He had bought the two for practically nothing and put them together. Now he glanced up at the western sky, wondering if Glenn Frasier would bring the plane back in one piece.

"Glenn's not the most reliable pilot in the world," he murmured.

"But he's been doing a good job, hasn't he?"

"Well, he's a hard worker and he's not afraid of anything—which can be bad." He suddenly smiled at her. "Men should be afraid of some things—like snakes and bad women and electrical wires."

Joelle laughed. "You class snakes and electrical wires in the same category with women? You must have had a bad experience."

"I'm just careful around all three of them," Luke said with a grin. He and Joelle had reached the point where they felt comfortable with each other, and it was a good feeling for Luke Winslow. He glanced again at the sky and said, "Watch out for Glenn. He thinks he's quite the ladies' man."

"Oh, he's already tried to woo me."

"What'd you do?"

"I pulled out a Bible and started preaching at him. He ran like a scared rabbit."

Luke laughed.

"Tell me some more about the women on your list," Joelle said.

"Too many to talk about."

"If you don't want to talk about that, maybe we can talk about this idea that I've had. You may think I'm crazy, but I've had this thought that I haven't been able to get rid of."

"What thought's that?"

"We've done so well with the Haven as a home for girls,

I've started to wonder if we should think about establishing a home for boys."

Luke stared at Joelle with amazement. "We're just barely making it with the girls and you want to start a home for boys?"

"I knew you'd think I was crazy, but the thought comes to me when I'm reading the Scriptures and when I'm praying and sometimes at night after I go to bed. So I have to wonder if this idea might be coming from God."

"Of course it's something you should pray about, but you know as well as I do how difficult it would be. Like I said before, the crop-dusting season is about over for the year. Once everyone has paid up for this month's services, there'll be no more income until next year. I don't see how it can be done."

Joelle reached up and ran her hand over her hair, a habit she had when she was thinking hard. "There was a great man of God named Hudson Taylor. Have you ever heard of him?"

"No. That name doesn't ring a bell."

"He was an Englishman who started a mission organization called the China Inland Mission. He didn't have any money. He didn't have anything really. He just got on a boat and went to China. Couldn't speak the language. Didn't have a dime. But he knew God had sent him there. I always liked one thing he said very much. He said, 'God uses men who are weak and feeble enough to lean on Him.' Well, at times I feel as weak and feeble as anybody."

Luke laughed.

"And another missionary," she continued, "William Carey, said, 'Expect great things from God; attempt great things for God.' That's what I want to do, Luke."

Luke squeezed her shoulder. "If this is something God wants you to do, I know He'll confirm it for you in your heart." They both looked up when they heard a plane coming in low. "There's Glenn," Luke said. "That engine doesn't sound good. I'm going to have to check it."

They watched as Frasier made a rough landing then taxied to a stop. He shut the engine off and scrambled out. Coming over to them, he winked at Joelle.

"Couldn't stay away from me, huh? I knew you'd come around." Frasier was a short burly man with coarse brown hair. His face bore signs of battle—mostly from brawls in bars. "I got the Thomason field done. Didn't wreck the plane. That oughta make you happy."

"It does."

"Tell you what," Frasier said. "Let's all three go into town tonight. We'll find some women for us, Luke, and we'll find a guy for you, Joelle."

She laughed. "I can imagine the kind of guy you'd pick for me. No thanks."

Joelle went into the house and Glenn turned his attention to Luke. "What about you? You need a little recreation."

"Never mind about that. I got a report you were coming in too low over the fields and nearly clipped a wire. Scared the farmer to death."

"Aw, he's an old lady."

"Just try not to crash and kill yourself, will you, Glenn?"

"Don't plan on it. I got too much living to do."

"We've got two more fields to do today. You take the Jennings place, and remember there's a radio tower just over a hill there. When you come up off of the field, you can barely see it."

"I could handle it better if I had a little drink first. Steady my nerves, you know. I fly better when I drink a little."

"No you don't. You just think you do. Remember our deal, Glenn. I catch you drinking on the job, no second warning. You're out."

"You're a hard man, Luke." He glanced slyly over at the house. "You getting anywhere with Her Majesty?"

"What are you talking about?"

"I'm an expert in these matters, Luke. You think I haven't seen the way you look at her when you don't think she's watching you?"

Luke frowned. "Don't be silly. I just work for her."

"That's what you say. I think otherwise."

"You're wrong, Glenn."

"Have it your way, then. Let's get this job done, and then you can go out with me. If you don't, I'm liable to get drunk and wind up in jail. You'd lose the best pilot on your extensive staff."

★ ★ ★

Luke finished his last pass and turned toward home. As always, he was enjoying the flight. Flying had always been a delight to him. Even in Spain, when there was danger behind every cloud, the flying itself gave him an exuberant feeling. Now he lifted the plane above the clouds and looked out at the fleecy floor that lay beneath him. His enjoyment was suddenly broken when a memory came to him, and he shook his head to clear it, but it would not leave. For several days Melosa had been on his mind, and the previous night he had had a dream about her. It had been one of those dreams that had seemed so real—the odors, the sounds, the sights were all magnified.

In the dream Melosa had been running across a field filled with wild flowers. They were the kind of flowers he had seen growing wild for acres in Texas. They were almost as high as her waist, and the blue of the blossoms was so startling it almost hurt his eyes. He was running after her, and he could hear her laughing softly at him. Finally he caught her by the shoulders from behind and turned her around.

And that was the part of the dream that troubled Luke, for in the dream when he turned the woman around, it was not Melosa but Joelle he was holding. He looked down at her in shock and confusion and suddenly cried out. And then he had awakened, aware that he had cried out in his sleep.

Now Luke came down through the clouds and headed for

the stretch of farmland they used for a landing strip. He brought the plane down and slowed it to a stop. As he got out and checked the plane methodically, his mind was still on Melosa.

For the rest of the day he went about his work mechanically, following the routine he knew by heart, and that night at supper the girls chattered, as always, but he paid little attention. When the meal was over, he got up and walked out of the house after thanking Joelle and the girls who had done the cooking.

The sky was already getting dark, for they had eaten late, and for a time he simply wandered, thinking about why he should have such a vivid dream about Melosa after all this time. He finally stopped by the fence and the horse came over, pressing his nose against Luke's hand, looking for a treat.

"Did you have a good day, Marshall?" He stroked the horse's soft nose.

"I brought him some apples."

Luke turned to see Joelle approaching, apples in her hands. She handed him an apple and a knife she had brought, and he cut the apple into quarters and fed them to the horse.

"These are a real treat for him," Joelle said. "I remember when he was just a colt. I was the first one to ride him. He must've plowed a thousand times for my dad."

"He's a good horse. Good-looking too," Luke commented. "It's a funny thing about animals. Marshall here is pretty old for a horse, but he probably looks as good as he did when he was a year old."

"He does. He was a handsome horse then and he still is."

"Not like men." Luke shrugged. "We lose our looks. When I'm as old for a human as Marshall is for a horse, I'll be covered with wrinkles and bald."

"No you won't. You'll be a dashing old man, Luke."

"You think so?"

"Yes. I'm an expert on things like that."

Luke smiled at her and turned his attention back to the horse, feeding it another slice of apple. Marshall ate it eagerly.

"Are you worried about something, Luke? You've been quiet all day. You didn't say half a dozen words at supper."

Luke did not answer for so long that Joelle finally said, "Sometimes it helps to talk about things."

"I'm not sure whether I ought to."

"You can tell me, Luke. What is it?"

Hesitantly at first, then with courage, Luke began to speak of Melosa. He could not believe he was telling Joelle about her. "There was a young woman in Spain," he said. "I fell in love with her. . . ." He told Joelle about his romance with Melosa and finally told about her horrible death. "She was so young and so beautiful, and she died before she could really live."

Joelle moved closer to him and put her hand on his arm. "It must have been terrible for you," she said softly.

"It was, but lately something else has been bothering me."

"What's that, Luke?"

"It's hard to explain. I guess like all men in love I thought our love was eternal. It would never change. After she died, I was positive I'd never love another woman because I had loved her so much." He hesitated, dropped his head, and looked down at the ground. "I thought I'd never even think of another woman, let alone love one. . . . But I do."

Luke's words startled Joelle. She moved to where she could look at his face. The light of the moon illuminated his features, and she asked, "What do you mean?"

"I had a dream last night. I dreamed I was chasing Melosa through a field. She was laughing, and I ran after her and caught her. I took her by the shoulders and turned her around, but when I saw her face . . ." Luke took a deep breath. "It wasn't Melosa. It was you, Joelle."

Joelle had long known she had deep feelings for Luke, and now she nervously waited for him to continue. When he did not, she said, "Does that mean you care for me, Luke?"

"I can't understand it. I thought my love for Melosa was forever, and here I find myself thinking of you all the time. That must mean I'm not much of a man."

"I don't think that's the way it works, Luke," Joelle whispered. "If a man loved me and I died, I'd want him to find another companion to share his life with." She saw the misery written on his face and then impulsively did something she'd wanted to do for quite some time. She put her hands on his shoulders, stood on her tiptoes, and kissed him. Then she said quietly, "You're a good man, Luke Williams."

Joelle's kiss had startled Luke, but her use of the false name that he had given himself jarred him even more. It all came racing back to him. What he had done and how he had deceived Joelle. He stiffened and said, "I don't know why I told you all these things."

Joelle felt Luke's withdrawal. She had expected him to finally show some affection, to admit his feelings for her, but it was as though a door had slammed shut, or perhaps more like he had put a sign around his neck saying *No Admittance—Keep Out*. She stared at him and said, "Is that all you have to say?"

Luke saw that he had hurt this woman, which was the last thing he wanted to do. "I'm sorry. I guess I'll have to work things out. I'm pretty confused." Quickly he added, "I've been thinking of a way to get money to build a dorm for the boys."

Joelle did not want to talk about future plans for the Haven at the moment. She wanted to know how he truly felt about her. But he continued to speak hurriedly. "The American Air Show takes place once a year in different cities. This year it's at Nashville. There are several contests, races, things like that, and there's some prize money. I think I'd have a shot at winning the aerobatics contest. I'm going to enter it, and if I win, we might have enough money to at least put up a building."

"That would be fine, Luke," Joelle said. She turned and walked away, her back stiff.

Luke felt miserable as he watched her go. *I've hurt her,* he thought, *but I'll make it up to her. I'll tell her the truth right after the air show. If I can win that contest and give her the money, maybe that'll help a little to make up for what I've done to her.*

CHAPTER TWENTY

THE TRUTH COMES OUT

★ ★ ★

Pushing the throttle fully forward, Luke flipped the biplane upside down. Beneath him the ground blurred, and he eased carefully down until he could almost feel the earth beneath him. This was the most dangerous move of his aerobatics and was one that he wanted to perform directly in front of the grandstands—particularly in front of the judges' stand. He had only a few seconds, but when he reckoned that he was in just the right place, he pulled up slightly and began to do rolls, with his wing tip coming breathtakingly close to the hard-packed ground each time. He pulled out and did the tightest inside loop the plane could handle. The abrupt turns and twists made it hard to keep track of exactly where he was in the air, and when he completed an outside loop, he felt the slightest nudge as the tip of his tail fin touched the ground.

Almost cut it too close that time. He took a deep breath, headed skyward, and did a series of intricate rolls and loops as he finished his program.

Joelle was standing on the ground beside Glenn Frasier. Both of them were staring transfixed as the crowd cheered at each maneuver he performed. Glenn had to shout to make himself heard. "He's going to get himself killed with that routine. Ain't no prize worth getting killed for."

Joelle felt as if she had an iron band around her chest. When Luke had told her about the daring routine he planned to do for the judges, she had pleaded with him not to put himself in that kind of danger, but Luke had paid her no heed. He seemed to be driven by some inner force that she could not understand. Once she had asked him, *"Luke, why do you take such terrible chances?"*

"All of life is a chance, Joelle," he had said, grinning back at her. *"You don't get anywhere without taking chances."*

The answer had not satisfied Joelle, and now as she watched Luke come in and land the biplane, she realized that her feelings for Luke had grown even stronger during the recent weeks. More than once she had thought about what would happen, what it would be like, if Luke were killed, and the very idea frightened her so intensely she could not sleep.

Now as she watched Luke pull himself out of the cockpit, she heard the crowd's roar and saw him smile. He pulled his helmet off, waved at the crowd, then leaped to the ground and came striding toward her.

Glenn stuck his hand out to shake Luke's hand. "Pal, you've got a death wish," he said. "It was great, but I'm glad it's all over."

"So am I," Joelle agreed. She found that her knees were weak, and she studied Luke's face looking for signs of fear but could find none. "I want you to promise me you'll never do that crazy routine again."

"I guess I can promise you that. It's all over now," Luke said. He glanced over toward the judges' stand to see if he could detect any clues to their impression. "No telling how the judges will think."

"When will they announce the results?"

"They'll announce all the winners after the last event." He checked his pocket watch. "I figure we have at least two hours to kill. Do you want to get something to eat?"

Luke took Joelle to an Italian restaurant he had discovered in Nashville, and the two were eating spaghetti with meatballs. The freshly baked bread had a delicious aroma and tasted every bit as good as it smelled. Luke had doused his spaghetti with hot sauce, and Joelle complained, "How can you even taste the spaghetti with that hot stuff on it?"

"This hot sauce brings out the flavor."

Joelle ate slowly, for the dangerous aerobatics that Luke had put himself through had frightened her. He didn't seem to be bothered a bit. "Aren't you ever afraid when you're doing those things?" she finally asked.

"No. Not at all. I was too busy flying to be afraid. That's the way it was in Spain. When I was on the ground thinking about it after it was over, I'd get scared. But during the action, you don't have time to be afraid. You're so busy just doing your job. That's the way it is with aerobatics."

"I don't like it, Luke. I don't want you to do that again."

"Why, it's just a job, Joelle. I've been doing it for a long time now."

"Luke, all it would take is one little mistake and you could be killed."

"I guess you're right." He looked down at his plate, then put his fork down and looked up, his eyes on hers. "Would that matter very much to you, Joelle?" he asked quietly.

"Yes, it would. You know it would, Luke."

She sat very still, for this was the most intimate moment they had shared in weeks. She had known for some time that she loved this man, but he had stubbornly refused to admit exactly how he felt about her. More than once she had been sure that he was about to speak to her about his feelings, and she longed to hear it. Like all women she desired to hear words of love spoken aloud, but although Luke would come close to such a moment, something seemed to stop him, a barrier that she could not understand and that she hated. Now, however, there seemed to be an openness about him, and she quietly waited.

"I haven't said much about how I feel about you, Joelle,"

Luke said softly. "But I can't hold it back any longer."

"Why should you hold it back, Luke? If you have feelings for me, you should tell me. What's wrong with that?"

"I've had a difficult life, Joelle. I don't have much to offer any woman."

"You've got yourself, Luke." She reached over and grasped his hand tightly. "You must know how I feel about you. I'm not much good at hiding my feelings."

He was silent for a moment, then said, "I love you, Joelle." The statement was simple, but his eyes revealed the intensity of his feelings, and she was acutely aware of the strength and warmth of his hand.

"Why haven't you told me before?"

"I just couldn't, but I can't hold it back any longer." The two sat there for a long moment, then Luke grinned and said, "After we win the prize, I'm going to ask you a question. Your answer had better be yes."

A great joy came to Joelle at that moment, for she knew she had found love after a long lifetime of searching. "I can tell you what my answer will be."

"Hold it until after the awards. I want to have something to bring you."

"It's the girl who's supposed to have a dowry."

"This time it will be me. If I don't win, I'm going to throw a fit. Come on. Let's go back. They ought to be announcing the winners pretty soon."

The two left the restaurant and drove back to the airfield. All the way there Luke held her hand. He did not say much, but the looks he gave her were enough—for now.

★ ★ ★

"And now, ladies and gentlemen," the voice said over the loudspeaker, "we will announce the winner of the aerobatic contest."

Luke reached out and put his arm around Joelle. "Here we go," he said.

"The winner is Luke Williams of Chattanooga, Tennessee."

A thunderous applause and shouts of agreement went up from the crowd. People were gathering around, beating Luke on the back, and Glenn Frasier said, "You did it, you son of a gun, you did it!"

"I'm so proud of you, Luke," Joelle whispered as he embraced her. She had to put her lips close to his ear to make herself heard, and he hugged her more tightly before making his way up to the judges' stand.

The chief judge came forward, holding a silver cup in one hand and a check in the other. He made the presentation of the cup first and then said, "We realize that you pilots don't care anything about money, but here's the cash award that goes with the cup anyway."

Luke took the cup and held it high. The crowd applauded and a photographer took his picture as Luke made his way back to Joelle. He handed her the check. "This ought to be enough to build whatever you need for boys," he said. His eyes were shining, and he was thrilled with his accomplishment.

Joelle took the check and said, "I'm so proud of you, Luke. It was a wonderful—"

"Why, Luke Winslow, you scoundrel!"

Joelle turned to see a tall, well-built man in his early forties coming toward them with a smile. She waited for Luke to correct the man who had called him Winslow, but when she glanced at Luke, she saw his face had frozen and the smile had dropped away. The big man gave Luke a mighty hug.

"I never expected to see you here," the man said. "I saw that name Luke Williams and never dreamed it was you. Why have you changed your name? Have you been a bad boy and gone incognito?"

"What's he talking about, Luke?" Joelle asked.

"This . . . this is Jack Thompson, an . . . an old friend of mine."

Joelle was filled with confusion. She saw that Luke could hardly speak and that he was looking at her almost wildly. "I wanted to tell you, Joelle—"

"What's it all about?" Thompson asked. "How come you dropped your real name and are running around masquerading as some stranger?"

Joelle saw that Luke was speechless, and she said, "Luke Winslow. Is that what you called him, Mr. Thompson?"

"Why, sure. We did our flight training together, didn't we, Luke? Had some pretty close calls there." Thompson put his eyes on Joelle. "Are you two married?"

"No," Joelle answered. "I want to know about this name Winslow."

Thompson suddenly looked embarrassed and cast a quick glance at Luke. "I'm sorry, Luke, I didn't mean to give anything away."

Something clicked in the back of Joelle's mind. "Luke Winslow . . . You're the one—" Suddenly it all came back to her. She had heard from others about how her brother had not been scheduled to take the flight he had been killed on. Rather, he had been filling in for a man named Luke Winslow who had been drinking and was in no shape to fly. She could see the guilt written all over his face. She thrust the check back at him, and when he didn't take it, she released it and let it fall to the ground. Without a word she turned and made her way blindly through the crowd, tears burning her eyes.

As soon as she cleared the crowd she started running toward the pickup. She could hear footsteps behind her and Luke was yelling her name. He grabbed her arm and turned her around to face him.

"I've got to talk to you, Joelle."

"You're the man who killed my brother," she said, and all of the anger and rage she had felt at the time returned. She had managed to put it out of her mind—or so she had thought—but now the sight of Luke and the discovery that he had deceived her was bitter to her very spirit.

"You killed my brother and you've lied and deceived me. Why did you do it?"

"I wanted to make up for what happened."

"You killed Roscoe," she said, and her voice was as hard as cool steel. "I don't ever want to see you again."

"Joelle, I was going to tell you who I was, but I didn't know how and then I fell in love with you. I was going to ask you to marry me. You know I was."

"I'd never marry you. You're nothing but a liar and a murderer! I don't ever want to see your face again!"

Luke felt helpless in the face of her anger.

"Give me the keys!" she demanded.

He dug into his pocket and handed her the keys, knowing that this part of his life was over.

She got in the truck and drove off, leaving him standing in a cloud of dust. He had often wondered what it would be like to be shot out of the sky back when he had been flying against the Condor Legion, and now he thought he knew. He had often escaped the bullets of enemy pilots, but he was certain that the hatred that filled Joelle's eyes was worse than any bullets he might have taken.

CHAPTER TWENTY-ONE

WISDOM FROM TROUBLED GIRLS

★ ★ ★

As Joelle worked on the books, she was suddenly aware that someone had come into the office. Looking up, she saw Sunny, who was looking at her in a sullen fashion.

"What is it, Sunny?"

"I want to know the truth."

"The truth about what?"

"About why Luke left." Sunny had been shocked when Luke had gathered his few belongings and left. Joelle had not witnessed the parting, but Sunny had come to her afterward and said accusingly, "Why did you run Luke off, Joelle?" Joelle had known it was futile to explain the situation to a thirteen-year-old, and she had put her off as best she could.

Now, however, Sunny was glaring at her with resentment. "You never tell me anything, and you lied to me about why Luke left."

"I didn't lie to you. I just didn't tell you all the truth."

"Luke was in love with you, and you were in love with him. Everybody knew it."

"That . . . that's not exactly true."

"What do you mean? You either love someone or you don't."

Joelle knew she owed it to the girl to attempt to explain. Sunny had always been fond of Luke, and he had spent a great deal of time with her. In a way he had become both the father and the brother she had never had, and now she was terribly hurt.

"Sit down here, Sunny. Let me try to explain."

Sunny sat on the edge of a chair, her resentment evident in every inch of her figure.

"It's true," Joelle began. "I had feelings for Luke, but I found out he wasn't the man I thought he was. He lied to me from the beginning. He didn't even tell us his real name. It wasn't Luke Williams. It was Luke Winslow."

"Why did he change his name?"

"Because . . . because he had done something very bad and he didn't want me to know about it."

"What did he do?"

"Sunny, can't you just take my word for it? The man I thought I cared for never existed. He did something that hurt me so terribly I can't even bear to talk about it." She twisted her fingers, locking and unlocking them, without realizing what she was doing. "It wasn't what I wanted, but we have to face facts. He did something terrible, and he tried to cover it up, and I couldn't feel the same toward him once I knew."

"So if I do something bad you're not going to love me anymore?"

The question caught Joelle with the force of a bullet. She realized that every one of the girls who were under her care had done something horribly wrong, yet she had given her life to them. Joelle tried desperately to think of some way to answer the question, but her mind was a confused jumble of emotions. She cleared her throat and said, "I'm sorry you're hurt, Sunny. I was hurt too. Sometimes people aren't as good as we think they are."

Sunny stood up. "That's right," she accused, "you're not as

good as I thought you were." She turned and left Joelle sitting there staring after her.

"That's not fair!" she whispered. "She doesn't understand. She's just a child."

In truth, in the weeks since Luke had left, Joelle had never recovered from the shock of her discovery. She had gone about her work methodically, even taking on more shifts at the hospital, trying to bury herself in work so she would not have time to think about the man she thought she loved. At night she would lie awake for hours struggling with her bitterness. She would think about her brother, Roscoe, and then she would think about how he had died, and Luke was always there to blame. The strain had caused her to lose her appetite, and she had lost weight. It affected her mental and emotional attitudes too. All of the girls, she knew, were aware of a change in her, for she had not been able to cover it up.

Joelle yanked open the desk drawer in front of her and took out an envelope. She removed the check from it. It had arrived in the mail three days after she had found out the truth, with a note saying, "This is yours. I'm sorry, Joelle, for everything. Luke."

She stared at the handwriting and remembered how bitter she had felt when she'd received it. She knew Luke was flying for a small transport company in a nearby town, for Glenn Frasier had informed her of that. As she stared at the check, she said to herself, *He thinks he can buy his way out of what he did, but he can't. I'll never cash it. I won't give him the pleasure.*

She kept the check in the drawer, half expecting Luke to come back to beg for forgiveness. If she had an address, she would mail it back to him. She had even gone so far as to write a letter to go with it. It was a harsh, bitter letter—short but as cutting as she knew how to make it. Now she stared at the check for a long time, then thrust it back into the drawer. "I'll never use his money—never!" she said bitterly.

★ ★ ★

"I'm sorry, Glenn, but there's just no work at this time of the year. I can't keep you on."

Glenn Frasier shrugged his beefy shoulders. "Yeah, I saw this coming. It's always that way with crop-dusting. You nearly kill yourself during the season, and after that's over you sit around and wait for the next year. Don't feel bad, Joelle."

"I'm sorry. I wish it were different."

Glenn had said very little to her about Luke, but now that he was leaving, he felt he had to say something. "Me and Luke have been out to eat together a couple of times." He watched her for some response but she was keeping all emotion out of her face. "I don't know what went on between you two, and he won't talk about it. You want to tell me what happened?"

"I found out that he's not Luke Williams. He's Luke Winslow."

"Yeah, he told me that. He's gone back to using his real name again. I asked him if he was running from the law. He just said no. He wouldn't tell me anything else."

Joelle felt the bitterness inside boiling over, and she found herself telling the entire story to Glenn.

He listened until she had finished and then he said, "Well, that was a bad thing. I know you loved your brother, but Luke feels terrible about it. Aren't you going to give him a second chance?"

"Who's going to give my brother a second chance, Glenn?"

He looked embarrassed, but he gave her a critical look and said, "Let me just say one thing, Joelle. You're putting Luke down pretty hard for something he did that was probably wrong. But you'd better be careful."

"Be careful about what?"

"Be careful that you never make a mistake. That you never do anything wrong. If you ever do, you might find out that we're all human. I ain't much of a person to preach. You're the expert at that, but there oughta be something in that Bible about a thing like this. Giving a guy a second chance."

"Good-bye, Glenn. Let me know if you need work again next summer."

"All right, then. I hope it works out. Luke's hurting pretty bad."

Joelle watched the man disappear out the door and then sat at her desk for a long time. She thought about what Frasier had said and knew that he was right about some of it. The Bible did speak about giving second chances. *Maybe I could forgive him, but I could never feel for him like I did before. He gave that all up when he decided to lie to me. I could never believe anything that he said.*

★ ★ ★

"Well, here she is. We caught her about to get on a bus."

Deputy Sheriff Anderson stood at Joelle's door, his hand on Audrey Carpenter's shoulder. "She hasn't broken any laws, but we kept an eye out for her, just like you said."

"Thank you, Deputy. I appreciate it."

Anderson turned to the young girl who stood beside him, eyeing him sullenly. "Audrey, you be nice. Don't make me have to run you down again."

"Next time you ain't gonna catch me."

The deputy shrugged. "You better keep her locked up for a while, Joelle."

"Thank you. I'll watch her pretty closely."

As soon as the sheriff had left, Audrey turned to face Joelle squarely. "You ain't no better than that no-account daddy of mine."

Joelle knew that Audrey Carpenter had been victimized by her father. He had beaten the girl severely and had been arrested for it. The girl had been removed from her family and wound up at the Haven.

"Come into my office so we can have some privacy, Audrey." The girl followed her down the hall.

"Go ahead and lock me up. That's what you're gonna do anyway."

"No, I'm not going to lock you up. I know that wouldn't work."

"Yes you will. That's what my daddy did, and sooner or later you'll beat me."

Joelle was aware that the girl had bitter feelings toward her father, who had failed her so miserably. She had talked with the girl before, but Audrey, who had been doing well in other ways, simply refused to listen.

"Let me just share one thing with you, Audrey," Joelle said as the two sat down in her office. "Out there in that world there are some dangerous things—guns and knives and drugs—things that can hurt you. But there's one thing that can hurt you worse than any gun or any knife."

"And what's that?" Audrey sneered.

"It's bitterness of the spirit. Something that's inside you. You see, Audrey, a gun is something outside of you. Somebody else has it and they can hurt you with it, of course. But bitterness is inside of you and it's like a poison. It can ruin your whole life."

"So I'm supposed to just forget all about the beatings my daddy gave me and all the other stuff?"

"I know it's hard, but if you don't forgive him, you'll be hurting yourself."

Joelle went on explaining the dangers of refusing to forgive, quoting several Bible verses. As she went on, Audrey's face gradually changed from belligerent to something else—confused, maybe.

"You believe all that stuff, Joelle?"

"Yes, of course I believe it."

"Then how come when you found out Luke had done something bad to you, you didn't forgive him?"

Joelle was so shocked at the charge she could not answer. Audrey saw this and took advantage of it. "Here you are preaching to me about how I oughta forgive my daddy who treated me like a dog or worse, and you won't forgive the guy you're supposed to be in love with because he done something wrong. How do you expect me to forgive somebody? You're the big Christian around here and you can't even forgive a guy who never lifted a finger to harm you."

Audrey's words pierced Joelle like a sword. On one level, she knew everything that Audrey said was true. She could quote endless Scripture verses about forgiveness and about the dangers of unforgiveness, but somehow that knowledge had not penetrated into the deepest part of her spirit. All she could think of was the wrong that had been done to her.

Now, like a blinding flash of light, Joelle understood that she had been completely wrong. She saw how her own pride had become a trap for her, and the truth of this suddenly caused her to break down. She felt the tears gathering in her eyes and felt her hands begin to tremble.

"Why are you crying?" Audrey demanded.

"I'm crying," Joelle whispered in a broken tone, "because the Lord has just used you to show me how wrong I've been. The way I treated Luke was entirely wrong. It's not the way I would want somebody to treat me. And just as I told you, I was hurting myself, Audrey. I'm so sorry. It's been a bad thing for me and a bad thing for you to see." Tears were running down her cheeks, and she began to sob. She put her arms on the desk and leaned her head forward, her shoulders shaking with convulsions.

Audrey Carpenter was one of the toughest girls who had ever shown up at the Haven. She sat watching the woman weep for a long time, and then finally something softened in her face and she did something that was totally out of character. Getting up and moving around the desk, she put her hand on Joelle's shoulder. "It ain't too late, Joelle. You can still make it right with him if you want to."

Joelle could not speak, but she reached up and covered the girl's hand with her own. Her heart was broken over the way she had behaved, but one thing was abundantly clear—she had a task to do that she could not avoid, even though it was going to be hard.

★ ★ ★

Luke had come in from a long day at work and thrown himself on the bed. Life had become a dreary round to him, an endless cycle of getting up, going to work—including all the overtime he could get—and then enduring a long and lonely night, which he dreaded.

He had lain fully dressed on the bed for half an hour when a knock caused him to start. "Who could that be?" he muttered. Getting off the bed, he went to the door and opened it. To his shock, Joelle stood before him, the light in the hallway illuminating her face.

"Joelle . . ." he said but could think of nothing else.

"I . . . I have to talk to you, Luke."

"Come on in. What is it? Is one of the girls sick?"

Joelle had a speech prepared that she had been practicing all the way to Luke's apartment, but her mind was a blank as she stood in front of Luke. She found herself trembling and afraid, but she had come for a specific purpose and started to speak from her heart. "I've been wrong, Luke, about the way I treated you."

She waited for him to respond and saw surprise wash across his face. "I knew better all the time. I knew I was behaving terribly, but it was . . . I don't know, it was like someone else was inside of me making me say horrible things. I never had anything like that happen before, but God has shown me the truth. You asked me to forgive you, and I refused to do it. The Bible says if you won't forgive those who hurt you, how can He forgive us? I was harsh and unforgiving and had a hard heart . . . and I was altogether wrong. So I've come to ask you to forgive me."

Luke knew what it had cost her to come here. Joelle was standing with her chin up and her shoulders squared as if she were prepared for a negative response. There was in her, as always, a strength and an imagination that he had always liked. He had guessed her depth from the time he had known her and saw in her a woman of great emotion. Now he had a view of the undertow of her spirit, and he felt a great wave of love for her.

"Let's forgive each other, Joelle," he whispered. He put his arms out, and she came to him willingly. She was beautiful inside and out, and she was rich in every way that a woman should be rich. Luke tilted her chin up and kissed her tenderly, and he could taste the salt from her tears as she returned his kiss. "This may be the wrong time to ask this," Luke said, "but I want you to be my wife. Will you, Joelle?"

She looked up at him with a tremulous smile on her lips but a light of joy in her eyes. "Yes," she said, "I will."

CHAPTER TWENTY-TWO

A NEW LIFE TOGETHER

★ ★ ★

Joelle came slowly out of her warm, restful sleep. The light from the window fell across her face, the warmth of the sun stirring her, and she smiled slightly. Slowly her eyes opened, and for a moment she experienced a touch of fright, but then she quickly realized that the face she was looking at belonged to her husband. It wasn't easy to get accustomed to awaking and finding a man occupying the space that had been empty for so many years!

Her sense of contentment grew, but she was somewhat puzzled by the expression on Luke's face. He was lying beside her on his side, his cheek propped up against his open palm, and his elbow braced against the bed. He was studying her in a thoughtful, meditative fashion that intrigued Joelle. "What are you looking at, Luke?"

"Just thinking about how blessed you are, wife."

Joelle, in the short period of her marriage, had become used to Luke's mild teasing. He would often say the most outlandish things in a most ordinary tone of voice. But he was also capable of speaking of his love for her in a way that was totally satisfying and pleasing. She saw that the corners of his lips were turned up ever so slightly, and she knew that he was concealing the humor that lay beneath the surface. "Why am I blessed?" she dared to ask, reaching out and touching his cheek, savoring the feel of the stubble of his beard.

"Why, to have such a handsome husband."

"Oh, you think so."

"Yes. I was just thinking about how many millions of women there are in the world who would dearly love to wake up and see a good-looking fellow like your husband in bed beside them."

Joelle grabbed at his earlobe and pinched it. "You are egotistical beyond belief!"

"Well, we have to face facts." Luke grinned. He captured her hand and pulled it away from his ear. He studied it for a moment and his eyelids lowered. "I'm thinking of taking advantage of you."

Joelle's eyes widened and then she laughed. "That's impossible!"

"No. I think I can do it."

"No you can't. To take advantage, I'd have to be resisting, and you are such a handsome fellow that I don't see how I could possibly do that." She pulled his head down until his face was only a few inches away from hers. "Say something sweet to me," she demanded.

Luke thought for a moment and then said, "Marshmallow."

Joelle laughed aloud. "You have no poetry in your soul."

"Yes I have. I'm writing you a poem right now. I haven't got it on paper yet, but it's going to be a great poem."

The two continued their teasing as they lay in bed, and Joelle enjoyed every minute of it. Suddenly she said with a more sober expression, "I always thought I'd be a maiden lady, as we used to call them."

"Not much chance of that. Not a good-looking filly like you."

Joelle wanted to get serious for a minute and explain to him how she felt. But where were the words to tell a man how a woman felt about him? How could she tell him about the strange fluttery feeling she got inside sometimes when she looked at him? How could she put into words the longing to see him again that came to her when he was gone for a few hours? And how to explain that the sight of him as he suddenly appeared lifted everything in her to a height she had never known? She wanted to explain how empty she felt whenever he was gone, but the words were too hard for her to say, at least for this early in her marriage.

"I've got to get up and make biscuits for you," she whispered.

"I didn't marry you to make biscuits." He grinned and then took her in his arms, and they both forgot about breakfast.

★ ★ ★

The sun was barely up and the girls were still asleep. Joelle was cooking breakfast and Luke was sitting at the table, reading from the Bible she had given him for a wedding present. Joelle enjoyed getting up very early every morning, before the house became filled with the noise of all the girls giggling and talking. She had grown to love the cobwebby hours of the morning that she shared alone with Luke.

"What are you reading, Luke?" she asked.

"I'm reading about you."

"What are you talking about?"

"I found these verses about you last night. I'm underlining them."

"What verses about me?"

"It says right here, 'Who can find a virtuous woman? for her price is far above rubies. The heart of her husband doth safely trust in her.' And then it goes on to say, 'She will do him good and not evil all the days of her life.'"

"Why, Luke, that's so sweet!"

"Why, sure it is. I've told you I'm a sweet guy. Used to win awards for it. I was elected the sweetest guy by my senior class in high school."

"I just bet you were. I bet you were a regular devil."

"You hurt me in the heart when you say that, wife!"

"You might be exaggerating a little bit. Are you sure you want this omelet with all this junk in it?"

"Junk! I made that recipe up myself. You put everything in there just like I told you."

"You really want jalapeño peppers in your omelet?"

"Yes, and those red peppers too. And those strong onions that came out of the garden."

Joelle followed his instructions and finished the omelet, as well as her own, which contained only cheese, and slid them carefully onto plates. She added four pieces of thick toast to his plate and put it down beside him. She sat down and they said a quick blessing. She watched as he took a huge bite of his omelet and chewed it thoroughly. She laughed when tears came into his eyes.

"You see, it's so hot it's burning your mouth."

"That's what makes it good. You can't get an omelet too hot or a wife too sweet. That's what I always say."

"You won't have any taste buds left. You'll burn them all out with your hot peppers."

They teased each other as they continued eating. When they were through, Joelle approached a subject she had been thinking about. "I've been meaning to ask you something, Luke."

"Go right ahead. Whatever it is you want, I'll tell you how you can get along without it."

"I don't want anything, but I'm wondering why you haven't called your family."

Luke suddenly grew serious. He took the thick mug that was half filled with coffee and took a sip. "Well, you've got me there. I was waiting until I could go home with some kind of a triumph under my belt, but I don't guess that'll ever happen."

"I don't know them, Luke, but I'll bet they're worried

about you. You've told me enough that I know they're fine people."

"Yes, they are."

"Do you think they'll like me?" she asked wistfully.

"If they don't," he said indignantly, "I'll cut them out of the will."

"Luke, be serious. I think you ought to call them. I feel bad that we got married without inviting them or even telling them."

"I expect you're right, but it's too late now to do anything about that. Tell you what. I'll write them this afternoon. Then we'll—" He broke off and twisted his head back toward the door. "Look out—here comes the thundering herd."

The girls came rushing into the kitchen, and Sunny cried out, "I want pancakes for breakfast."

Audrey Carpenter shook her head. "No. We had pancakes yesterday. I want oatmeal."

Sunny made a face. "Oatmeal. That's for horses and cows."

Joelle put an end to the argument by saying, "We're having omelets and toast today. Or you can have scrambled eggs if you prefer."

"I'll have scrambled eggs," Shirley said. She sat down beside Gladys, and the two began talking about the movie Joelle had agreed to take them to the previous weekend. "I think Errol Flynn is the handsomest man that ever lived," Shirley said.

"Well, you must need glasses," Luke said, winking at Joelle. "You haven't looked at me lately, have you?"

"You think you're better looking than Errol Flynn?"

"Why, that poor fellow is as ugly as a pan of worms when he lines up next to me."

The girls all screamed at this, and Sunny, who was sitting next to Luke, began to beat on his shoulder with the heel of her fist. "You're not as good-looking as a movie star."

"Well, you are, Sunny. You're so pretty I'll just have to give you a reward." He leaned over and kissed her on the cheek.

"That don't make you any better looking," she said with a giggle.

The girls all pitched in and, with Joelle's help, soon had their breakfast on the table. When they sat down to eat, Sunny was once again at Luke's side. She was obviously fascinated with Luke, and Joelle listened to their conversation with amusement.

"How do you like being married, Luke?" Sunny asked.

"Why, it beats sliding down a forty-foot razor blade into a vat of alcohol, I reckon."

"Ooo, that's awful!" one of the girls cried.

Luke glanced over at Joelle, who was pretending to glare at him. "I was just teasing. I like it fine. A fellow needs a woman. Needs somebody to wait on him and tell him how handsome he is and stuff like that."

"If you're not careful, you're not going to get any *stuff like that*."

Ignoring Joelle, Luke turned to Sunny and the girls. "All you girls listen to this now. I'm going to tell you how to have a perfect marriage."

"I'd like to hear it," June said. "I don't think there is any such thing."

"That's because you've never seen anybody practice the Winslow formula for having a perfect marriage. It works every time. Why, people who follow my formula live happily ever after, just like in the storybooks."

"I'd like to hear it myself," Joelle said, cocking her head and turning a critical eye on him.

"I'm talking to Sunny here. You've already had a taste of the method—not quite enough yet, though."

"What is it, Luke?" Sunny said.

"Well, girls, if you want to have a perfect marriage, as soon as you get a man all married up, then you treat him like a grandmother treats her favorite grandchild."

"What do you mean by that?" Sunny asked with a puzzled look.

"Haven't you ever watched grandmas with their favorite

grandchildren? Whether it's a boy or a girl, grandmas spoil them to death. The instant they start crying, they go pick the kid up and give him whatever it is that makes him stop crying. They bring him presents all the time. They just devote their lives to making that grandchild happy. So that's the way to have a perfect marriage," Luke said, looking as pious as he could. "When you get a husband, just give him everything he wants as soon as he wants it. As a matter of fact, try to figure out what he wants and give it to him before he asks for it. Why, it'll work every time! He'll be so happy you'll stay married to him until they carry him off to the cemetery."

"Don't pay a bit of attention to him," Joelle said. "He's making all that up."

"Now, wife, you know how you're always telling me when we're alone how wonderful I am and how perfect I am and all that."

Joelle flushed. Sometimes Luke's teasing embarrassed her. She opened her mouth, but Luke beat her to it. "I won't tell any more secrets about how you make a big fuss over me. Just remember, girls, give your man whatever he wants, and he'll be sweet and good—like me!"

★ ★ ★

At the end of the day, Joelle found herself weary, as she often did. The joy she had found in her marriage did not diminish any of the work required to keep the Haven going, and by the time the girls were all in bed, she was tired to the bone. She heard the clock in the parlor strike eleven, and hanging up the dishrag, she went into the parlor and found Luke listening to the late news on the radio.

She sat down beside him, his arm around her, and listened to the news. The situation in Europe was sounding more ominous than ever. The Nazis were pounding British cities with air attacks, and a new problem had arisen between the United

States and Japan. Luke and Joelle listened as the announcer spoke with an ominous tone.

"Tensions are mounting between the United States and Japan as talks between representatives of each nation seem to be deteriorating. Earlier this month Prime Minister Tojo of Japan assailed American and British exportation of the Asiatic people and threatened that they must be purged with violence."

"The news isn't good, is it, Luke?"

"It's not bad in one sense. The Germans have gotten bogged down outside of Moscow. You know, attacking Russia was the biggest mistake Hitler's ever made. It'll be his downfall too."

"Do you think we'll ever get into the war?"

"No way of telling," Luke said. "It's possible. Roosevelt has been warning us to get ready. He's been sending supplies to England undercover—old naval vessels, things like that."

When the news broadcast was over, Luke reached over and turned the radio off, and Joelle could see that he was deep in thought. "What are you thinking about, Luke?"

"I've been thinking about your dream."

"What dream is that?"

"You know. To build another facility for boys."

"I think God wants me to do it, but I don't see how. We've got enough money with your prize from the air show to build some kind of a structure for them to live in, but it would take every penny."

"I don't think it's a good idea to put the boys' unit on this property."

"Why not, Luke? We've got land here to build on."

"I know, but boys with problems right next door to girls with problems?" He shook his head doubtfully. "I don't think that would work."

"What could we do?"

"You know the Mackelson place?"

"You mean the one six miles down the highway?"

"That's the one."

"It's been for sale for a long time. You're not thinking we should buy that, are you?"

"Well, it would do fine for a haven for boys. That old house must have a number of bedrooms. It's a huge thing with the addition they built onto it. And it's got enough land to raise some animals, plenty of room for gardens . . ."

"It's probably more than we can afford."

"We'll have to check into it. See how much they're asking. If this is something God wants us to do, He'll give us the means to do it. I think we should look into it."

Joelle was stunned by the proposal. The two sat there talking about the possibilities for nearly an hour, and finally Joelle said, "Luke, that would take a lot of faith. We just barely manage to hang on to this place. And you're talking about buying another one. We would have two mortgages."

"Well, it may be hard for you and me, but it won't be hard for God." He reached over, gave her a hug, and kissed her cheek. "We'll pray about it and see which way God is leading us. I reckon God may just want to rear back and work a miracle!"

CHAPTER TWENTY-THREE

HOME TO LIBERTY

★ ★ ★

Sunny was watching Joelle pack her suitcase. The thirteen-year-old had a sad expression on her face and had been unusually quiet.

"How long will you be gone, Joelle?"

"Not more than a week."

"That's a long time."

"No it isn't." Joelle turned and saw that Sunny was unhappy. "It'll be over before you know it."

"I don't want you to go."

"Oh, Sunny, I thought you'd be happy for me."

"Well, I'm not," she said defiantly. She looked down at the floor and mumbled something that Joelle could not make out.

"What'd you say, Sunny?"

"I said I don't think you'll ever come back."

Joelle was shocked at the child's attitude. "Of course I'm going to come back! I've explained all this."

"I know, but I still don't want you to go."

Joelle was aware that Sunny, like all the other girls at the Haven, had deep-seated anxieties. She also knew that most of the girls had formed an attachment to her, and more than one of them had experienced cruel separations in their life. Quickly she went over to Sunny, put her arm around her, and drew her down to sit on the bed. "I don't want you to worry about this. I have to go meet Luke's family. It was bad enough that we didn't go there to meet them before we married, but now they're having a reunion. That's all it is."

"What's a reunion?"

"That's when the members of a certain family come together from all over to meet one another and spend some time together."

"You promise to come back?"

"Of course I do." Joelle leaned over and kissed the girl on the cheek. "You're going to have a good time while we're gone."

"Aren't you afraid they won't like you?"

"That who won't like me?"

"Luke's family. They might not like you at all. They might be mean to you."

"Now, why would you say a thing like that?"

"Because when my mama died I went to stay with a different family. They didn't like me at all."

"I sure can't understand why. There must be something wrong with those people. Everybody here loves you, Sunny."

"But aren't you afraid Luke's folks won't like you?"

For a moment Joelle hesitated, but she had determined to always tell the truth to the girls. "Well, I am a little nervous."

"You see! That's the way I feel."

But Joelle laughed and said, "It's all foolishness. They'll like me and I'll like them, and then I'll come back and it'll be just like it was before. You won't have to—"

At that moment a small herd of girls appeared in Joelle's room. They all got as close to Joelle as they could and were pumping her with questions. June, who had reformed to a great extent after Phyllis had run away, sat as close to Joelle as she could get. The other two, Gladys and Shirley, crawled onto the bed, leaning around to watch Joelle's face. It gave Joelle a good feeling to know that she had bonded with these girls. She was very proud of the progress they had made.

"We bought you a going-away present," June said, mischief dancing in her eyes.

"You shouldn't have done that."

"It was my idea," Gladys said. "I thought of it myself."

"What a nice thing to do."

"I woulda thought of it if she didn't," Shirley said.

"We all put all our money together," Sunny told Joelle. "And we went down and picked you out a present at the store."

"Here it is," June said. "You better like it."

"I'm sure I will." Joelle began to unwrap the package. "Somebody did a good job of wrapping."

"I did that," Shirley said. "I'm the best wrapper here."

"You are not," Sunny said. "I can wrap as good as you."

"Now, don't fuss, girls. Let me see what you got me." Joelle untied the ribbon, opened up the colorful paper, and lifted the garment out. For a moment she could not speak. Her cheeks grew red, and she said, "Why . . . what a . . . nice present."

The garment she was holding was a thin nightgown of sheer black silk. It was designed for a more daring woman than Joelle had ever been, and she knew she would be embarrassed to even put it on and see herself—much less let Luke see her in it!

"We all voted on it," June said. "Gladys wanted to get you a vacuum cleaner, but we didn't have enough money for that. Besides, a bride needs a nightgown like this."

"It's very pretty."

"Look, you can almost read a newspaper through it," Sunny said. "Why don't you put it on and let us see how it looks."

"No. I'm not going to do that," Joelle said quickly. She looked around and saw that they were all waiting expectantly, and despite her inhibition, she knew she had to show the proper response. "It's the most beautiful nightgown I've ever seen," she said, holding it up against herself. "It's just beautiful and I'll treasure it forever. Thank you so much, girls."

"You gotta keep a man interested," June told her, "and that gown oughta do it."

"I'm sure it will," Joelle said, thinking, *If this won't do it, nothing will.*

"Who's gonna look out for us while you're gone?" Sunny asked.

"The Taylors are going to stay here until we get back." Ted and Irene Taylor were favorites of the girls. They were farmers in their middle forties and had no children of their own but had been very helpful with the girls. Anytime Joelle had to be gone for more than a few hours, she could call on the couple and they would come at once, and the girls all loved them.

"That's good," Sunny said. "I can make Ted do anything."

"I doubt that," Joelle said. "At least I hope not."

"Irene can't cook as good as you can," Gladys said, "but I'll help her."

"That's good, Gladys."

At that moment Luke's voice drifted up from downstairs. "All right, wife, I'm leaving without you if you don't come down right away."

"I've got to hurry." Joelle started to close her suitcase, but Sunny said, "Wait a minute. You haven't put your present in it."

"Oh, that's right." Actually Joelle had been hoping to leave the nightgown behind, but she knew that would not do. Quickly she opened the suitcase and put the gown inside. Then the girls began to argue over who would carry the suitcase downstairs. June, being the largest and the oldest, won the battle and carried it down triumphantly.

"Are you ready for the big trip?" Ted Taylor asked. He was a big man with a weathered face from years of farming.

"All ready, Ted. I thank you and Irene so much for helping with the girls."

Irene, Ted's wife, was a small woman with quick mannerisms. "It'll be fun," she said. "Now, don't you worry about a thing."

"Come along," Luke said cheerfully. "You can say your good-byes while I get the plane warmed up."

All of them followed Luke outside and watched as he stored their luggage and then got in and started the engine. As it was warming up, Joelle went around to each of the girls and said a personal word and gave her a hug. Then she went over to thank Ted and Irene again.

Luke came out of the plane and was careful to go around to each of the girls. He had discovered that they were very jealous and somewhat insecure. So he spent equal time, as far as he could manage it, and when he had hugged them all and given them a kiss on the cheek, he winked at Ted and said, "That's your last chance to hug a good-looking man until I get back."

"I'm glad you borrowed that closed airplane from Mr. Morrow," Ted said.

Luke had made a deal with Jim Morrow, who owned hundreds of acres of farmland. He had borrowed Morrow's closed Cessna in exchange for spraying his crops when the next season started. "It's a little bit too cold for open cockpits, Ted. Well, you and Irene take care of everything here, and I'll take care of everything in Arkansas. Come on, wife."

Joelle got into the plane as Luke held the door open, slammed it shut, then came around to climb in beside her. He reached over and fastened her safety belt and grinned at her. "Safety first. It's been hard enough to get a wife. I don't want to have to go to the trouble of getting another one."

Luke took off and then he wheeled the plane over to give Joelle a good look at the Haven. All the girls were looking up and waving, and she waved back.

"They're such dear girls," she said. "You know, Luke, sometimes it breaks my heart when I think that there are girls everywhere who could be helped just like these."

"Boys too."

"Yes. Boys too."

"Well, we put it before God and now it's up to Him. He'll see to it that there'll be more than one Haven." He leveled the plane off and climbed to a higher altitude. "I'm looking forward to seeing the folks. And I'm especially looking forward to showing you off."

"I wish they could have been at the wedding, but it was all so sudden."

"You wanted to get married so bad that you just couldn't wait. We'll just have to make it up to them."

"*You* were the one who wanted to get married so bad."

"Was it? I knew it was one of us. But anyhow, it's done now, and anyway, I liked having such a small, intimate wedding. And I know my family will like you. They've never thrown out a Winslow bride yet." He laughed and lifted the nose of the plane higher into the air.

★ ★ ★

The flight was a delight to Joelle. Before this, she had only flown in the open plane with the engine roaring and the wind tearing at her hair. Being enclosed in an airplane with the engine somewhat muted permitted more talk.

On the first leg of their journey, they hit snow flurries, but as they moved west, the weather warmed up. By the time they were over Little Rock, the sun was shining brightly. Luke pointed ahead to the town of Liberty. "There it is. My old hometown. Let me give you a tour."

"A tour?"

"Sure. Show you some of the high points of the misspent life of Luke Winslow." He banked the plane and in a short time pointed down. "There's where I went to high school—and there's the football field. I wish I had a dollar for every forward pass I've thrown down there."

He skimmed over Liberty, pointing out different sights, and finally mischief twinkled in his eye. "Now I've got something really important." He flew over a wooded area that surrounded a small lake. "There's Lovers' Lake," he said. "That's where I used to bring girls to point out the beauty of nature," he said. "You'd be surprised how beautiful nature is on a moonlit night on a lake like that."

Joelle had become accustomed to Luke's mild teasing, and she said tersely, "I don't want to hear about your old girlfriends."

"There was Mabel Matthews," he said. "Now, Mabel really appreciated the beauty of that lake."

Joelle turned and hit him sharply on the arm. "Hush up! I don't want to hear about it."

"I've kept it all in my diary. I'll let you read it sometime if you're good."

"I don't want to read your old diary!"

Luke laughed and banked the plane. "Oh well, then. I'll show you the home place."

He dropped the nose of the plane down and finally banked and pointed. "Look. There it is right there. That multicolored brick with the white windows."

"What a beautiful house and beautiful lawn too."

"I hated that lawn when I was growing up. Five acres and I had to cut every bit of it."

"Didn't your brother help you?"

"Well, every now and then, I guess."

Suddenly Luke grinned. "Let's give them a thrill."

"What do you mean?"

"We'll announce our coming."

"What are you doing, Luke?"

"I'm going to give them a buzz."

Luke slowed the plane down, but he flew dangerously close, it seemed to Joelle. The wheels almost seemed to skim the top of the house, and then he banked again and began circling.

"You're going to hit the telephone wires or those trees."

"An old crop-duster like me? Why, I could fly through the front door and straight out the back." Luke laughed. "Look. They're coming out."

Joelle looked down and saw that, indeed, people were coming out of the house.

"There's Dad—and there's Mom. Look, they're pointing up."

"They're probably talking about how crazy you are."

"You're probably right. Dad will have a word or two to say to me about this." He reached over and pulled Joelle close. He gave her a quick kiss, and his eyes were dancing with fun. "But I'm giving him a beautiful daughter, so he won't stay mad very long."

"Don't you think it's about time you landed this thing?"

"I guess you're right."

Soon Luke was bringing the plane down on the municipal field. After he cut the engine, he said, "Welcome to Liberty. Are you anxious to meet my folks?"

"I guess so."

"You're not nervous, are you?"

"A little bit. They haven't even met me, Luke. We shouldn't have gotten married before I at least met them."

"We didn't have time. They'll love you." Luke got out, came around, and helped Joelle out of the plane. After grabbing their bags, he made arrangements with one of the employees to take care of the plane and asked the man where he could find a telephone. He found the phone and called for a cab.

"Did you just get in?" the driver asked as he got out of the cab.

"Yep—just flew in from Tennessee."

"Let me help you with the bags." The driver stowed the bags while Luke and Joelle got seated.

"Where can I take you?"

Luke gave the address, and the driver blinked with surprise. "I've been hauling people there for two days now. What's going on?"

"A family reunion. The Winslow family."

"Are you a Winslow?"

"A minor one. I'm Luke Winslow."

"Hey, man, I remember you. As a matter of fact"—he grinned crookedly—"you gave me this busted beak."

Luke stared at the man. "Don't guess I remember that."

"Don't you remember when Liberty played North Little Rock for the big championship?"

"I sure do. Were you in that game?"

The cab driver laughed. "I'm Mike Connelly. I played guard for the North Little Rock Wildcats."

"Hey, sure I remember you! I ought to." He grinned. "You caved in my ribs pretty well, smacking me down that day."

"That was the hardest game I ever played in."

"Me too. What have you been doing with yourself, Mike?"

"I run this cab company. One of my drivers has been sick for the last couple of days, so I've been filling in for him." He reached over and Luke shook his hand.

"I'm sorry about that nose, Mike."

"And I'm sorry about the ribs. Well, it's good to see you again."

Joelle listened as the two men chatted about their high school days. She was actually more nervous than she wanted to admit, and when the cab pulled up to the Winslow home, she was almost ready to turn and go back to Tennessee.

Luke got out and helped Mike get the bags out, paid the fare, and then gave him a healthy tip. "Good to see you again, Mike. That was a great game, even if we lost."

"I guess somebody's got to lose. Look. Here's my card. Call me if you need a lift while you're here, Luke."

"I'll do that."

Mike drove away, and Luke picked up the suitcases and started up the walk. They had not gotten to the porch when the door opened and his parents came out, smiling broadly. His mother came down the steps and gave him a big hug. "The bad penny's home again, Mom."

Peter Winslow had waited to give his wife first chance, but then he grabbed Luke and hugged him. "Good to see you again, son."

"Dad, it's good to be here. Look. I brought you a present. A new daughter."

"I'm so glad to get to meet you at last," Jolie Winslow said. She embraced Joelle at once, which immediately helped Joelle feel more comfortable.

"I've been longing to meet you too."

"Well," Peter said, putting his arm around Joelle and giving her a hug, "it's good that Luke now has somebody who can make him behave."

"Wait a minute," Luke said. "I'm the boss of this family."

"We can argue about that later. Come on in. Part of the family's here. They're anxious to meet you."

"Oh, and I'd like to say a few words about your buzzing the house," Peter began. "I don't want—"

"Save your sermons, Peter," Jolie said, digging her elbow into his side. "I could say a few words about the way you drive that car of yours."

As they moved into the house, Joelle was suddenly surrounded with people. She tried to remember their names, but it was impossible. She was greeted warmly by Tim Winslow. This, she knew, was Luke's younger brother. She remembered Luke saying Tim had wanted Luke to work at the family factory when he first came back from Spain.

Tim was all smiles now as he took his wife by the arm. "This is my wife, Mary, and these are our children, Gerald and Carolyn."

Joelle squatted down to greet the kids but was almost immediately interrupted by a woman who looked a lot like Luke's father.

"I'm Priscilla," the woman said, "Luke's aunt. It's so nice to finally meet the woman who managed to snag Luke's heart."

"It's wonderful to meet you too, Priscilla," Joelle said.

"You must be tired. If you want to follow me, I'll show you to the room you and Luke will be staying in."

Joelle actually was glad to get a break for a moment. She followed the woman up the stairs and into a room that boasted a double bed. "Let me help you unpack. It's madness down there with people coming and going all the time. Most of them aren't here at the house at the moment. There must be a hundred Winslows in town."

"I'm so glad to be here, Priscilla. Luke tells me you're a teacher."

"That's right."

"What a wonderful vocation."

"It's hard work, but I love it. I know I'll miss the kids when I retire in another year or two. Now, tell me all about you and Luke."

"What do you mean?"

"About your romance, I mean. Luke never was much for staying with one woman."

"Did he have lots of girlfriends?"

"Oh, he was very popular. He just never got serious about any one girl."

"I want to hear all about when he was a boy growing up," Joelle said. "You'll have to tell me everything." She opened the suitcase, and Priscilla's eyes widened. "That's some night-gown there."

Flustered, Joelle said, "It was a gift from the girls who stay with me at the Haven."

"How old are those girls?"

"They range in age from twelve to sixteen." She reddened and said, "It's not the kind of gown I would have bought for myself."

Priscilla's eyes danced and she laughed aloud. "Maybe it's really more of a present for Luke."

At that moment the door opened and Jolie came in. "You girls can talk later. Come on down." She turned and smiled. "Everyone wants to meet you, Joelle, and it's almost time for supper."

★ ★ ★

Joelle was sitting next to Wesley Winslow, who had brought his wife and three teenage children. The extended family was crowded around the huge dining table, waiting for supper to be served, and the room was filled with conversation and laughter. "I've admired your photographs for a long time, Mr. Winslow."

"Thanks very much, but please use my first name."

"I remember the first time I saw one of your photographs in *National Geographic*. It was absolutely beautiful."

Wes Winslow winked at his wife and said, "I'm a little hard of hearing. Will you tell me again how wonderful I am, only louder so everyone can hear it?"

"Never mind that," Leah Winslow said. "He's vain enough as it is. We don't want your head to get any bigger, Wes."

"That's right." The speaker was the Baptist minister Patrick Winslow, who was sitting across the table from Joelle. He grinned as he said, "We don't want to talk about you, Wes. We want to talk about me."

His wife, Seana, sat next to him, and their three children were on the far end of the room.

"It looks like we're starting a town for boys around here," Patrick said, looking around the room.

"You fellows are trying to repopulate the earth, it looks like," Luke said. "I'm sure glad the kids all favor their mothers instead of their dads."

"You wound me when you say that," Patrick said, gripping his chest. "If you want to see one proud grandfather, wait until my dad gets here tomorrow."

"Your father is Barney Winslow, right?" Luke asked.

"Yes, that's right."

"I've read the biography about him. I'm in awe of missionaries—especially him."

"So am I," Patrick said. "He's quite a man."

The talk ran around the table, and finally Luana and the other women who had been hired to help out for the weekend started bringing out trays of food.

Luke grabbed Luana's arm as she went by. "All those bad

habits you taught me when I was growing up . . . I've told my wife it's all your fault."

"Bad habits, my foot!" Luana exclaimed. "I did everything I could to keep you straight."

"Luke, you're awful," Joelle teased.

"What . . . you mean I got my bad habits all on my own?"

Luana shook her head as she went back into the kitchen for another tray.

"Can I have your attention, everyone?" Peter stood up, raising both arms. When the room became quiet, he said, "Let's say a word of thanks for this meal."

After he prayed, Peter sat down and said, "Now, Joelle, we're all dying to hear about how you and Luke met."

"It was just like in the movies, Dad," Luke said. "She took one look at me and fell in love. Her knees got so weak I thought she was going to faint, and she told me that if I didn't marry her, she would die. So I had to marry her to keep her alive."

Cries of indignation went up, and Jolie said, "You hush, Luke. We want to hear Joelle's side of the story."

Joelle turned to smile at Luke. "It wasn't exactly like that. It was freezing outside and snowing, and Luke hitchhiked to our house, to the Haven, but his last ride didn't get him all the way to our place. He was sick and so weak that he fell down and couldn't get up. He nearly froze to death."

"She saved my life and nursed me back to health. So she had to marry me," Luke said.

"You made a big leap from nursing you back to health to getting married!" Jolie maintained.

"It wasn't quite as smooth or fast as he makes it sound," Joelle said with a smile. She went on to tell them about their friendship and how it eventually became love.

"If it hadn't been for Luke, the Haven would no longer exist. The bank was going to foreclose, and he fixed up an old plane that my brother had and made it into a crop-duster. He made enough money dusting crops to keep the wolf from the door."

"Tell us more about the Haven," Luke's brother, Tim, said. "It sounds like a great ministry."

For the next fifteen minutes, with her eyes glowing, Joelle told the group about how God had spoken to her about wayward girls and making a home for them. She told them about the first girl who had lived with her at her folks' place and how it had grown from there. Finally she said, "I'm talking too much."

"No you're not, my dear," Peter said. "We're so happy to have you in the family, and looking at Luke, I can tell he's a different fellow."

"She's made me what I am today," Luke said with a sigh. "I hope she's satisfied." He grinned at his wife.

★ ★ ★

Luke and Joelle finally made it to their bedroom, and Luke quickly climbed into bed. They could hear the sounds of merriment downstairs, for not everyone had gone to bed.

Joelle was brushing her hair in front of the mirror. "I love your family," she said.

"And they love you too."

"They're all such wonderful people."

"I guess I was the only black sheep."

"You're not a black sheep anymore."

Joelle had an idea, and she walked over to the chest of drawers where she had put her clothes. She took a long flannel gown out of the drawer. "I didn't know how cold it would be here, so I brought this old flannel gown," she said as she held up the gown.

"It's not as cold as I thought it might be, but that ought to do."

For a moment Joelle hesitated, and then she said, "You know . . . the girls gave me a going-away present. I don't think you saw it."

"That was nice of them. What is it?"

Joelle pulled out the black silk nightgown and held it against herself. “What do you think?”

“Well, now,” he said, his eyes wide, “if the girls went to all the trouble of buying it, the least you can do is wear it, I guess.”

“You are impossible! It’s too cold for this gown.”

“There’s another blanket in the closet. I’ll get it while you slip into that.” He turned and winked at her. “After all, you don’t want to disappoint the girls. I’m willing to make the sacrifice.”

Joelle laughed and disappeared into the bathroom.

CHAPTER TWENTY-FOUR

A REUNION TO REMEMBER

★ ★ ★

All morning the skies had been a leaden gray with the threat of snow ever present, but by noon the sun had come out and brought with it shoppers to the streets of Little Rock. It was still three weeks till Christmas, but the shoppers all seemed in a holiday mood.

Luke and Joelle had come to nearby Little Rock to do some Christmas shopping as well. As they walked down the main street, Joelle turned and smiled up at Luke. "Do you hate shopping like most men do?"

"I love shopping! I spend all of my spare time at it when I have the money. There's nothing I enjoy more than walking until my feet hurt and looking at a hundred items in order to buy one," he said with an earnest look. "It's my favorite thing, wife."

"You're just being silly." Joelle reached over and pinched Luke on the arm. They were both carrying sacks full of gifts they had already bought. "We won't be here for Christmas, so I want to get everyone presents and leave them here. It'll be less expensive than mailing them."

"I suppose that's true, but it's hard to buy anything for my family."

"It was never hard to buy for mine," Joelle said. "We sometimes didn't get anything at all."

"You had a hard time growing up."

"We never had much money, but we were happy and we did just fine."

"You make me feel like a greedy bureaucrat swollen up with riches. What were your Christmases like?"

"Let's see . . . we usually tried to make gifts for each other. My mother would sew a skirt for me or make a pair of pajamas for Roscoe, or my father would make toys for us out of wood. I remember sewing a potholder for my mom once and knitting a scarf for my dad. We didn't have to spend much money to make each other happy."

"Did you have a tree?"

"Daddy always went out and cut down the biggest tree that would fit in the living room, and we made a lot of decorations. We'd pick red berries and string them on thread—just like you did—and we'd make ornaments. We only had one string of lights, and of course when one bulb went out they all went out."

"We had the same troubles with our tree."

"Most of our friends were in the same boat. We didn't know anyone who had much money. But we had each other."

Suddenly Luke stopped and said, "Look. There's another Salvation Army bucket. They're all over town."

Joelle fished a dollar out of her purse and put it in the bucket suspended beneath a tripod.

"Merry Christmas, miss," the man ringing the bell called with a smile.

"And merry Christmas to you too."

"That's the sixth Salvation Army pot you put money in. Don't you ever get paid out?"

"They do such good work. They go places nobody else can."

As they continued down the street, Luke started thinking about the way his family had celebrated Christmas when he had been a child. "Tim and I were totally selfish about Christmas," he told Joelle. "I don't think we had the foggiest idea for a long time that Christmas had anything much to do with religion."

"Didn't you have Christmas pageants?"

"Oh yes, we did. I forgot about that. Tim and I were usually shepherds. That was the high point of our Christmases."

"Did you get lots of presents?"

Luke laughed. "Mom and Dad both loved to buy presents for us. When it got close to Christmas, every day we'd get up and come rushing down the stairs to see if there were any new presents under the tree. We'd count them and make sure Tim and I each had the same number. If Tim had five, I had to have five too. It had to come out even. One time Tim got two more presents than I did and I beat him up."

"You didn't!"

"The old Christmas spirit."

"Well, I trust you've become a little more generous since then."

"Oh yes. I hardly ever beat Tim up anymore."

"What do you want for Christmas this year?"

"You don't have to worry about that. We're buying my present today. I was here yesterday and I picked it out." He stopped and winked. They were in front of the Gus Blass Department Store. "Come on. I'll show you."

"You can't pick out your own Christmas present. It's supposed to be a surprise."

"You know how bad my memory is. I'll probably forget all about it by tomorrow. The only way I can be sure I'll get what I want is to get it myself. I've always done that."

"You are awful, Luke Winslow!"

He led her to the second floor, where all the newest radios were prominently featured, and pointed out a portable record player. "That's what I want right there."

"I've never seen anything quite like it," Joelle said as she peered around all sides of the device. "How does it work?"

"You just put your seventy-eight on the spindle there and then crank it up with this handle."

"So you can have music wherever you are?"

"That's right."

A clerk came over and said good morning. "I see you have your eye on this record player. A nice machine, it is. Bought one myself."

"And does it work as advertised?" Luke asked.

"Sure does. I'm real happy with it."

"All right, then," Luke said. "Can you wrap this one up? It's going to be a surprise for a very dear friend of mine."

"I'll wrap it up myself. Just put it in a sack," Joelle said with resignation, "if you have one that's big enough." Luke grinned and paid for the record player.

"This record player is going to come in handy," he said as they strolled through the store.

"We can keep it in our bedroom."

"I thought I'd keep it in my plane when I'm dusting. It gets boring up there just flying back and forth. I can get some Harry James or Tommy Dorsey seventy-eights. A little entertainment for the pilot."

"You're teasing me again. The needle would be jumping all over the record every time you changed direction."

Luke grinned. When they passed the lingerie department, he suddenly grabbed her arm. "Now let's buy your Christmas present."

Joelle gave him a startled look. "You're not buying any lingerie for me."

"Sure I am."

He pulled her through the lingerie department, commenting on different garments, and Joelle protested all the way. "I'm not going to let you pick out my lingerie and that's final!"

"Why, I let you pick out my underwear. Good old Fruit of the Loom shorts."

"That's different," she said, her face flushed. "Come on. We've got to get something for your parents."

"I've told you they have everything."

"There's one thing they don't have. A picture of you and me together. I've made an appointment with a photographer. They'll love it."

* * *

Peter picked up the nutcracker and cracked a pecan. The paper shell fell off, and he picked out the kernel without breaking it. "It takes a real genius to pick pecans like I do," he said. He popped one half into his mouth, chewed it with pleasure, then ate the other half.

"If you don't stop eating those pecans, you're going to get as fat as a pig," Jolie scolded.

"No I won't. Pecans are good for you. They've got lots of vitamins or something. Gives you healthy corpsuckles."

"That's corpuscles."

"Whatever."

"You're eating more pecans than you're putting in the bowl."

Peter winked at her and grinned. "I don't see how you can rebuke me, Jolie. I've been a perfect husband all these years. Now you throw a fit when I eat one or two little pecans."

"One or two! You've eaten two dozen."

"Well, I'd eat them anyway on top of that pie you're going to make."

Jolie could not help but laugh. "When did you decide you've been a perfect husband?"

"I can tell by the look of excitement in your eyes when I come into a room. You're so proud of me. Everybody says the same thing." He cracked another pecan, glanced at her, then put both halves into the dish, which was half full. "There. You see how perfect I am?"

"What do you think about Luke?" she asked, changing the subject.

"I've never seen a man change so completely. He told me he was going to get baptized as soon as they get back home. He wants to join the local church there in Chattanooga."

"Joelle told me about that. She said he hasn't missed a service since he's been saved. He's singing in the choir too."

"He can't sing any better than I can."

"Joelle says he makes up in volume what he lacks in pitch and tone."

Peter cracked another pecan, and catching Jolie looking down at her own bowl of pecans, he put them in his mouth. "You know," he said thoughtfully, "I almost gave up on Luke a few times. But you never did."

"No. We gave him to the Lord when he was just a baby, and I knew God was going to do something with his life. I don't like to give up on anybody."

At that moment Priscilla came in. She reached down into the bowl and picked up a handful of the shelled pecans in front of Peter. She bit down on one and nodded. "That's good."

"Hey, I've worked like a dog on those things! You can't just eat them."

Priscilla ignored him. She sat down and said immediately, "What are you going to get me for Christmas?"

Peter glanced at his sister and, as always, could not help teasing her. "I've given that a lot of thought, sis, and I think you're really going to love it. You can't have it until Christmas, though."

"And you won't tell me what it is, will you?"

"If I told you now, you wouldn't have a surprise on Christmas."

"I know, but I'm so curious with those sly looks you've been giving me."

"Well, if you're sure you want to know already, I'll tell you."

"So tell me already!"

"Your car needs a new set of shocks. I picked them out for you and Jason at the garage. You'll have to pay to have them put on, though. I can't afford that."

"Peter!"

"I'll have Jolie wrap them up and I'll write a nice verse to go with them."

"You're such a good brother. Just what I wanted—a nice new set of shocks. What are you going to get Luke and Joelle?"

"I can't tell you because it's a secret."

"I won't tell anybody."

"Yes you will. Women can't keep secrets like men can." For a while he teased her, and finally he said, "Well, Jolie bought them some little things they can use in the house, but we also bought a van that's got a few miles on it but is in perfect shape. I'm having it overhauled inside and out, and it'll carry ten people. I'm having *The Haven* printed on the side."

"Why, that's a wonderful idea!" Priscilla said, smiling brilliantly. "Joelle told me how hard it is to get all the girls into the truck to go anywhere. Most of them have to ride in the bed."

Priscilla helped Peter and Jolie crack pecans while they chatted about the family.

"Everything's set for the big banquet tonight," Peter said when they had finished the job. "That's going to be the biggest mob of Winslows ever gathered under one roof."

* * *

Joelle was squeezed into the corner next to Luke as they rode in the back of the car.

"Can you move over a little, Luke? You're squashing me!"

"I can't help it, woman. I'm like one of those butterflies that can smell a female butterfly twenty miles away."

Peter laughed. "You two are still on your honeymoon, I see."

"I plan to make it last at least forty or fifty years—just like yours, Dad."

Both Jolie and Peter laughed at that.

"That's a joke," Luke said, "but I don't think there are many women with husbands who say such nice things as you do, Dad."

"It gets me what I want. A lesson for you, Luke. You don't have to spend a lot of money on presents to make a woman happy. Just tell her she smells good or her elbows are pretty or something like that. Anything, as long as it's nice and sweet."

They continued their teasing, and five minutes later they pulled into the parking lot of the Marion Hotel. The party was going to be in the banquet room on the top floor. They left the car with the attendant and went inside, where they saw one of Peter's cousins waiting for the elevator.

"Barney, it's good to see you," Peter said.

"Peter, good to see you too." The two men shook hands. At age seventy-one now, Barney's hair was silver, but he still looked strong and healthy, his face weathered from the African sun. He had been a missionary in Africa for many years and was the most famous of all the Winslows. "How have you been?" he asked. "You know my daughter, Erin, and her husband, Quaid Merritt?"

Peter shook hands with Quaid and greeted Erin and then pulled Luke and Joelle into the introductions.

"Oh, Mr. Winslow," Joelle gushed to Barney, "I've read your biography over and over again."

"Well, don't believe everything you read in it. It was written by my son, Patrick. I think he sort of gilded the lily."

The door opened, and when they got on the elevator, Barney said, "You know, Quaid and Erin are both pilots. They're both serving as missionary pilots in Africa."

Quaid Merritt was a tall, lean man with a pair of keen, observant eyes. "Say, Luke, I heard about your service in

Spain. We could use you in Africa."

Peter grinned. "Luke and Joelle already have a mission field."

"That's right," Jolie said. "They're working with girls who are in trouble and need a place to stay."

"That's a wonderful thing to do," Erin Merritt said. She had been a famous stunt flyer who was talented and beautiful enough that she had received offers to act in movies in Hollywood. She had walked away from it all when she married Quaid.

"What do you think about this matter of Japan?" Quaid asked. "They've been rattling sabers over there."

"I read in the paper," Luke said, "that their ambassadors are meeting with our State Department. I hope it will work out."

"I think we'll have more trouble with Hitler than Japan," Quaid said as the door opened. They all stepped outside, and Barney whistled in a low tone. "Look at all the Winslows. I never saw such a mess of them. . . ."

* * *

The banquet was sumptuous. It was impossible, of course, to meet everybody, but Joelle was entranced by those who were in their immediate vicinity during the meal. Luke had introduced her to the couple on her right. "This is Lewis Winslow and his wife, Missouri Ann. You have to be very respectful of Lewis. He won the Medal of Honor in the Spanish-American War."

Lewis Winslow was getting on in years but still looking vigorous.

"Did you make that charge up San Juan Hill?"

"Actually, it wasn't San Juan Hill. It was Kettle Hill. The history books have got that all wrong." Lewis smiled. "Yes. I was with Teddy."

"How exciting! Were you afraid?"

"It took more nerve to start a second family than charging up that hill with Teddy Roosevelt." He gave his wife a sly grin. "Missouri Ann here scared me half to death."

Missouri Ann was much younger than her husband. She was a large woman, full of energy, and she loved to laugh aloud. "It was the strangest courtship you've ever heard of. Lewis was out hunting and broke his leg out in the middle of nowhere. I took him to my cabin, set his leg, and told him God had sent him to be my husband. It nearly scared the daylights out of him."

"I was too old to start a new family." Lewis grinned. "At least, I thought so."

"But you weren't. We've got three healthy children now—triplets, mind you—every bit as handsome as his first family."

"It was a funny courtship. I didn't have any chance at all. What do you do when a woman just up and tells you that God has sent you to be her husband?"

"Now, why didn't I think of that?" Joelle said, winking at Luke.

The woman sitting across the table from Joelle tapped her fingernail on the table to get Joelle's attention. "I'm Barney Winslow's sister, Esther Krueger. This is my husband, Jan."

"Esther is a very famous photographer," Lewis said. "Does marvelous work."

"I don't do much of that anymore. I have to take care of this husband of mine."

Jan Krueger had a foreign look about him, and his accent revealed that English was not his native language. "I think I'm easy enough to take care of."

"He's spoiled to death," Esther said. "I had to give up my work just to pamper him. He's a famous heart surgeon now, and he gets so swollen with pride it takes half a day to bring him down to earth."

Joelle was fascinated with the Winslows. It seemed there wasn't a run-of-the-mill person in the whole bunch.

"I want you to meet a real hero," Luke was saying. "This is Logan Smith and his wife, Danielle. He was an ace in the Great War."

"I'm so glad to meet you, Mr. Smith."

"Most folks just call me Cowboy, at least they did in France when I went to serve over there."

"Did you ever see the Red Baron?" Luke asked.

"Oh yes. I met the scamp. Nice enough fellow."

"What do you think about the new planes, Logan?"

"Well, from what I've read, that Me-109 the Germans have is going to be a tough cookie. They're giving the Spitfires fits over in England."

"I'd sure like to get into one of those P-47s that America's turning out."

"So would I," Logan said. "It's shaped almost like a jug. Big huge airplane. You know, if I'd had one of those P-47s in France, I think I could have wiped up the entire Luftwaffe."

The conversation was cut off when Peter Winslow stood up. He was sitting at the head table with Barney, and when he got everyone's attention, he said, "It's a dangerous thing to let a preacher speak at a banquet, but I have Barney's promise that he'll save the sermon for the Sunday morning prayer breakfast tomorrow. We hope all of you will come. As I think most of you know, Barney Winslow has been an intrepid missionary in Africa for many years. His brother, Andrew, is a fellow missionary, as are several of his family. I'm going to ask him to come say a word about the Winslow family. Barney, it's your show."

Barney Winslow rose, and his voice was still clear, despite his age. He stood looking over them and said, "Last night I was reading the journal of Gilbert Winslow. I think you all know that he was the first of our family to come over on the *Mayflower,* of course. His brother Edward came also, and he was one of the early governors of the colony. Gilbert was an amazing man. My favorite part of his journal is the part that he wrote while he was in prison at Salem. Let me read a few lines of it:

> "It appears that I will not be able to serve the Lord in this world much longer. We are all to be executed within a week. Strangely enough, I feel no fear, which is of the Lord's doing. No man can face death without fear unless God helps him.
>
> "I am an old man now, and I have lived to see my son serve the Lord Jesus. We are privileged to be servants of the living God, and if today is the day we are to die, I shout hallelujah, for we will be ushered into the presence of the great King.

"Those words were written by a man on the threshold of death. Obviously Gilbert Winslow did not die within the week, as he had expected, but went on to serve God in many ways. He was the first of the Winslows to make his mark on America, but there have been others. Some have been college presidents, some have been plumbers, and some have been governors. There is an admiral with us tonight who bears the name Winslow. We've had our villains and our weak men and women, but the Winslows have served the country and have served the Lord God faithfully throughout the years."

Joelle and all the rest of the Winslows listened attentively as the old man talked for a long time, mentioning the names of Winslows who had come down through history. Joelle had not heard of most of them, but she was thrilled at the stories that he told.

Finally Barney grinned and said, "I promised that I wouldn't preach a sermon, and I won't tonight. But tomorrow I want every one of you back here in this very place. We'll have a great breakfast and then I'll preach you a sermon that'll curl your hair."

Peter Winslow rose and grinned. "I always wanted curly hair. We'll all be here, Barney. Now I have an announcement to make, a very wonderful announcement. I'm going to ask my new daughter-in-law, Joelle, and my son Luke to come stand with Jolie and me here."

Joelle found herself nervously getting to her feet, following her husband to the front. "What is this about, Luke?" she whispered.

"I have no idea. Dad always likes surprises."

When the two of them were standing in front of Peter, he was grinning widely. "My spiritual gift," he said loudly, "is meddling. Jolie and I have practiced this gift to perfection. The Winslows, as Barney has been pointing out, have always been in battle for the Lord. Because Jolie and I want to do our part in the battle, we have decided, Luke and Joelle, to join your ministry to wayward young people. Several of us have been working all week to set up a foundation called the Haven Foundation. A board has been selected to handle the finances. We're going to raise money from every Winslow we can find, and here is the first check from the Haven Foundation to be used to start a residence for boys and young men. We Winslows don't like to lose, so we're expecting God to establish Havens all over this country."

Luke took the check and held it so Joelle could see it. Joelle began to cry.

"That's the way it should be," Peter said, smiling. "Now let's give a big hand to the directors of the Havens, and may there be one in every major city in this country to help the young people who need it."

Joelle felt Luke's arm go around her, and she whispered, "I'm so proud to be a Winslow, Luke!"

★ ★ ★

The next morning, nearly everyone who had been at the banquet the night before returned for the prayer breakfast. Joelle had been able to meet all of the Winslows who would be on the board of the Haven Foundation, and she and Luke had made an appointment to meet with the board before they left town.

Barney was wrapping up his remarks. "I told you I would preach a short sermon and that's what I've done, even though it goes against the grain for me." Mischief danced in his eyes. "The Masai don't have any respect for a sermon that lasts less than three hours, but I can see that this crowd doesn't have that kind of stamina.

"This has been a real pleasure for me," he went on. "It's wonderful to see so many in this family of ours serving God, and I hope we gather like this again before I get my promotion to the throne room. But if—"

Barney broke off as his brother, Andrew, burst into the room calling his name. "What's the matter, Andy?"

"The Japanese are attacking Hawaii! They're bombing the fleet in Pearl Harbor!"

A total silence fell over the room and then everyone began speaking at once. "Are you sure, Andrew?"

"They're talking about it on the radio."

Someone from the back of the room yelled, "There's a radio back here in the corner. Let's see if we can hear something."

Andrew turned the radio on and turned the volume up so everyone could hear.

". . . attack was completely unexpected," the announcer was saying, "for the representatives of the Japanese Empire were in Washington for peace talks. The first reports are that the American fleet has been decimated. Many lives have been lost. This, of course, means that America will be at war with Japan."

"How could they bomb Hawaii?" Peter asked loudly. "Japan is thousands of miles from there."

"Aircraft carriers," Luke said grimly. "No other way they could have done it."

Luke's words were verified, for as they listened to the newscast, they learned that the Japanese carriers had brought the bombers and fighters to the attack. The one piece of good news was that none of America's carriers were at Pearl Harbor.

"That means we still have a chance in the Pacific," Luke said. "If they had gotten the carriers, there would be no stopping the Japanese."

"What will happen, Luke?" Joelle whispered.

He took her hand in his own. "A lot of people are going to die." He looked around the room with troubled eyes, then added, "And some of them will be Winslows."

CHAPTER TWENTY-FIVE

CHRISTMAS SURPRISES

★ ★ ★

Joelle was sitting in the kitchen talking to Jolie. They spoke mostly of the war, for in the three days since the attack on Pearl Harbor, the Winslow household, like practically every other household in America, was filled with talk of nothing but the tragedy. The two women were sipping coffee, and Jolie was speaking softly, her eyes full of grief.

"The whole world seems to have been turned upside down, Joelle, in just a few days."

Joelle nodded. "I read a poem one time. The poet said that once he stooped over to pick up a shoe, and when he straightened up his whole world had changed completely. I didn't understand that poem until December the seventh. Now I don't think anyone can have the same life they had before that."

"I believe you're right. I never thought of it that way."

"I've been thinking about all those poor men who died on the *Arizona*. They got up that morning, I suppose, and had breakfast and had no idea what was going to happen. That before the day was out they'd be taken out of this earth."

"It's an awesome thought, but you know, Joelle, it's true of us every day. Not just the sailors on the *Arizona* but every one of us. When we wake up in the morning, we ought to think, *I may not live to see bedtime. I may be in the presence of the Lord tonight.*"

"You're right, of course," Joelle agreed. "We never know when our time will come." She took a sip of her coffee. "I've heard that several of our family have already enlisted. One of Wesley's sons enlisted in the navy. Just yesterday. I talked with Wes and his wife and they were saddened by it, but at the same time they understood that it was going to be that way."

"There was a picture in the paper yesterday of one of the enlistment lines in Little Rock. The same thing is taking place all over the country. All the young men are rushing to arms."

Suddenly Joelle lifted her head. "I hear the front door."

"It's probably Peter. He usually comes in about this time."

The two women turned to face the door, and Peter came in, accompanied by Tim.

"Hello, dear." Peter kissed Jolie and smiled at Joelle. "What have you two been doing all day?"

"Nothing much," Joelle said. "Luke went out on some business. Hasn't been here all day."

"I was hoping he'd be here," Tim said. "There's something I want to talk to him about."

"What are you so excited about, Tim?" Jolie asked. "You never could cover up your feelings too well."

"The greatest thing has happened, Mom." Tim's face was flushed, and his eyes were dancing with excitement. "Dad and I have been talking all day to government officials."

"Talking about what?"

"About the company. It's great, isn't it, Dad?"

Peter did not seem as excited as his son. "I suppose it could be called exciting, but it's sad too."

"Sad? How could it be sad? It's a great opportunity for the Winslow Company."

"What are you two talking about?" Jolie said. "What were you talking to the government about?"

"Mom, they want our company to make carburetors for army vehicles. Of course nothing's signed yet, but they're positive that we can get a contract. Why, it'll be the biggest thing that our company has ever done. We'll have to put up a new building to take care of all that business."

Jolie glanced at Peter and saw that he did not seem entirely happy. "Aren't you in favor of this, Peter?"

"I guess so, but it's going to mean a lot of changes."

"What kind of changes?" Joelle asked.

"We'll have to enlarge the factory, and it's going to be harder to get help. All the young men will be going off to fight."

"We'll find the help," Tim said confidently, "and we'll be doing a great work too. You know—we'll be doing our part for our country."

"This whole country has got to gear up. We've got to build an army. We've got to build tanks and planes and ships. It's going to be the biggest effort this country has ever made," Peter said.

Tim turned to Joelle and smiled excitedly at her. "All the time we were talking to them, I was thinking of you and Luke."

"Of me and Luke? Why would you think of us?"

"We're going to need all the help we can get. This expansion might work out perfectly for the two of you."

"I don't see what it has to do with us. We'll be going back to Tennessee to continue with the Haven and to start looking into expanding to take in boys."

"I realize that, but here's what I was thinking," Tim said. "Why couldn't you establish the headquarters for the Haven Foundation in Little Rock?"

"Why here? Why not in Tennessee?"

"Because, don't you see, Joelle, if your office was here, you could run the Haven—and Luke could go to work for the company."

Joelle glanced at Jolie and then shook her head. "We've already got plans."

"Everyone is changing their plans. This war has changed everything. You can still do the Haven work. With the money that's coming in, you can hire a director to take Luke's place, and he can plunge right in here. It's an opportunity of a lifetime."

"I don't think of it like that," Peter said heavily. He seemed depressed. "It seems wrong to take advantage of a terrible thing like a war to make money."

"Dad, the carburetors have to be built. We'll be serving our country." Turning to Joelle, he said, "Would you agree to it if Luke does?"

"I suppose so," Joelle said reluctantly, "but I don't think he will."

"I'll talk to him," Tim said. "Did he say when he'd be back?"

"No. He just said he had some things to take care of."

"Tell him to come see me in my office first thing in the morning, will you, Joelle? I'll run all the numbers by him."

"I'll tell him, Tim, but don't get your hopes up."

★ ★ ★

Joelle was getting ready for bed when Luke finally came in. "Where have you been all day?"

Luke began to undress. "You sound like Mom, always wanting to know where I've been."

"Well, I can't help but be curious. You left this morning and I haven't seen you since then."

"I've been up on top of Mount Pinnacle."

"Where's that?" she asked as she climbed under the covers.

"Just west of town here. It's the highest spot in this area. You can see a long way."

"Why did you go up on top of a mountain?"

Luke was slipping into his pajamas. He got into bed beside her and reached over to kiss her. "I just needed a good place to think, and that was the best place I could come up with."

"Why, it's freezing out there, Luke."

"You're right about that. The wind cut right through me up on top of the mountain."

Joelle studied his face carefully. "I guess you had a reason for going, but I can't imagine what it was."

"When I was a young fellow I used to go up there by myself. It was so quiet and peaceful. I was always busy with something or other, and at times I just wanted to get away. It was a little cold today, but I wanted to think about what all has happened to this country and about us."

"Couldn't you think here?"

"I suppose I could, but I just wanted to get away for a while. You're not mad at me, are you?"

"You know better than that." She reached over and touched his face. Smiling, she said, "You'll know it when I get mad."

"What have you been doing all day?"

"Nothing much. Been listening to the radio. The news gets bleaker all the time. They keep talking about how we lost our fleet except for the carriers. Now the Japanese can just walk right over us. Is that true, do you think?"

"I'm afraid we're not going to win any battles for a long time. Congress has cut back on the military until practically all we've got is a peacetime army and navy. All the equipment is pretty well worn out. We'll have to start from the ground up to fight this war."

"That reminds me. Tim came by with your father today. Tim was so excited."

"He's always excited. What is it this time?"

"He was telling us how he and your father have been talking to someone from the government. He says that the government wants the Winslow Factory to build carburetors for military vehicles."

"Wow, that'll be great for the company."

Joelle hesitated, then said, "He wants you to go talk to him tomorrow about an idea he has."

"Tim's full of ideas. What's this one?"

"He wants us to move the central headquarters for the Haven to Little Rock."

"Wait a minute. Let me guess. And he wants me to come back to work at the factory, doesn't he?"

"Yes, he does. He's very excited about it."

"Well, I'm not. I've already got something to do."

"What will you tell him? He's going to be terribly disappointed."

"I'll just tell him I have other plans."

Joelle gave a little cry and reached out and threw her arms around Luke. "I'm so glad."

"Glad I'm not going to work for the factory?"

"Yes. I wanted us to work for the Haven together."

"And that's just what we'll do, so you can forget about my going to work at the factory. That's just Tim's idea."

Drawing back, Joelle said, "You know, I'm enjoying my visit so much. It's been so good to meet your family—but I'm ready to go home now. I miss the girls and there's so much to do."

"Only another day and we'll be on our way. I feel like you do. There's a lot to do."

★ ★ ★

"I'm sorry you have to go so soon," Jolie said. The four were standing outside the hangar at the airfield. The plane was warmed up, and they were saying their final good-byes.

"It's been such a wonderful visit," Joelle said, smiling, "and now that the Winslows are behind the Haven, we're going to see great things for God."

"I hope Tim's not too disappointed by my not coming to work at the factory," Luke said.

His father shrugged his shoulders. "He was pretty disappointed. He's a stubborn fellow, but he'll get over it."

"Well, this is good-bye for a while," Luke said. "We'll keep in touch."

Joelle hugged Luke's parents, and then she followed Luke out to the plane. He helped her in and shut the door, and then went around and climbed in beside her.

Joelle turned and waved as Luke taxied out toward the main strip. He picked up speed and then they were off the ground. Joelle waved again and saw Peter and Jolie waving at her. "I feel like I've got brand-new parents."

"You do. They're crazy about you."

As Luke gained altitude, they discussed their plans for expanding the Haven to include a boys' facility. "You know," Joelle told him, "as our place gets bigger, I don't want to become just an executive in an office somewhere. I want to know these young people."

"You probably won't be able to know them all, but you'll always know some of them." Luke grinned and reached over and squeezed her arm. "It's going to be great, honey. Better than anything you've ever dreamed of."

★ ★ ★

Sunny was full of questions as she helped Joelle peel potatoes. More than once Joelle had asked her to try to make her peelings thinner. Sunny was more interested in fishing for information about Joelle's trip than she was in peeling potatoes. She had fired questions as fast as she could speak, and finally she said, "Did Luke like the present we gave you, that nightgown?"

Joelle laughed. "Yes, he liked it."

"I thought he would. Men like frilly underwear on women."

"How in the world do you know that?"

"I read it in a magazine."

"What magazine was that?"

"I don't remember. Just one that Shirley found."

"Well, I've got something better for you to read than magazines about underwear."

Sunny suddenly dropped a potato into the bowl and turned to Joelle. Her face was lit up, and Joelle thought about how she had changed since the first time she had met her. When Sunny had first come to the Haven, she had been depressed, sullen, and uncommunicative. But now the girl had an inner glow that was so good to see. "You know what, Joelle?"

"What?"

"Luke's going out to get a Christmas tree today, and he told me I could go with him. It'll be just him and me."

"That'll be wonderful."

"He said I could pick out the tree."

"You be sure to choose a good one."

"I will, but you know what? I just love Luke!"

Joelle reached over and pinched the young girl's earlobe. "So do I, honey." She grinned. "So do I."

★ ★ ★

The living room was a pile of papers on Christmas morning. The girls had ripped into their presents, throwing the wrappings aside as they expressed their delight at their gifts.

"Christmas sure is a lot of hard work—buying all these presents and wrapping them."

"Oh you," Joelle said. "I did ninety percent of it."

"But I had all the mental anguish." Luke grinned at her.

The girls were examining their presents and chatting excitedly about what they had received. The foundation board had instructed Luke and Joelle to spend part of their first check on the girls, for they had predicted that some of the girls wouldn't be getting anything from their own families. Twelve girls were living in the house now, and that was the upper limit of what the old house could hold. There were plans afoot to erect a new building not only for the boys but one for the girls as well. They were hoping for a new facility that could house as many as fifty girls if necessary.

"It's been a wonderful Christmas," Luke said. "Best I can remember. If you'll stay right here for a minute, I've got one more surprise for you."

The girls all turned to look at him and Joelle.

"What kind of a surprise?" Joelle asked.

"You wait right here. Nobody move until I get back."

As soon as Luke left the room, the girls began peppering Joelle with questions. "Do you know what it's going to be, Joelle?" Sunny demanded.

"I have no idea. You know as much as I do."

They speculated on the nature of the surprise until they heard Luke starting down the stairs. Joelle's eyes opened wide as Luke appeared.

He was wearing the uniform of a captain in the Army Air Force. He stood there tall and straight and proud, and his eyes met with Joelle's. "I've been trying to come up with a way to tell you about this, but I thought this might be the best way."

The girls were all crying out and jumping up as they ran to Luke. He was surrounded by the entire group, trying to answer their questions, and finally he pulled himself loose and went over to stand beside Joelle. "I just didn't know how to tell you."

"Will you be leaving soon?" Joelle asked, knowing the answer.

"I'm afraid it won't be too long."

Joelle wanted to protest, but she knew what she had to do. "I'm proud of you, Luke! You'll be the pride of the air force!"

★ ★ ★

The girls were all in bed, and Joelle sat with Luke in front of the fireplace. He had pulled the couch around so they faced it, and now he got up and poked at the logs. They shifted and sent swirling sparks up the chimney. Putting the poker back, he came back to sit beside her. He put his arms around her and after a moment of silence said, "You're not angry with me, are you?"

"Of course not."

"That was what I went to Mount Pinnacle for, to think about this. I got to thinking about my life, how little I'd done."

"That's not true."

"Well, it seemed like it to me. Then I started thinking about how the air force is going to need experienced pilots, especially those who've been in combat. So I went to Little Rock and talked to Major Crandall, the enlistment officer, told him about my experience in the Spanish Civil War."

"What did he say?"

"He called Washington and talked to some general about my experience. They gave me a commission, and my job will be to train a squadron of pilots, all young fellows who have never seen any combat, of course."

"You'll do a wonderful job, Luke."

The two sat there talking for a long time, and finally Joelle turned, her eyes luminous. "I guess I have to tell you I'm afraid, Luke. War's a terrible thing."

Luke nodded and pulled her closer. "It is, but I suppose all over America, wives and mothers and sisters are worried about their men going off to war. I'm sorry to do this to you, Joelle, but I feel I have to go."

She put her arms around his neck, her head on his chest. "Promise me you'll come back to me."

"You know I will, sweetheart."

Joelle pulled back and looked into his face. Something danced in her eyes, and she said, "I have a present for you."

"You've already given me a present."

"This is different."

"All right, give it to me, then."

Joelle's face lit up, and her lips parted with a delighted smile. "I can't give it to you until July or maybe August."

Luke stared at her with a puzzled look, but then suddenly

his eyes flew open wide. "Does that mean what I think it means?"

"Yes. We're going to have a baby."

Luke gave a delighted cry. "I promise you one thing. When my son is born, I'll be here for that."

"Maybe it'll be a girl."

"So much the better." He kissed her then and held her tighter. "Thanks for the present, darling!"

CHAPTER TWENTY-SIX

THE KNIGHTS FLY AGAIN

★ ★ ★

The ancient transport groaned at the seams as it nudged into the dock at Portsmouth. Luke had heard about the fog in England, and here was the reality. It was August 3, 1942, and Captain Luke Winslow stood in the bow beside his second-in-command, Lieutenant Hal Harkness.

Harkness was a highly excitable young man, one of the best pilots Luke had ever flown with and one that had the complete and utter confidence of the men in Wolf Squadron.

Harkness moved impatiently. "It seems like ten years since we met at Walnut Ridge to organize the squadron," he said.

"Well, we made it, Hal."

"There were times I didn't think we were going to. This last year has been hard."

Indeed, the year had been hard. Luke had gained the reputation of being a tough man, but he had known that these young men the government had put under his command needed toughness. They would be facing some of the most skilled pilots in the world in the Luftwaffe, and Luke was determined that they would be able to hold their own.

The months had passed slowly, and only the birth of their

son, whom Luke and Joelle had named Peter after Luke's father, had broken the routine. Joelle had managed to come and stay with him at the training station, and they had been fortunate that Ted and Irene Taylor had once again agreed to stay at the Haven during Joelle's absence.

The training had been demanding, and more than three-fourths of the men had failed to make it through. More than Luke liked to think about had been killed in training accidents. At times it seemed that the training program was as dangerous as combat itself, but raw young men jockeying P-47s made mistakes, and these mistakes were sometimes fatal.

"Can't see a thing in this fog," Hal commented. "I wonder how in the world we're gonna fly in it."

"We'll find out, Hal."

He laughed. "We managed to get here in one piece, but you earned the reputation of being the meanest squadron leader in the whole air corps. For a while there, some of the men hated you."

"I realize not everyone likes me. But if I didn't push them in training, they would never be prepared for what they're gonna be facing now that we're finally here."

The two men stood at the rail watching the sailors perform their duties. "If it wasn't for little Pete and Joelle, I don't know how I would have made it through these past several months."

"I know you're going to miss them. I'm glad I'm not married. I've got big plans about making the women of England happy."

"I'm not sure how much time you're going to have for women, Hal. You're going to have plenty to do."

"That's right. I'll be taking on the Luftwaffe. I'm awfully glad I'm not going to have to fight you up there. You're the best pilot in the service."

"I hope General Eaker thinks so."

"I hear he's about as hard-nosed as you are."

"He had to be. They sent him over here last February with

nothing. No airfields, no planes, and he's supposed to create the Eighth Air Force. I don't think anybody but Eaker could have done the job. Well, we better get our things ready," Luke said, and turning, he went belowdecks to make preparations.

★ ★ ★

Ira Eaker rose when Luke and Hal walked into his office. Coming over, he saluted the two and then offered his hand. "You'll never know how glad I am to see you boys," he said with excitement.

"We're glad to be here, General. This is Hal Harkness, my second-in-command, a hot pilot if there ever was one."

"Excellent. We need all the hot pilots we can get over here."

"When will we be going out on a mission, General?" Harkness asked eagerly.

"We don't have the American planes here, but they're on the way. It'll be September."

"What are we going to do until then, General Eaker?" Luke asked.

"Don't worry. You'll be busy. I'm assigning the squadron to fly cover for the English bombers."

"When will we start flying?"

"When can you start?"

"As soon as they get the airplanes uncrated and put together. A week maybe."

"The sooner the better."

"What are the missions like?" Hal asked, bubbling with curiosity.

"Well, they're not perfect. None of our planes have the range to escort the bombers all the way to target. The Spitfires can go halfway, but then they have to turn back before they run out of fuel. From then on the bombers are on their own. They've been taking a terrible beating."

"The British bomb at night, don't they?"

"Yes, they do. They tried it at daytime and said that losses were too great. As a matter of fact"—he grinned ruefully—"they think I'm crazy for wanting to bomb in the daylight. They say it'll never work." He gave Luke a studied look. "I've read a lot about you, Captain Winslow. I understand you've taken a number of 109s down."

"That's true, but I hear they've improved them since I was last in combat."

"How good are the German pilots?" Hal asked.

Eaker frowned. "They're plenty good." He gave Luke a pointed look. "I hope you haven't lost your touch."

"Oh, he hasn't, General," Hal spoke up eagerly. "He's the hottest pilot—"

"That's enough, Lieutenant," Luke said. "General, I've been reading the newspapers. There's an old acquaintance I'd like to look up. Colonel Erich Ritter."

"You know Ritter?"

"He was with the Condor Legion in Spain. As a matter of fact, I shot him down."

"Well, apparently you didn't kill him. Maybe you could do a better job this time. He's their leading ace, you know, and his pilots are among the most feared in the Luftwaffe."

"I'll be looking for him."

"The pilots all report he's easy enough to find. He flies a 109 painted black with a knight fighting a dragon on the cowling."

"That's exactly what he did in Spain. General, with your permission, I'd like to decorate my plane a bit."

"What kind of decoration?"

"I'd like to have it painted white with a knight on the side. That was like the one I flew in Spain. Of course, it wasn't a P-47."

"Why do you want to do that? You want Ritter to find you?"

"No, sir. I want to find *him.*"

"Good! You paint that plane any way you want to." Eaker suddenly snapped his fingers. "I know what. We'll publicize this thing. I'll have it put in the papers. Maybe we'll even get a mention on the radio."

"You think they read our papers?"

"You bet your boots they do! And they must have all kinds of people over here. Lord Haw-Haw comes on the radio and tells us stuff about our base I don't know myself. Why, yesterday he said that the clock in the officers' bar was five minutes slow, and you know what? It was!"

"Who would have guessed."

"Anyway, you two get to it. Get those planes ready to go, and as soon as they are, you can fly cover for the Brits."

★ ★ ★

Erich Ritter had just gotten back from leave. He was on his way to General Hoffmann's office to report for duty when he saw planes coming in from a mission. He knew his own squadron had been out, and he assumed they were returning. He counted the planes and saw that it was not a full squadron. "The boys must have had some losses," he muttered.

He waited until he saw his second-in-command, Wolfgang Began, approaching him.

Began saluted Ritter and muttered, "Glad to see you back, Colonel."

"Was it a bad mission, Began?"

"The worst!"

"What happened?"

"We were just beginning the attack when all of a sudden a flight of P-47s dropped out of nowhere. They came right out of the sun. Three of our boys went down on their first pass and then it was just a dogfight. It was like a swarm of wasps. Those 47s are tough airplanes. A few bullets won't stop them. They just keep coming at you. They're *devils*, sir!"

"How many did we lose?"

"Six in all. It was that squadron leader, the white one with the knight painted on his ship. He got Willie with one burst, and then he got on Franz's tail. Franz couldn't shake him off. That White Knight shot him all to pieces. Poor Franz," Began said, shaking his head and plainly disturbed. "He didn't have a chance. His plane burst into a fireball."

"What did you do then?"

"I called the squadron back. We were outnumbered for once, and that demon in the white plane—I had to get away from him!"

"You ran away?"

"Yes, sir, I ran away."

"Well, when I get the White Knight in my sights, I won't run away!"

Ritter talked to all the men in the squadron as they came in and saw that they were disheartened. Anger began to burn in Erich Ritter as he envisioned what had happened that day. After encouraging the men, he left and made his way to General Hoffmann's office.

Hoffmann rose as soon as Ritter walked in and saluted him. "I'm glad you're back, Erich," he said warmly. "We've missed you."

"I was just talking to Began and the other men. We lost six planes today."

"Six! How could that happen?"

"They say they were hit by a squadron led by a man who calls himself the White Knight. His plane is white with a knight painted on the side."

Hoffmann looked troubled. He chewed his lower lip and said, "I want you to hear something." He walked over to his desk and turned the switch on a piece of machinery Erich had never seen before. A voice broke the silence, and Ritter listened intently.

"This message is for Colonel Erich Ritter. My name is Luke Winslow. Colonel Ritter and I are old adversaries. Colonel Ritter, I'm sorry you were not with your squadron today. The last time we met, I shot you out of the skies, and it was my intention to do the same today. Please try to be with your men the next time they fly. The Wolf Squadron will be glad to furnish the reception. You'll recognize me. I'll be flying the white plane with the knight on the side."

The voice faded, and Hoffmann saw shock on Ritter's face.

"I have no idea how he got your name, Ritter."

"He flew against me in Spain, General."

"You know about him, then."

"He shot me down there. I should remember him." Ritter was remembering his encounter with Luke Winslow. Ritter had almost fond memories of the man who'd had every opportunity to shoot him and yet didn't, but now he knew he was matched in a battle with an adversary he had to kill.

"You can't let this go, Erich," Hoffmann said. "It'll be in all the papers. He'll be the hero and you'll be the coward if you don't meet him."

Erich Ritter nodded vigorously. His voice was harsh as he said, "I'll face the White Knight, General Hoffmann. Don't you ever doubt that, and he'll go down in flames this time!"

CHAPTER TWENTY-SEVEN

CHECKMATE!

★ ★ ★

The date was October 5, 1942. The aide outside of General Hoffmann's office twisted his mouth at the sound of the angry voices that emerged from the general's inner office. "Don't cross the general today, Max," he said. "He's not in a good mood."

"I'm surprised Colonel Ritter's making such a fuss. Listen to him. He's shouting like a crazy man."

Indeed, Ritter was shouting. He had burst into General Hoffmann's office unannounced and startled the general, who was not accustomed to such behavior from his men.

Hoffmann sat back in his chair staring at the finest pilot in the entire Luftwaffe. He had never seen Ritter lose control like this, and he knew he had to handle the matter delicately. He simply sat there and waited while Ritter stormed at him angrily.

"The orders are insane, General!" Ritter complained.

"They were handed down to me from high command."

"Those idiots don't know what's happening! The orders are to wait until the American fighters run out of fuel and have to turn back. We can't attack before then."

"It's the wise thing to do. We're after the bombers, Erich."

"The same men who are flying these fighters will soon have planes that have long-range fuel tanks. I can't imagine why the Americans haven't done it yet. When they do, it'll be these men we're letting escape now who'll be flying. I say we kill them now before they have a chance."

"We can't afford to lose any more fighters than we have to." Hoffmann shook his head. "It's not general knowledge, but our factories have been letting us down. The British are turning out Spitfires like crazy, and the Americans are shipping P-47s and other fighters over daily. Every time we engage in attack, we risk losing precious 109s."

"I don't care about that. When I'm up there, I see American fighters down below and I know we can get them. But the orders keep me from attacking. My honor is being questioned and even my courage."

"You're talking about the broadcast Winslow put through."

"Yes. He mocks me for running away and for not meeting him in battle."

"You've proved your courage to me," Hoffmann said. "You don't have to prove it to anyone else."

"Yes I do. My men are beginning to doubt. Winslow's Wolf Squadron shows up and we watch them and don't attack. What do you think the men are thinking?"

"It's orders, Erich."

"They're stupid, idiotic orders! Winslow's gotten to where he hangs around now when the rest of the planes go back and challenges me to come down and meet him in a single duel. And I hang around and wait until he runs low on fuel. I tell you, General, my honor's at stake. Something has to be done."

"I'll talk to Göring about it."

"Good! He's an old fighter pilot. He should know what it's like. I've got to go now. It's time for the mission."

Ritter left the general's office and went at once to the field. He made his way to where his plane was being prepared and said, "Is she all ready to go, Neudorf?"

"Yes, Colonel. All ready and in fine shape."

"You always do a good job."

"Thank you, Colonel." Neudorf hesitated, then said, "I hope you get that blasted White Knight, sir. I know you could shoot him down if they'd just let you fight."

Ritter stared at his mechanic, and suddenly something changed in his features. A smile appeared on his thin lips, and he asked, "Did you ever disobey a direct order, Neudorf?"

He grinned. "Several times, sir. Did you?"

Erich Ritter thought about that and then said enigmatically, "Not yet. . . ." He climbed into the cockpit, and after he was strapped in, he closed the canopy and moved the 109 forward. He saw the rest of the squadron coming after him and led them out for the takeoff. He waited until they had gained their proper altitude and then said over his radio, "If we see the Wolf Squadron, I'm going to have a crack at that White Knight. It shouldn't take long. Shultz, you're in charge until I return."

The competition between the White Knight and the Black Knight was well known to the pilots in Ritter's squadron. The second-in-command said, "Isn't that against orders, Colonel?"

"Yes, it is, but I can't put up with him any longer."

A cheer came over the radio, and all the men in the squadron shouted words of encouragement.

"Let's go get them, and I hope the White Knight is there with them!"

★ ★ ★

General Eaker had come out to watch the Wolf Squadron take off. He chomped on his cigar and shook his head. "I wish we had long-range fighters and could stay with the bombers all the way to the target."

"It's hard to leave those fellows in the bombers, General," Luke agreed. "When will we get belly tanks for our planes?"

"I don't know. There's some kind of problem with the P-47. The drop tanks aren't working right." He turned and said, "You've seen Ritter several times, I understand."

Luke's face was grim. "Yes, sir. Those krauts know our range, and they don't attack until we turn back. Several times Ritter has shown himself, but by that time I'm low on fuel and have to turn back." A smile creased his lips. "But I have a plan."

"A plan to do what?"

"How to get him."

"I'd like to hear about it."

"I've been thinking about this for a long time, General Eaker. We use a lot of fuel just gaining altitude and flying at high speeds. Today, since I don't have an auxiliary tank, I'm going to let the squadron go on without me. I'm going to fly as slow as I can at low altitudes. By the time the rest of the planes have to return, I'll get to where the bombers are. I ought to get there about the time Ritter makes his attack after he sees the rest of our planes coming back. When Ritter and his men attack, I'll go up and meet him. I won't have a whole lot of fuel, but all I need to do is get on his tail for a few bursts."

Eaker liked the idea. He was a daring man himself, and he had complete confidence in Luke Winslow. "That's cutting it pretty fine. If you run out of fuel, you'll have to bail out over Germany. I wouldn't like to spend the rest of the war in a prison camp."

"If my plan works, I'll wipe out the Black Knight and then scoot for home."

Eaker sucked on his cigar and blew out a thick cloud of smoke. "Sounds like a bad novel, Winslow, but I hope it works."

★ ★ ★

Flying slowly at very low altitudes was boring. Luke kept track of the squadron by listening on his radio but did not use his own. Finally he looked up and saw the squadron coming back. He counted them and muttered with satisfaction, "Good! They're all there." He calculated his fuel and saw that he had quite a bit more than usual at this stage in his flight. Finally up ahead he saw the contrails of the bombers, and increasing his speed slightly and gaining some altitude, he was soon able to see that the bombers were under heavy attack.

"They were just waiting for our boys to leave," he muttered. "Now if I can just find Ritter. . . ." He headed for the bomber formations, and the B-17s already showed gaps. He saw one B-17 get shot down in flames. Luke anxiously watched the plane head for the ground and waited until he saw the parachute.

The fighters would not be expecting a P-47, nor would they be looking at him to come from beneath. He had always come from above, out of the sun, which was a good aerial tactic. Finally his heart gave a lurch as he saw a plane painted black. Straining his eyes, he could finally make out the knight and dragon on the side.

"All right, Colonel Erich Ritter, it's payoff time!" He gunned his engine to full speed and pulled rapidly. Ritter had made a pass at a bomber, raking it with his guns. But as he shot by it, he was completely unprepared when suddenly Luke caught him in his sights. Pushing the firing button, Luke saw the tracers reach out but was disappointed to see that only a few of them struck the 109.

Ritter had excellent reflexes, and he gave the 109 a sharp twist. Bringing it around, he was headed straight for Luke, who had little time to change direction. As he flipped the P-47 over, he felt bullets raking his ship. Suddenly the control felt loose in his hand, and he knew that something vital had taken a bullet.

Ritter had been totally shocked to see the white plane with the knight on the side. He knew that his own plane had escaped serious damage, and when he saw the white plane break away and head for home, he knew this was his chance. "I've done him some damage. I'm going to get him now. Shultz, take over," he said over the radio. Then he shoved the throttle forward and took off after the P-47, leaning forward with anticipation. "I've got him," he said as he saw smoke trailing out of the white plane's engine.

The trip home was a cat-and-mouse affair. Luke's plane was so damaged he knew he could not engage in a dogfight with Ritter, so he did his best to dodge him, hiding in clouds when he had the opportunity, but he was unable to shake Ritter. He was becoming almost desperate when he looked out and saw the English Channel beneath him.

"At least I'll be over England if I have to bail out," he breathed with relief.

He looked down and saw that his fuel gauge was almost empty. The control still felt loose, and once again he heard the stammer of Ritter's guns and wrenched the plane to one side. As he did an idea came to him. With his plane damaged he could not outperform Ritter, so he would have to use the element of surprise.

Glancing up in the mirror to his left, he saw Ritter striving to get on his tail. It was the thing he had tried to avoid, but he had one chance. He allowed Ritter to come up behind him and as soon as he did, instead of increasing speed, Luke cut the throttle back to zero and at the same time wrenched the stick back. The plane nosed upward, and Ritter, caught off guard by the decrease in speed and the sudden rising of Luke's plane, shot past Luke. As soon as he did, Luke dropped his nose and had Ritter in his sights. He pulled the trigger and the guns of the P-47 shook the entire plane. He saw he had hit the black plane, doing massive damage. As he followed, he expected Ritter to bail out, but he did not.

Ritter's engine had been hit and was smoking, and he knew now that he had no chance. Reaching up to shove the canopy back, he realized one of the bullets had struck it and it would not move. He struggled, but it was too late. His plane was losing altitude, and he knew he would have to do his best to land it with the little control he had left.

He spotted a field far ahead. "If I can make that field," he muttered, "I'll be all right." He brought the plane in and it bounced several times, then flipped over, wrenching Ritter's hands from the controls. His head struck the windshield as he was thrown forward, and he knew nothing but blackness.

Luke watched Ritter land and saw the plane flip over. He suddenly remembered how Ritter had been a gallant adversary, despite their differing opinions over control of Spain. He did not have enough fuel to get to another field so he made a quick decision. He brought the Thunderbolt down, jumped out, and ran over to the black plane. The cowling had been raked off, and Ritter was hanging by his safety belt. Pulling out his knife, Luke cut the safety belt and caught Ritter as he fell. He dragged the man frantically, for he knew very well what could happen.

When they were less than a hundred yards away, the German plane burst into a fireball, the impact knocking Luke down. He struggled to pull Ritter's limp body farther away as the flames roared.

Luke collapsed to the ground, panting, while he watched the fire of the burning plane.

Ritter's eyes opened, and he looked around wildly. He saw the plane, then turned to see Luke Winslow supporting him. Ritter was a man of great courage, and he knew exactly what had happened at that moment. "I guess you've won the game, White Knight. I seem to be checkmated."

Two British soldiers were rushing across the field, weapons at the ready. The English were accustomed to German planes being shot down and were alert to opportunities to capture them.

"You're going to enjoy our prison camp, Erich. I hear the food is good, and you can dig potatoes for recreation until the war's over."

EPILOGUE

★ ★ ★

December 1942

Joelle was giving little Pete a bath. They were calling him Little Pete to distinguish him from his grandfather Peter. The baby enjoyed his bath immensely, but his favorite trick was slapping the water and cooing with delight when it splattered everyone in the vicinity.

Joelle heard the door close and thought it was one of the girls who had gone to the grocery store. "Just put the groceries on the table, Shirley."

"I don't have any groceries."

Joelle's heart gave a leap. She turned and saw Luke standing there, a big grin on his face. "Luke!" she cried, and he came to her and his arms went around her. She clung to him frantically, and he kissed her passionately.

When she could pull herself away, she asked, "What are you doing home? Why didn't you tell me you were coming?"

"I didn't know I was coming home, but I'm here because I have a new assignment."

Joelle's heart filled with joy. "You mean you won't be flying combat anymore?"

"Nope. Just training missions here in the States. Got to train a new crop of pilots."

"Where will you be stationed?"

"In Texas." He held her and kissed her again. "Do you think you'll like Texas?"

"Pete and I will like it fine."

Luke turned his attention to the fat baby, who was staring at him owlishly. The baby raised his arms and cried out, splashing water everywhere. Luke was almost deluged. He laughed and went over to the tub, giving Pete a kiss on his head and rubbing his silky back. "Little Pete," he said, "I've been missing you."

"Can Pete and I go with you to do the training?"

"I threatened to quit if you couldn't come with me." He put his arms around her then and said, "I promised to come back."

Joelle Winslow clung to her man and whispered, "I knew you would!"

SPECIAL ACKNOWLEDGMENT

Bethany House has been gracious beyond my desert throughout the history of the Winslow series—especially Gary and Carol Johnson. And a special thanks to my faithful editor and friend, Dave Horton.

More Riveting Historical Fiction!

When Olivia Mott sails to America with the daughter of her former employers—the Earl and Countess of Lanshire—she ends up in the company town of Pullman, Illinois. Using a forged reference letter, Olivia obtains a position as assistant chef in Pullman's elegant Hotel Florence. As her status in the town grows, so does her web of deceit. But when her traveling companion reveals a secret of her own, Olivia must either admit to her real past and accept the consequences or deny the truth to preserve her comfortable new life.

POSTCARDS FROM PULLMAN Book 1:
In the Company of Secrets **by Judith Miller**

Michael Phillips' bestselling Civil War saga traces the efforts of two Southern girls fighting to stay safe during the chaos of a divided country. Born into two different worlds, Katie—the daughter of a plantation owner—and Mayme—a slave freed by the war—must unite their efforts to keep Rosewood plantation from falling into the wrong hands. But as Rosewood becomes a beacon of hope to those ravaged by the war, an evil force threatens to overtake all the girls hold dear.

SHENANDOAH SISTERS Series:
Angels Watching Over Me
A Day to Pick Your Own Cotton
The Color of Your Skin Ain't the Color of Your Heart
Together Is All We Need

Born from the memorable characters of the popular SONG OF ACADIA series by Janette Oke and T. Davis Bunn comes a new series about their brave descendants. Spanning American and British history, the HEIRS OF ACADIA series follows courageous men and women as they struggle for freedom and faith in the face of tyranny.

HEIRS OF ACADIA Series:
The Solitary Envoy
The Innocent Libertine
The Noble Fugitive
The Night Angel
Falconer's Quest **(April 2007)**